# CREWSHIPLIFE

*CRUISE SHIPLIFE IS LIKE A SOAP OPERA, YOU CAN EITHER WATCH IT, BE IN IT OR IN THIS CASE DO BOTH.*

*THIS IS THE BEGINNING OF A LOVE STORY ABOUT CHANGE.*

## TOBIAS BIDDICK

CONNECT
www.amazon.com/author/tobiasbiddick

Although based on real events, this is a work of fiction. Characters are either part of the Authors imagination, or if real, used fictitiously without any intent to describe their actual conduct.

Copyright ©2015 by Tobias Biddick
All rights reserved

# CREWSHIPLIFE

Dedicated to Mum and Dad for putting up with me
for all those years and my supportive and loving wife…
I found you eventually.

*To Brian and Carla you guys rock thanks for being awesome*

# From the Purser's Desk....

Well this is amazing, this time last month I was working in a hotel in England worrying about the bad weather, filling room nights, demanding stakeholders and an unhappy girlfriend. Thirty days later, I am standing at the bows of the largest cruise ship on the planet doing my best Leonardo DiCaprio impression sailing out of Port Everglades waving to happy strangers and listening to Enya through the outside speakers. What a difference enthusiasm, willingness to learn, and a well-prepared CV can make. I have been extremely lucky to be onboard for a three-week training course, which has been an amazing help, I could not imagine working on the front desk without that invaluable training, even though many people do. I now feel fully equipped to deal with passengers and answer their questions in a calm, confident, and convincing manner.

Of course, my new life at sea as a junior assistant purser is not without its pressures. There is the art of balancing a $15,000 float, lost luggage reports, angry passengers that tell me that I have ruined their cruise because there is a lifeboat in front of their porthole and getting used to the rocking of the ship.

Nevertheless, the pros far outweigh the cons and life on the desk is fast, busy, enjoyable pressure and promotes comradeship amongst both passengers and crew. Being new to sea, I am finding it far more social than I first imagined, from the regal atmosphere of the Commodores cocktail parties to cheering on Keegan's army on the big screen in the crew bar.

Our cruise ship will be soon crossing the Atlantic for an exciting itinerary of five days at sea, which is supposedly best suited for the hardest seafaring passengers and crew. Never has there been a better time to test out those sea legs. This will be followed by deploying to the Mediterranean and the many fresh challenges that will bring in our role. But all of these experiences are character building, I am learning something new every day and the fact of the matter is that we are all in the same boat - sorry cruise ship.

Already in my brief time at sea, I have seen so many changes especially to the shape of the crew. This seems to be the only sad part about cruise ship life thus far, the building of very powerful relationships in a short period of time, and then having to say goodbye just as swiftly.

# TABLE OF CONTENTS

Chapter 1: History of a Broken Heart.............8
Chapter 2: The Great Escape.............12
Chapter 3: Arrival.............18
Chapter 4: Cozy cabin.............29
Chapter 5: The Training Team.............34
Chapter 6: Sail Away.............41
Chapter 7: First Working Day.............46
Chapter 8: Learning the Ropes.............57
Chapter 9: Tour Dispatch.............65
Chapter 10: St. Maarten.............72
Chapter 11: Mad Morning.............84
Chapter 12: Turnaround Day.............91
Chapter 13: Falling.............101
Chapter 14: Sailing free.............114
Chapter 15: Costly error.............122
Chapter 16: Our Fate.............136
Chapter 17: Cutting the Cord.............152
Chapter 18: Crew Cabin comforts.............161
Chapter 19: Off to the Mediterranean.............171
Chapter 20: Close call.............177

Chapter 21: Crossing over ............................................. 188
Chapter 22: Atlantic Sea Days ..................................... 197
Chapter 23: Shift changes ............................................ 201
Chapter 24: My name is Luca ...................................... 210
Chapter 25: Lonesome Lisbon ..................................... 217
Chapter 26: Canadian Progress ................................... 226
Chapter 27: Reconciliation .......................................... 237
Chapter 28: Down to Business .................................... 247
Chapter 29: Honored ................................................... 254
Chapter 30: Overland .................................................. 261
Chapter 31: Gladiators ................................................ 270
Chapter 32: Barcelona Freak Out ................................ 277
Chapter 33: Back to Earth ........................................... 283

ABOUT THE AUTHOR ................................................ 291

# Chapter 1: History of a Broken Heart

So far, I cannot complain about my life really. It was average for a 28-year-old, but I felt that something was missing. I had a decent enough job as a manager of a busy seaside hotel. I was getting up to enough mischief to enjoy myself. I had a good number of people who I could call close friends whom I trusted, and generally, life was good. So, what was wrong with me that I had an urge to do something different from the everyday routine? Could it be that I did not have a gap year? Actually it could be that I never actually made it to university. Or it could be my irritating inability to commit in a relationship. I do not totally blame myself for this, though, as I had just not found the right partner yet. This is a story about that journey.

    I shamefully admit that I was fairly shallow and inexperienced in relationships. I had been in love once and had my heart broken. I was 23 years old, and from the first moment I saw Marie, I knew I just had to be with her. That was a very strong motivating feeling, and one that I had not yet experienced in life. She was a waitress in the hotel where I was assistant manager. My strategy was to try to be cool, build trust, and then ask her out. I slowly, but subtly, stalked her and got to know a bit about what made her tick. She had just completed her A-levels and was set to go to University in September to study French.

By chance, one week the hotel working schedule had blessed Marie and I with the same day off. I made my move on a Sunday evening after dinner service. I was brave and just asked her out, albeit with a slightly awkward and shaky voice. I asked her to have lunch with me on our day off; my cunning plan was to take her to France for lunch. Our first date was a day trip through the Euro Tunnel. It was one of the coolest dates I had been on, and actually, it was probably one of the only dates I had been on. I had been a slow starter when it came to girls. I preferred to just hang out with my mates, and I had no motivation to have a girlfriend. Until I met Marie. For some reason, all those previous doubts and lack of interest and motivation for a girlfriend had dissipated, and I wanted to be with her more than I had ever wanted anything else in the world. What a turnaround I had experienced from meeting just one girl. I guess it must have been love at first sight.

I had hired a blue Ford Escort for the day trip and picked her up at first light from the cute little bungalow where she lived with her mum and dad. She seemed as excited as I was about our impending adventure. The first thing she said to me as she slammed the car door shut was that she had brought everything—even a little first aid kit—and we were off. One of the biggest issues with living on the Isle of Wight is that you are surrounded by water. To travel anywhere, you have to factor in extra travelling time and about fifty notes for the ferry. Once we hit mainland England, the drive was nice, but long, except a slight detour to Yapton as I took a wrong turn, which made us both laugh. We were getting on well and talked as we drove, getting to know each other a bit better.

The Euro Tunnel was fun and we eventually found ourselves in France. It had just dawned on me that I had no idea where I was going or what to do once we got there. I drove to a little French village, and we parked and went for lunch. We drank some rose wine that could only be described as diesel in both look and taste.

During the Euro Tunnel return journey, I finally made my move and leaned in and kissed Marie for the first time. That kiss seemed to last for the entire journey through the tunnel. The first date had been a triumph, and after that day, we became a couple. That summer was amazing. We took things slow and got to know and trust each other. We met friends, attended family functions and spent all our time off together. We fell in love, and I floated through the months. It was the strongest I had ever felt about another human being, and I was on top of the world. This was love and happiness to me, Marie was the first girl I had said 'I love you' to, I had never felt so fulfilled.

As the summer was coming to a close, Marie was accepted into Swansea University and would soon be leaving. In my naivety, I had no idea what sort of an effect this would have on our relationship. I thought that everything would be okay, as we were in love and nothing could break that. But I was wrong, very wrong. As the months went on after she had left, communication from her was less and less, and I eventually received a "Dear John" letter, with all the classic lines including "it's not you but me." She had finished the relationship, and I was left behind and all alone. I went through every textbook emotion: denial, anger, bursting into tears at inopportune moments, and complete lack of sense of humor. I was no fun to be around. I had a broken heart and had to deal with a massive lonely struggle for about six months. It was the darkest of times.

## Chapter 2: The Great Escape

Five years later, and my twenty-eighth birthday was upon me—probably the best birthday in my life so far as I had decided to throw myself a party. I had moved off the Isle of Wight and was the manager of a hotel on the seafront in Eastbourne with 40 staff reporting to me. I had a slight addiction to bacon with fried eggs on toast, strong coffee and I operated with a constant hangover most days due to a decent social life. Mustering up a birthday bash wouldn't be much trouble. I had been working in the hotel for over three years and had many highs and many lows, but I was getting the feeling that I needed to do something with more variety—possibly travel, to feed my hunger for a fresh challenge.

The venue for my party was a classy bar just a few doors from the hotel. I had become close with the management there. They came into catering with very little experience and winged it with heavy financial backing from what I thought were the "catering mafia" and most probably were.

I hired karaoke from the bloke who dressed like a cowboy at a dodgy local pub, laid on some food, and provided a subsidized bar. About thirty friends came, and we all really enjoyed the night, which was the whole point. It was the October before the millennium and things were changing...

By February 2000, after some soul searching, I discovered "a way out" of the regular routine. A way that included travel without compromising the comfortable lifestyle I was accustomed to. I needed to see more of the planet. I did not want to go backpacking though, and I needed an income of sorts to service the small amount of debt I had. After months of pondering, the answer was staring me in the face in a magazine called The Caterer. I would not very often buy the magazine but instead would flip through the pages in my local newsagent. But on that day, I was committed to the purchase. It was about two and a half quid, which I normally would not squander on reading about the latest developments in hotels and restaurants, but this was different.

The situations vacant section had an advert for junior hotel managers working at sea for a cruise company. Finally, I felt my ship had come in. This could be the answer to my problems and a way to change my lifestyle. I sent off my CV and cover letter and hoped for the best. I had a feeling this was the key to my dream life and change I had been searching for.

My prayers were answered when I was granted an interview, 10:00 a.m. at the head offices in Southampton. I took the day off work and drove down with my interview suit hidden from any inquisitive hotel staff members' prying eyes. I had left in plenty of time to ensure that when I inevitably became lost I would not be late for the actual interview. I actually did get lost in Southampton, but managed to ask a kind local for directions. By that time I was experiencing that sick feeling of panic in my stomach where I thought I would be late and compromise my chances for a decent first impression. However, I managed to get there with enough time to sit in the car park and reflect for a short period before entering the large tower office building. I reflected on what a work up it was to get ready in the morning, shower, shave, and suit as well as travel to an unknown location. I was stressed out and emotionally drained before I even started the interview. I would have to remember that the interviewer would not take the fact that I actually arrived on time as a huge plus—just a matter of course and expectation.

The interview was with a group of twelve other hopefuls and started with an overview of what the role entailed. A white uniformed purser came in to talk on the way things work onboard and the different roles within the floating hotel for a junior assistant purser. We were shown a short film on the different nationalities, some points of code of conduct onboard, and safety and security regulations. I found it all fascinating and had a very open mind. I embraced all this extra information on my potential new lifestyle floating around the oceans for six months at a time. After this group session, we all were placed in a holding room and were called in one at a time for individual interviews. I was slightly nervous because I wanted this so much, but once my turn came, I allowed my natural enthusiasm to take over and gave it my best shot in front of the two interviewers. I left the building after three hours feeling excited that I might have just had a life-changing interview. Only time would tell if I had been successful or not.

I went back to my hotel post in Eastbourne and got on with my life and job without telling any of my friends, staff, or my girlfriend what I had been up to. A month and a half passed and a letter came with the cruise company postmark. I held so much in my hands. It was either going to be a "yes, you can change your life" or "no, carry on with what you are doing." I took the letter into my room and opened it with the same trepidation and care as Charlie did when he was carefully opening the Wonka bar of chocolate that contained the golden ticket. I quickly scanned it for key words, and they were there in the form of "we are pleased to ..." "congratulations" and "joining instructions to follow." To say that I was overjoyed is an understatement. It was a lifeline and in my eyes not dissimilar to winning the career lottery. I was going to work abroad on a cruise ship. It sounded romantic, exciting, and wonderful. I was told it was not all glamour during the interview, but I did not care. This was the best thing that had happened in my life so far, I was proud and very happy, and it was exactly what I had wanted and needed.

    A few weeks later, the official joining instructions arrived accompanied with a large A4 binder containing the WAVES manual. This would be my new bible and in it was the guide to ship life and my new role. I would join "The Grand" in eight weeks in Miami for a three-week onboard training course. This information made everything seem very real. I had a joining date and my flight details would follow with full joining instructions. This dream was only getting better: Miami, biggest cruise ship on the planet, and an actual training course to get used to the new life! I had to pinch myself. The Grand was the most expensive cruise ship ever constructed, costing $450 million, and twice the cost of the Pathfinder Explorer mission to Mars. I was officially excited.

I still had a bit of housekeeping to attend to regarding my current life. I had to give a months' notice to my current employer, which I am sure would go down like a cup of cold sick. Not to mention telling my girlfriend that I would not be around for the next six months—this would probably go down just as well. But personally I felt that this job was lifting a huge weight off me; it was just where I was at with my life.

The housekeeping was done as tactfully and as sensitively as possible, but was never going to be news gratefully received by either party. Before I knew it, I was packing up my room and life of the past three years. I sold my car, ensured my financial affairs were in order for a six-month absence from the UK, and moved back in with my parents for the last week of my freedom before I was due to fly off to America.

I was going from a big fish in a small pond to a small fish in a big pond, and who knew how I would get on. Would I hate it? Would I get seasick on the first day? Would I be able to continue with my habit of drinking cold beers every night? Would I be any good at the work? Would I be happy? These were my main concerns at that point.

The day before my flight, I travelled up to London to stay with my best friend, who would be dropping me at the airport for my flight; he worked at the airport for British Airways. He was currently living with his fiancée and her parents in Hammersmith and the whole family had been wonderful friends over the years, and I had spent a lot of time with them. The next day, nursing a significant hangover, I found myself at the departures gate, saying goodbye to my friend. I was now on my own and made my way through security. All of a sudden, I felt very alone and scared. This was the point of no return. I was about to start the journey for a new life. It was just me, myself, and I. I just had to be strong and get on with it.

## Chapter 3: Arrival

The flight was not memorable. I watched a few movies, drank as many beers as I was allowed, and tried to sleep in my cattle class seat. Upon landing in the late afternoon and after a very long baggage claim wait, I was met by a man with a handwritten Cruise company sign. I politely introduced myself, shook his hand enthusiastically and presented my joining papers; these actions were greeted with a dismissive nod. He told me to stand to the side whilst we waited for another ship joiner from that flight who was being transferred to the same hotel. The other joiner arrived swiftly and looked as grumpy as the meet and greet representative. Undeterred I enthusiastically introduced myself to this person, who I felt I had so much in common with and with whom I wanted to share my eager initial thoughts, fears, and feelings with. I was stopped in my tracks though because this joiner did not share my excitement. He just moaned about the bad seats during his flight and the fact that we were being transferred to a hotel that he knew was not the best one available. I knew no different and was doing my upmost not to let his negativity ruin my rose-tinted glasses view of my situation. I had just gotten a free flight to Miami; I had the night in a hotel and was joining a cruise ship in the morning. How could that be turned into a negative?

The transfer dropped us both at the hotel where check-in was very busy. My moaning fellow traveler went straight to the reception desk to advise the staff member that he would not be sharing a room, stating that he was a two-striped engineering officer and he was entitled to it as part of his contract. I cheerfully approached the desk and just took what I was given and was grateful. I was listed down to share with someone, but that person had not yet checked in. I was given a room key card, a $15 meal voucher for the restaurant, and told that pick up would be at 6:30 a.m. to transfer me to the ship in the morning. That was it. I was in. I had a very welcome hot shower to wash the flight off me, a quick inventory of my belongings, which seemed in order, lie on the bed, and shut my eyes and drifted off. I awoke startled and realized that luckily only an hour had passed, the last thing I needed was to nod off without eating. Doing so would mess up my sleep pattern. I would need to keep myself awake at least until early evening so I would have a proper night's sleep and be correctly adjusted for the next big day of joining the ship.

    I explored around the hotel and surrounding area but found very little of interest. I defaulted to the bar to cash in my meal voucher for a rack of BBQ ribs and French fries. After my hearty American bar meal, I was relaxing and having a few beers, excited about the coming months. But I also was quite scared. I was in the total unknown and way out of my comfort zone.

    I cannot remember who said hello first, but I began talking to the guy on the next barstool. His name was Clem and we both thought it was the biggest coincidence in the world that we were both joining the same cruise ship the next day. We celebrated by downing as many beers as we could. Clem was around my height at 5'10 and had dark curly hair not unlike a soft Elvis. He said "alright" and "okay" a lot, in recognition of what I was talking about and he just naturally seemed very cool. The conversation flowed, as did the beer, and I could just tell that this guy was a special person from his soft spoken, caring manner and having an aura cooler than Johnny Depp. He lived in Las Vegas and played classical guitar for a living, enjoyed the company of women, and seemed to drink as much as me. We were going to be friends. This was not the first ship Clem was to join. He had been aboard another ship previously and was back for more, however, he still gave the impression of someone who was on their first contract.

    We drank and talked until the bar closed and then realized that we had a 6:30 a.m. pick up. The last thing I needed on the "first day of the rest of my life" was a massive hangover, but it was too late for such worries. The damage was done from the initial hotel bar excitement, and I would have to hope that fear would awaken me. It did, and I was up on time, dived into the shower and dressed for action. The hangover was there but fear and nerves were the bigger emotions, I looked at myself in the bathroom mirror and asked myself what on earth I was getting myself into. I had my moments where I lacked confidence, but generally I just wanted to offer a high level of customer service and naturally attend to the needs of guests; I had a feeling that I would be perfect for this role. I was a fresh blank canvas for this company and totally moldable, ready and willing to be brainwashed.

    Clem and I were not the only ones joining the ship at that hotel; about 25 crew members of varied nationalities had assembled by the coffee station. Everyone was polite because no one really knew each other. It seemed that people from all over the planet had travelled to join. I spotted a shaky hand Clem, and we stood together while we awaited the shuttle pick-up to take us to our new home. The bus arrived and we loaded our personal effects into the bottom of the coach. The drive was about 45 minutes, and I enjoyed the early morning sun and calm before whatever was about to hit. The coach approached Port Everglades at Fort Lauderdale and things were becoming more military with gates to get through and barriers and dock security checkpoints to pass. I had a feeling of trepidation in my belly, but I had to hold it together like everyone else. A few questions ran through my head: Was I doing the right thing? Was this all one big mistake? It all sounded very glamorous when I was telling all my friends that I was off to Miami to join a cruise ship in the Caribbean for six months. But now that I was there, I was all alone with no clue of what to expect. The dream was becoming a reality.

    An astonishing vision greeted us at the next turn, as 109,000 tons of glorious white stared at me in the glimmering morning sunshine; The Grand was totally breathtaking and like nothing I had ever seen before. Sure, I had seen pictures, but this steel beast close up was a sight to behold and one that would stay with me forever.

She stood an impressive 201 feet high, which is 60 feet higher than Nelson's Column, and 951 feet long, which was 151 feet longer than the height of Canary Wharf Tower in London. The glass on the outside of her gleamed a magnificent super-sharp blue, and she boasted more private balconies than any other ship afloat; 80% of all outside staterooms had balconies, 710 in total.

The coach drew closer to the dockside and you could really tell those that had not worked on board before because they continued to draw breaths when the ship got closer. The Grand is 159 feet wide, wider that the entire width of the UK's M25 motorway, and 43 feet too wide to fit through the Panama Canal; she was impressive. As our coach pulled up, we all got off and sorted out our various bags from the four pick-ups from various hotels, which I later learned were determined based on rank and availability. The new joiners were held together in the waiting area for an hour while the formalities of paperwork and passports took place. It looked like the person dealing with us was wearing the white uniform that I would be donning in my role, but then I noticed lots of them about the area walking very quickly and organizing the day.

We were led onto the busy dockside and up a steep gangway, struggling with our luggage. We were instructed to drop our belongings in a corner of a very long, crew area that was referred to as the "M1." This was the main working corridor on Deck 4, which seemed to have multi purposes: offices, doorways to crew quarters, and the main loading and unloading areas for ship stores and luggage. Once we were parted from our luggage, we followed the officers in white along the very busy M1 corridor and through doorways and up shiny white stairways. I had no clue where we were going or had been; I was about three-quarters from the front of the line of new crewmembers. We made our way forward and up about 12 flights of stairs, all in crew areas, until we finally were led into the closed crew bar. "Well at least they had a crew bar" I thought, considering my constant raging thirst for hops, malt, and barley.

As we sat down, we joined about 40 other awaiting crew members that had already been there for about a half an hour. Here we were told what would happen next. It was turnaround day and that meant all the passengers were getting off and another load were boarding, as well as new crew members. The whole ship's company seemed to be in a tremendous hurry and all walked with purpose, talking as if they all knew each other. The Grand sailed with around 1,100 crew members and had the capacity for just over 2,400 passengers; we were on weekly cruising every seven days, so this operation happened once a week. It seemed like a lot of work just talking about it. The crew bar seemed like a quite dreary place. It smelled of stale smoke, the carpet stuck to your feet, and the taste of stale beer hung in the air. I was looking forward to finding out all about it.

We were then divided into departments. There were about 60 or so new crew members in the crew bar being signed on, and I ended up sitting with a little group of seven trainees. These were my fellow junior assistant purser trainees (JAPs), I politely said hello and we all introduced ourselves. There was Sebastian Taylor-Wright who was a captain's step-son and seemed to be trading off that fact already. He did not seem to have the social skills to back it up though, which was obvious from how he acted and he seemed to be expecting special treatment. He was not really getting it, though, as this industry thrives on hard work and a good attitude. It seemed that Sebastian would have problems with both.

There was one chap, Martin, missing from the manifest. He was apparently flying from Australia, and we were told he had problems with his connections, and he would join us later.

There was a nice couple from New Zealand called Steve and Jane. Steve was over six feet tall, and Jane was about five feet tall. They were both very jolly and positive and they smiled a lot. They were totally in love, but it seemed they were taking a gamble on their relationship. After all, there was no guarantee they would end up on the same ship after the three-week training course.

Then, there were the girls. Debbie was a well-rounded American girl who formerly worked in the head office and was testing out her sea legs. She seemed nice enough at this stage, but not someone I would get too involved with. Claudia was South African and many would find her very attractive, I would come to realize that she was a kind and warm person. Just reaching 30 years old, she was at a crossroads and like me, probably looking for some answers. Then came Stef, also South African. She was bubbly, with particularly large breasts and seemingly slightly low intellect, but she already seemed very popular; we would become friends.

This group sat in the crew bar in our civilian clothing about to undertake a three week training program to become junior assistant pursers. I had a manual that gave instructions on how it all worked, but I had no practical idea on what it took to survive personally and professionally. The small talk amongst the seven of us seemed more significant than normal small talk. We had all made the decision to move away from conventional lives and try something totally different; that took something special, so we already had common ground.

A cheery chap came up to our group of seven and asked what we did and if we had been onboard before. He was Canadian, very friendly, and appeared similar to Robin Williams in his nature and the way he talked. We told him we were the pursers department's new trainees. He responded by saying, "Ah—the elite." That alone made us feel somewhat special and this guy was very friendly. Almost suspiciously over friendly, but he was just was a genuine nice guy.

My turn came as my name was called by the two white-uniformed pursers running crew arrivals. I walked up to the makeshift desk in the middle of the sticky dance floor and gave my passport over, signed the ship's articles, and was given my joiners pack, which included a map of the ship.

Once all seven of us had followed the same process, we were introduced to our trainer for the next three weeks who had arrived to pick us up and get things started with our transformation from normal civilians to "shippies." This would turn out to be no mean feat, as a few of us had no idea on what to expect. Alison was around 30 years old and immediately gave us the impression that she was in charge and that she knew what she was doing. She was confident, smart, and dressed in white with two gold stripes on her shoulders, depicting that she was an SAP (senior assistant purser). It was a great job but she now had to babysit eight trainees for three weeks and get them through the WAVES exam. She was British, so I thought that would give me some advantage in becoming pursers pet.

We were welcomed and given a brief talk on what the day and the next three weeks would involve. Alison was quite tall, spoke very well, and ran the room with efficiency. I already had the impression that she would take no nonsense; we were led from the crew bar, still staying behind the scenes of passenger areas. The stairways, and crew areas where very shiny and clean, but not that warming to the eye. It was all quite clinical. The stairs were blue with white glossed railings to guide you down the stairs. We were going to take the lift, as we were going from Deck 7 to Deck 3 to get sized up for our uniforms. Alison suddenly turned to us as we were waiting for the lift and fired a question, "What does C-R-U-I-S-E stand for in the manual?"

I fired the answer back in record time because it was one of the very few things I had memorized. It was quite simple and rolled off the tongue as if I had been saying it for years: Courtesy Respect Unfailing in Service

Excellence. As the elevator arrived and we all squeezed into it around Debbie, another question followed. This one I was not so sure on, so I held back to give the others a chance for glory. We were required to repeat the CRUISE Credo, which were the rules that we would live by while on board. Slowly the group painfully churned them out, but it was apparent that we were all a little rusty on this important aspect of the work. "We Smile. We are on the stage. Our Uniforms are immaculate. We never say no. We smile as we are on stage. We always speak English in passenger areas. We never pass a passenger with our greeting them." These were just some of the CRUISE credo highlights.

We had them finally churned out, with a little help, by the time we arrived at the uniform stock room. It was built around a huge cage with racks and racks of various clothes for all the many departments—from officers to bar staff to entertainment staff to cabin stewards. There were all shapes and sizes, and I was sure we needed them all. The Filipino in charge was busy bossing around an assistant; they were like a pair of wedding planners on speed. They already seemed sweaty and stressed, however things were about to get a lot worse for them. They had seven new junior assistant pursers to kit out from scratch. We were not first in the line; there were a few photo staff members and waiters before us, but the storekeeper could see us in the queue and his level of grief were growing, especially as he eyed up Debbie, who did not look like a regular size to him. Eventually, we were served and each of us was measured and given many different pieces of kit from formal shirts to our half stripes. The storekeeper jokingly flashed the commodore's four stripes and rising sun at us, saying that was what we would be aspiring to achieve. "Wrong department mate. But nice thought." Debbie was unfortunately a problem and her sizes could not be accommodated, and they would have to special order a uniform for her. This was going to be quite embarrassing for the poor girl as she would be the only one with no whites, and it would not take long for the crew members to work out why she was the odd one out. We were told to get changed into our uniforms as soon as possible and report to the desk for a briefing.

## Chapter 4: Cozy cabin

It was time to discover where we would be living for the next three weeks during training, so we reported to the main reception desk to pick up our cabin keys with uniforms in tow, still wondering about the whereabouts of our luggage. We were told it was safe down on the M1.

It was apparent that I would get lost a great deal while on this ship. I did not have a great sense of direction at the best of times but was really struggling to work out the front or back or which deck I was on. I was currently on Deck 5 amidships in passenger areas, waiting for our cabin keycards to be printed so we could access our cabins. I was told at the interview that I would have to share a cabin, which I felt slight trepidation about. I was 28 years old and had never really shared a room, except with the occasional waitress, so it was a bit of a gamble. My immediate choice would be the Australian that had not yet arrived; maybe he was having second thoughts so I would be able to have the cabin to myself. No such luck. There were four boys and four girls, and to our horror, we would be four to a cabin. We were handed D320 D for Dolphin Deck 10; we were told that we were lucky as they were passenger's staterooms and that we should count our lucky stars we were not on Deck 2 or Deck 3. We were given an hour to sort ourselves out and get ready to work. Off we went to find our luggage down on the M1, the main crew area corridor on Deck 4. The crew office and crew cabins were hidden behind the bulkheads and this corridor was always busy. It was especially busy on turnaround days with passenger luggage being offloaded and loaded by the accommodation teams. Fellow crew members were hugging goodbye at the end of their contract and people were moving fast with purpose. The floor was shiny red gloss and walls had the same look in clear bright white.

The crew luggage was located in the gun port door crew area near the crew office, and I was pleased to see my case was there. Everyone grabbed their belongings and followed Steve, who seemed to know his way around already, up to our room D320. Upon arrival outside our stateroom none of our key cards were working so we had to call a nearby room steward to assist. This guy was ultra-friendly. His name was Ricky and was polite, helpful, and spoke fantastically good English. He let us in with a smile and wished us good luck on our training course.

Once Ricky was out of assumed earshot, Sebastian said, "Thank you flip flop." I had no idea what that meant but I saw Ricky turn and look at who fired the comment at him. Whatever it meant, it was not good news as we piled into the cabin. There were only two single beds in the room, so had to try to locate the other two. Sebastian went searching through the only other door and it led to a small bathroom with sink, water closet, and shower. He certainly did not impress anyone so far with his arrogance and ignorance.

Steve leaned over the single bed and pulled down a top bunk—oh great, bunk beds. What are we nine years old? We all knew what the next conversation would be:

top or bottom? Time was ticking away already and I did not want to be late for Alison, so we made some executive decisions. I would be the bigger man and go for a top bunk because Steve was too tall for it, and I had no inclination to argue with Sebastian about it. Once sleeping arrangements we sorted, we all changed and sorted out in our confined space. Staterooms are of ample size for two people with their luggage for one cruise of a week or 14 days, but three, soon-to-be-four, blokes with six months' of supplies and three sets of new uniforms to live with was no joke. It was like some kind of sick game of Twister; within ten minutes, the room looked like a whirlwind had hit it. We all took turns in the bathroom and did our best to get our uniforms on. There were four different costumes to choose from and we had no idea what trousers went with what shirts. There were black pants, white shirts, white and black jackets, and a black tie and bow tie. Out came the WAVES manual to try to help us dress by looking at some pictures of crew in uniform. The rest of the ship seemed to be wearing the white uniform, so we decided to go with that. Our hour was almost up, and we were going to be late on our first shift—not a great start and first impression. I was big on first impressions, and this was not one I was going to be proud of.

    We all managed to get our white uniforms on and realized that we desperately needed to iron the shirts as they had come straight out of a packet and were creased. We needed to find the laundry room quick. Steve said he saw one down the corridor, and we all rushed out the cabin to grab the iron first. The laundry room was nearby, as Steve had rightly stated. Sebastian managed to grab the only iron first and made it obvious that he had not used one, ever. He probably made his servants do it for him at home, Sebastian was getting more and more upset with the aspects of ship life already. I think he thought he could call the room steward and he would iron his shirt for him, which was not the case here. We were workers and not passengers. We left Sebastian to struggle with the iron and went in search of the second closest laundry. It was just up a deck. We walked through what seemed to be endless corridors with no passengers and just a few room stewards with their fully loaded trolleys working to get the rooms ready for the next passengers. The ship had a slight calm feel about it, except us three Muppets running around half dressed. I had no shoes on and Steve had his shirt off ready for the iron. It was the calm before the storm, though, with over 2,000 travelling passengers joining the vessel preparing to embark.

    The time was ten minutes past eleven, and we were already late. Our shirts were finally ironed—quite badly ironed all the same—but we went back to our stateroom to realize we had all left our key cards inside. We were locked out. Sebastian looked around in a panic for Ricky, who was nowhere to be seen. Great. Steve knew his way around best and had shoes and socks on, so he would have to go in search of cabin entry. This took him down to the pursers desk where we were due to be meeting to start our seafaring careers twenty minutes earlier. Steve returned and we managed to get into the room and finished getting ready in record time.

All smartly dressed in our whites, we made our way to the back office to learn of our new roles. The girls and Alison were already there, and we made of first excuses for being late. Debbie was still in her own clothes while the rest of the girls were in their white shirts and skirts. We were shown around the back office and introduced to some people before lunch. The back office was a busy place normally, but it was currently in the lull before the storm, as embarkation did not start until 12:30 p.m. The atrium was empty, with just the piano tuner playing a single note at a time, which would drive us mad over the coming weeks on turnaround days.

The back office of the Grand is on split levels—Deck 5 and Deck 6—with a connecting stairway all out of passenger view. Deck 5 had four workstations with computers and chairs, paper-based information and blank forms for lost luggage, lost persons, and lost and found. There were large heavy brown drawers by the printers on the floor and a longer wider drawer for the float box above it. Around the desks were documents containing the answers to every question ever asked by a passenger. Deck 6 had five workstations and two offices hidden behind a large screen: one for accounts and the other a spare office that connected to the casino cash cage. As we were introduced to the ships company differing ranks, I was slowly learning of the jobs and stripes. Luckily for me everyone had a name badge; remembering names was second on my list of things I struggled with, just behind finding my way around.

# Chapter 5: The Training Team

We were currently trainee junior assistant pursers, and if we successfully completed our three-week training program, we would become "Junior Assistant Pursers," or JAPs. JAPs assisted in the running of the hotel side of the ship's operation, including the desk, crew office, night manager assistant, casino cage assistant, tours office, and business center. JAPs did an average of four or five contracts before they were possibly promoted to "Assistant Pursers," becoming a one-stripe officer with their own cabin, an extra $1,000 a month, and more responsibility. "Assistant Purser" jobs included night manager, crew office (depending on ship size), passenger administration, and head casino cashier. The real elite were the next level up, the "Senior Assistant Pursers," or SAPs. Ask any first purser or purser what their favorite past rank was, and they will 99% of the time say "senior assistant purser." The money increases to $3,600 per month, a double bed cabin, and two gold stripes and huge onboard respect. On the Grand, the senior assistant purser positions were SAP crew, SAP hotel services (weddings), SAP public relations (complaints and luggage—ouch), and SAP accounts (all the onboard money, millions of dollars).

Everyone reported to James, the first purser with three Stripes. James was very British, well-spoken, and seemed fun. Top of the Tree was PSD or Passenger Services Director (purser, four stripes) who was a very busy fast talker, fast walker, fast worker, and fast drinker.

It was time for our first meal onboard; we were all quite hungry and were lead like obedient ducklings toward the officers' mess. Once again it was evident that I had no sense of direction and if required to find my own way around I would really struggle, even probably starve, so as per normal I followed the crowd. The Officers mess was a lot smaller than I imagined, but it was neat and clean and had about twelve well-kept clothed tables spread around made up with four to eight people per table. We had the privilege of windows, so we could observe the Fort Lauderdale dock area activities. It was clear that certain departments and ranks favored certain tables. We all sat on two tables and helped ourselves to the buffet area presented from steaming silver bay marines. The selection was unimpressive, but this was mostly due to the fact that it was turnaround day and feeding officers and crew was not top of the agenda for the Food and Beverage (F&B) department. They were busy on the dockside loading the supplies for the next cruise. I was still quite nervous and in the very early stages of getting to know my new peers, feeling like that first day at school and school dinners.

Lunchtime conversation was light as we got to know a little about each other's backgrounds, likes, dislikes, and reasons for being on the ship. Most reasons were similar to mine—to get to see a bit of the planet in a comfortable environment. Sebastian stated that he was there for career reasons, but I already had his number, he probably could not hold down a proper job in the real world. Steve and Jane just wanted to experience something together, but again, they seemed to be playing a dangerous gamble. We could all end up on different ships at the end of the training. That would certainly push a nail into the coffin of even the strongest relationship, and their relationship seemed strong. I hoped for them to be able to stay together, but we were all aware that they could be sent to different ships in three weeks.

Claudia seemed to be escaping land life reality on this adventure. Stef was just very happy to be here and seemed amazed that she had this officer status where she had deck privileges. She said it must have stemmed from her traditional South African feeling of pessimism. Debbie was getting out of her job and life at home, but I was not too sure what she was looking for or even if she would find it. As for the missing Aussie Martin, he had not even arrived onboard yet.

As lunch ended, our host and leader told us that we would begin our official training the next day in the main dining room at 9:00 a.m. Next up would be a ship tour hosted by a member of the cruise staff, after which we would spend time at the desk learning what the JAPs did and how they did it. We would experience the embarkation of over 2,000 passengers during the afternoon.

We made our way to the back office which I was convinced was a totally different route than we took before, I was dreading having to find my way anywhere on my own. At that point, I made a conscious decision to always be with someone who knew their way around. I elected that person to be Steve—lucky him. By the time we were at the desk, passenger embarkation had begun and many lost Americans were walking around aimlessly staring at the bars, the closed shop windows, and public areas. It was the year 2000 and the cruise market had just exploded in the States and The Grand was an amazing ship with a unique stern accommodating the passenger disco, she was one of a kind. Many people came on to experience what she had to offer and to tell their friends where they had been. I felt very lucky to be onboard. I considered what I had been doing the previous month and felt excitement about being in Miami on this amazing vessel about to set sail around the Caribbean. I felt like it was some surreal dream and someone would wake me up at any moment and I would be back in my old life.

    In the back office, there was a lot more activity with more officers around. We met the SAP Passenger Relations who seemed most underwhelmed to meet us and made us feel that our presence was an inconvenience to her work and life. Great start. The next SAP we met was a grumpy-looking Brit who looked like he did not suffer fools gladly, he seemed someone I certainly would not like to meet in a dark alley. I secretly hoped that underneath that savage outer demeanor was a loving, kind, and caring customer service advocate. Then, we went to the upper level of the back office and met SAP Accounts, who was extremely gay and friendly. All the SAPs were busy and could not spare much time. The other SAP was Kathy, who looked after all aspects of crew paperwork and payment, a great job for keeping out of the way of the passengers but sometimes the crew would be even more of a problem, as I would learn in time.

    The time now was about 3:00 p.m. and it was time for a guided tour of the ship. The cruise staff members were the entertainment officers made up of mostly gay men and bubbly hot women. They were led by the cruise director, quite a misleading title in my opinion, as it sounded like he was the director of the cruise, but he looked after the entertainment. Those duties included all the dancers and guest entertainers and coordinating all of the entertainment aspects onboard, so it was no easy feat. Our tour was to be conducted by self-titled character Number Two—as he liked to be known. He was British, very camp, and on the prowl for fresh young meat, which I had no I idea I was. Number Two was a brilliant assistant cruise director and had ambitions to climb the ladder as fast as possible. The tour took us through the glorious atrium and showcased the bars, public areas, show lounges, and eating establishments. The main interesting bars were The Wheelhouse, classic leather seated, marine decorated, members bar, without the required membership, it was best for cocktails and post- or pre-dinner drinks. The Voyagers' lounge had a stage that bands entertained on and art auctions were held there. The Outlook lounge was at the aft end of the ship and a nice enough bar with a stage for the second most popular productions and artistes. The main theatre was at the front, or bow, of the ship called The Grand Theatre. It was impressive and would give most land show lounges in the

UK a run for their money in terms of décor and sound and light technology.

On the ship, in total there were about 14 different places to buy a drink, many on the outside decks in the sunshine. The disco was at the aft of the ship right at the top giving the ship the look of a shopping trolley. Our tour ended back at the atrium, and I was still at a loss with ship directions. All the others seemed to be getting the hang of it, and I began to think I had missed some direction orientation or possibly was missing the "sense of direction" gene.

It was time for the first of our inductions, which are required of each crew member on each new vessel. Induction One was held in the crew bar where the accommodation department had set out forty or so chairs facing a desk with a couple of chairs behind them.

Our names were all checked off by the first officer and those missing crewmembers were chased by phone to attend. We took our seats as near the back as possible. We were shown a fifteen-minute video about safety at sea, which seemed set in the '80s detailing what to do in an onboard emergency, including fire and man overboard situations. It seemed many of the Induction One attendees had seen it all before and one even slept. He was woken by first officer, making him look a fool in front of everyone. He made an excuse about being very tired from the flight from Manila. Once the video ended, the first officer introduced us to the Commodore (Captain of the Captains). The Commodore was a very tall man who spoke very slowly and very clearly with a posh accent. He told us where to buy drugs in St. Thomas (behind the 7-11, apparently), but if we were caught we would face criminal charges and be sacked. He also shouted at us about sexual harassment. It was quite an interesting talk and certainly held everyone's attention; no one dropped off asleep during the Commodore's speech.

Straight after the end of the induction we were led down to Deck 2 for the first officer to show us how to open and close a water-tight door. These were steel doors that slowly slid closed to seal off an area in the event of a water threat. When opening and closing, there is a very loud beeping noise to alert everyone around that they are closing. The first officer managed to scare us into listening to him by relaying a story about a crewmember that lost his leg trying to get through a water-tight door and not allowing enough time. We all paid attention; knowing how these monster doors worked could save our lives one day or could cause serious injury if we did not know how to use them properly.

## Chapter 6: Sail Away

We were led into the back office past very long queues of passengers on Deck 6; embarkation was now at peak, and it was only under two hours until we sailed. Most of the noise at the desk was from the passengers asking about their luggage or chancing their arm asking for an upgrade. In the back office, our leader had produced a work schedule for us with details of what we would be doing for the next three weeks. It included spending time with each department and covering many aspects of ship life as well as plenty of desk time. It had allocated time for classes in the dining room out of catering hours, tour of the bridge and engine room, as well as accommodation department, crew office, food and beverage sector, and safety.

Alison had word come through that the purser was ready to meet us and say a few words. Mike was the Passenger Services Director and had a large office on Deck 5 behind the tours desk. We were led through the back door into an office with a large table in the middle and a desk at the end. A four-striped officer sat behind it, looking very busy and important. He spoke very quickly and with purpose; we introduced ourselves to him one by one. Debbie received the weirdest look in her jeans. Purser gave us a brief speech about ship life being different from land, paying attention to safety and security, looking after the passengers, and enjoying it. I had felt excited to have met the highest level of management that could be reached onboard and hoped that I made a decent enough impression.

We returned to the back office before that the whole ship, including passengers, had to attend a drill called GES (General Emergency Stations), which is part of maritime law. On everyone's life jacket was a letter denoting which muster station they had to attend in order to muster for life jackets in the event of an emergency. We were told that we were not assigned crew alert positions for drills, so we would muster with the passengers in the Theatre Deck 7 forward. That suited us as we felt we had done enough for the day already. We sat in the theatre as the crew took up their positions at stair ways and doors to clearly direct passengers to their designated muster stations. As we sat in a line of seven in the theatre, it filled up with passengers, holding their life jackets and looking like they needed directing. It did not take long for the whole place to fill up. The assistant cruise director, Number Two, was on the microphone talking to the passengers and keeping the room informed on what was going to happen during the next twenty minutes. The freckled faced, bubbly Brit was a good communicator who controlled the room well.

At that point, the bridge made an announcement advising all stairway guides to go to their muster stations, and a few minutes later we were joined by photographers, shoppies, and casino staff, all in uniform wearing their life jackets. They all took up a set position in the theatre, took off their life jackets, and stood waiting for the voice of the Commodore over the public address system, welcoming us onboard as well as giving a 10-minute talk on what to do in the event of an emergency. He advised us the crew alert signal of constant singing of the ship's whistle, man overboard, and passenger alert of seven short and one long blasts. I was from the Isle of Wight and had heard similar broadcasts on the car ferry during my trips across to the mainland and back.

On completion of the drill, we were dismissed to return to enjoying our cruise and returned our life jackets to our cabins. The boys returned to D320 and had a chat on our thoughts so far. I found it all very exciting, with never a dull moment, and I was looked forward to setting off on our first cruise.

The ship and crew was preparing to set sail, and we met up on Deck 7 forward, the crew bar, as a trainee group and sat with our mentor Alison. We talked about what was coming up in the next three weeks and our training schedules, which would begin with WAVES training the next morning. We had to take an exam at the end of the three weeks, so I would really need to concentrate; exams were not my strong point. The crew bar opened at 6:00 p.m. and we were already there; great start, I thought, as I did enjoy the occasional scoop. If truth be told, a lot of my life had revolved around the acquisition of malt, barley, hops, and water. Corona was the order of the day for me, and it gave me the chance to use my special account number for making purchases in this cashless society. There was no way of using cash onboard to make purchases for either passengers or crew, so you either put cash on a card through a "datacol machine" on the wall in the crew bar or hit the account number and then settled up with the crew office for those expenses on payday.

Our leader stepped in and brought the first round, and we made a toast to a successful course and future, I sat with Sebastian and Steve. Martin was still absent and clearly going to miss the ship due to delayed connecting flights; at least we had an extra berth and space in our stateroom for now. We all went out of heavy side doors, which led to outside Deck 6, which went all the way round the front of the ship. We had a full view of what was going on. The mighty Grand was making her way from the dockside and somehow seemed to move with great grace and ease. The Commodore spoke on the public address system and told us we were on our way and gave a weather update on the coming days. He also said that the sail away party was going on in open deck area with the cruise staff dancing and supervising the waving off of Fort Lauderdale. A few other crew members appeared to watch us set off as well. Clem appeared by my side very coolly, which made me happy to see a friendly face outside of the training group. Clem and I had a good talk about our first day so far, and I introduced him to the rest of the group, who seemed surprised I had made friends so quickly outside of the department. I had a really good feeling about what was in store for me over the coming months, combined with the sense of freedom at completing our first day. Being unleashed on this amazing cruise ship, just to wander around where I chose was a liberating sensation.

The Grand made her turn and started to glide down the gauntlet of condos and seaside homes out into the open sea. Many people were outside their homes waving us off, some displayed flags, and the sounds of Enya and her track "Sail Away" filled the air throughout the outside decks of the ship accompanied with the occasional sounding of the ship's horn. This was a moment I would always remember, that sail away seemed to mark the end of one life and the start of another. Exciting changes and opportunities were just round the corner with a new job, friends, and a lot to learn. This was the beginning of a great adventure.

# Chapter 7: First Working Day

Before I knew it, we were out in the open sea. There were two sea days before arriving at St. Thomas, St. Maarten, Prince Cays, and then another sea day before returning to Fort Lauderdale. We were seven-day cruising out of Fort Lauderdale and filling the ship up with Americans every week. Where they were coming from I had no idea, but the United States must have had a lot of people willing to part with their money to cruise. I had no idea at the time, but what I actually was witnessing was the beginning of a rolling snowball that was about to get bigger and bigger. The first night of the cruise was normally quite a quiet affair I was told. Most crew members were tired from a very long hard day's work, so below decks was not the hive of activity I was expecting after an exciting sail away. We ate in the officer's mess around 8:30 p.m., and then we went for a walk on decks before hitting the stateroom. I had arranged to meet up with Clem for a catch up at 9:30 p.m., so we met in the crew bar, which had picked up a little. We decided to drink vodka and cranberry and reflected on the fact that this time yesterday we had just met for the first time in that hotel bar. It felt like such a long time had passed, but it was only 24 hours. We were both on good form and spoke to loads of different people. I seemed to get on well with a bunch of five or six photographers, and we started drinking together. I called Clem over to meet them, people were already assuming that we were gay and granted I do have some androgynous characteristics. The photogs were good company and certainly drank well. I seemed particularly drawn to two girls who shared a cabin, Claire, a Kiwi, and Suzanne, a South African. Clem and I sat with them for the rest of the night and talked about our new adventure; both girls were on their second contract and knew how things worked, so I drained as much information as possible from them. The first night onboard drew to a close and Clem and I shut the crew bar down. A great partnership had been born, and we just hit it off immediately. I staggered back to my stateroom around 1:00 a.m. and woke up my cabin mates in the process of putting myself to bed as I stumbled about in the darkness.

    Our meeting time for our first morning's training was in the restaurant at 9:00; it was a sea day and our first full day onboard. I awoke to the taste of cranberry juice gone wrong in my mouth; the cabin mates took turns in the shower. Showers at sea are great. They are hot, powerful, and you just don't want them to end. As for the toilet, it seemed to be powered by a suction system developed by NASA. When you press the flush button, it produces a noise so alarming and sharp that you feel that if you were still sitting on it your insides would be sucked into the bowl too. We donned our whites and made our way to the mess for breakfast. I did not feel 100%, so did not opt for much food, just coffee—strong coffee. We met up with our fellow trainees in the restaurant and Alison was already there. Stef looked very rough, and she had experienced a rather enjoyable night in the company of the safety officer who had wooed her at drills. The other three girls looked ready to learn. My hangover was fading fast with the prospect of having to concentrate. We all sat down around a large round dining room table with our oversized WAVES manuals (our new bibles) and started to go through the principles of CRUISE, the credo, and what our new roles would mean.

Alison was no nonsense and spoke with decent common sense and purpose. She talked and we listened, well except for Stef who felt the need to interrupt every 15 minutes with irrelevant questions. Not sure if it was just her hangover talking or just a need for attention, but it certainly was slowing us up. Alison pulled her up on it after a few hours, stating that we needed to crack on if we were going to cover all the topics. Her job was to prepare us all for the WAVES exam in under three weeks' time. We all had to pass it if we wanted to work for the company.

The hours of learning passed and before we knew it, we were off to lunch in the officer's mess. Lunch in the mess on a sea day was a busy affair. The general working shift pattern seemed to be start work at 8:00 a.m. until 12 p.m., then back at 3:00 p.m. until 7:00 p.m. On sea days, most of the ship's company would go for a nap, sunbathe, read, or watch a movie, depending on relaxation choice. We were given until 2:00 p.m. off, so we all decided to find the crew deck on seven forward for a dip in the crew pool and catch a few rays. We went off to our cabins to get our swimming gear and met at the crew bar area to find the crew pool. Again I would have never found this place without help from the others; there were what seemed to be secret doors that lead up above the crew bar to the open deck area. The bright sea air and sunlight hit us as the heavy metal door was opened and released us out into the incredible day outside. The crew pool area was not massive and was overlooked by the imposing and allowing officers of the watch an eyeful of shoppies and dancers in their swimwear. There were plenty of blue plastic sun loungers for us all to relax on and a very small pool and normal sized Jacuzzi, but at least it was something. There was only about half a dozen other crew members there; the whole area could probably only hold about 70 people in comfort, which is not many when there are over 1,100 crew members onboard.

    The boys braved the small cold pool while the girls sat and talked in the sun as the ship cut efficiently through the water, for me this was another defining moment in my life change. Just comparing this day to a month earlier in my old life in Eastbourne was amazing. My new colleagues and I were splashing about in the sun on the front deck of one of the world's biggest and most spectacular cruise ships; it certainly felt like an achievement. I felt free and happy; the future held untold excitement and opportunities. After an hour or so we had to go in and get ready for our afternoon work, which would be followed by our first formal night.

    Once we were changed back into our uniforms after our pool break, we made our way through the ship's corridor and atrium areas; it was apparent that most guests were getting ready for formal night. The desk was quiet for the first time this cruise and photogs were getting backdrops set up at key locations for formal photos. As part of our training schedule, we were due for some desk time and were assigned a buddy to shadow and learn from. My buddy was a petite, pretty American blonde girl called Grace; she was the best JAP on the desk and knew most things that were required for the job. She had pride of place at the busy part of Deck 6, and I sat and watched and learned from her for the next two hours. She coolly and calmly dealt with each passenger in a professional and fitting manner, I immediately liked her and we got on very well. I was a very keen and enthusiastic student and soaked up her knowledge as fast as she could give it. I really wanted to be a success at this job and shine to show the senior officers that I was worthy of respect. Most passengers had questions about the ship, admin, lost luggage, upgrade enquiries, noise complaints, and complaints about different services and occasional crew members.

  On formal night there were two welcome cocktail parties hosted by the Captain: one for first sitting dinner and one for second seating dinner passengers. The passengers would gather in the atrium and enjoy a free cocktail whilst the captain would make a speech and introduce the senior officers. After that, passengers would go on their merry way to have a formal photo and dinner before the entertainment. The first formal cocktail party was at 6:00 p.m. and before then all JAPS on the desk had to change into 12A uniform, which consisted of black trousers, black jacket, white long sleeve shirt, and black tie. But if you were on duty to attend the cocktail party, which we were as trainees, we had to change into our formal rig, which consisted of black trousers, white formal shirt with bow tie, and white jacket with stripes. So I had to change from the whites into 12A for two hours on the desk and then change into formal rig for the cocktail party. It's not too confusing if you know what bits go with what and are not sharing a cabin with two other blokes and their luggage.

There we all were in D320 with bits of different uniforms scattered all over the place. I needed the 12A uniform to get back on the desk and the other two boys needed formal rig as they were attending the first sitting of the Captain's cocktail party. I would be attending the second party. We finally managed to fit the uniform jigsaw together and set off on our allotted tasks. Walking through the busy atrium, I bumped into one of the photogs that Clem and I had been drinking with the previous night. The South African girl, Suzanne, had been sourcing extra supplies of camera film and was on her way to her Deck 5 backdrop. She looked totally stunning in a semi see-through sequined number that clung to her tiny frame with incredible detail. We spoke for a few minutes and flirted quite heavily with each other. I did not know it yet but that first formal night, with us meeting and flirting, her dress, and our conversation would stick in my mind for years to come as the start of something special and another defining moment. I wanted to kiss her there and then, and I had a feeling that she pretty much felt the same way. It was quite an exciting sensation when that kind of electricity occurs between two people that do not know each other that well. It certainly gave me a warm fuzzy feeling inside, and for the rest of the evening, I would be floating. Talking to girls back on land did not seem that easy or pleasant.

    I managed to find Deck 6 and the front desk on my own for the first time and placed myself next to Grace, who was dealing with a passenger that needed to hire a tuxedo. I was amazed at all the guests and how they had transformed themselves into such a smart looking bunch. Gents were in full tux mode and ladies in flowing gowns and little black numbers. The atrium was the heart of the ship at this particular time and certainly the place to be. The photogs were taking shots of smiling couples on different backdrops. I flashed a smile over at Suzanne and Claire who were shooting the atrium stairway pictures with their new supply of film.

    I put my mind back to the job at hand, which was watching and learning the master at work. All I needed to do was mirror what Grace was doing and I knew I would be a success. The desk was quiet as the main focus for the passengers at this time was on the free cocktails and canapés being offered by the smartly dressed bar stewards and the string quartet playing on Deck 5. After about 10 minutes, the Cruise Director (CD) appeared on the Deck 6 balcony area and gave a brief welcome speech before introducing the master of the ship and Commodore of the fleet. Everyone applauded as the tall imposing figure stepped out and took the radio mic from CD. All he was missing was a sword by his side and he certainly gave the impression of a man in control of his fleet.

The Commodore spoke for about five minutes giving detail of the ports to come, weather outlook, and numbers of different nationalities of passengers onboard. Each group of guests cheered when it was their turn to acknowledge their part of the world or state. It was a nice touch but obviously one that had been used before and would be used for many years to come.

Once the Commodore introduced the senior onboard officers for their bow and applause, the crowds dissipated into the various dining rooms and the atrium areas were quiet again in readiness for the second sitting guests and their Captain's cocktail party. This was the one that I would be attending premiering my formal mess kit. Grace sent me off to change and get ready for the event, so back off to D320 I trotted to make my third costume change in the space of just a few hours. The other two lads were back in the room and gearing up to go for dinner, but I managed to con them into attending my cocktail party too for a second drink, so we could all eat together afterwards. I threw on my mess kit and we all went off to the atrium to be seen by our leader Alison who was in attendance with fellow SAP, Kathy. She had coached us that our main role at these parties was to be visible, chat with the passengers, and mingle. So we all split up to try to find someone half-sane to chat with. I bumped into Stef and the girls. Debbie had substituted her jeans for a ball gown, as her uniform was not arriving for a few days due to the size issues. We chatted for a few moments before awakening to the fact that we needed to be talking to guests and not each other and could feel a stiff telling-off coming from Alison if we did not comply. There were a lot of senior officers about so we needed to shine as fresh enthusiastic, keen trainee JAPs.

I became very aware that I had no idea what to say to any passenger, and my knowledge of anything nautical was minimal. I latched onto a group of four smart looking guests and tried making polite chit-chat, but they were busy in their own group, so I failed to impress and manage a full conversation. I then found an old couple and they took pity on me, and I managed to talk to them for what seemed ages but was only five minutes. This was more difficult than I had imagined. I grabbed a passing cocktail; I had always managed to hold a better conversation with a glass in my hand for some reason. The drink I was holding tasted as bad as it looked; it was some sort of fruit cocktail, but it did have some alcohol in it, so as it hit my nerves I made my way toward a group of ladies. They seemed a lot more interesting and, for some reason, they assumed I was a deck officer, so I had to attempt to astound them with talk of the bridge and navigation and what the first officer was like. Their attention was, luckily for me, diverted before I went into too much detail of things I had no idea about, as several senior officers with a lot more stripes than me had arrived, so I made a break for it.

The next person I bumped into was Clem in his tuxedo, he resembled James Bond, but only cooler. We were very pleased to bump into each other and made a plan to hook up for a few beers later on that night. Seeing Clem gave me a feeling of just how small this massive ship was at times and certainly gave me a warm feeling that it all seemed quite local and similar to a small village. I was not going through this alone. Clem gave the impression that I had been friends with him for years and was extremely laid back and cool, but at the same time, on the inside he seemed to lack some element of self-confidence. I felt he was searching for something. I could not put my finger on it, but he was just very open, honest, sharing what he felt, and that brought out a sincerity and kindness in me that I had not explored for a very long time.

 Back at the cocktail party, I made a walk past the desk to throw a wave a Grace and show off in my tux, even though everyone was wearing one. She seemed as impressed as I feared she would be. The Commodore made his speech and the cocktail party came to an end again. We trainees made our way to the mess for dinner where most of the conversation revolved around the occurrences of the day.

 The wardroom was where officers and petty officers could go and drink. It was just above the mess and had a small well-stocked bar, including a friendly barman, cream leather chairs, and small sofas. There were two big windows overlooking the sea right at the aft end of the ship. We had a perfect view of where we had just been by the churned up sea from our propellers. The wardroom also had a powerful music system, a dart board, and the room looked like it could only fit about 30 people in, but I have been assured that it fit several hundred on party nights. This was no such night, and it was quiet with the exception of about five British engineers who sat at the bar in their formal wear.

Our entire group made our way around the sofa area and ordered up. I stepped up and got the first round, I was still in amazement at how cheap the drinks were: $1.10 for a Corona and the same for a vodka and sprite. The mood was relaxed and The Red Hot Chili Peppers "Californication" was playing on the stereo. Suzanne and Claire came up and had a quick scoop in between printing formal photos in the lab on Deck 4. The cruise staff came in for a quick one in between hosting doors at the theatres, and dancers popped in and out for water between shows. Clem arrived and we stepped up the drinking pace. By this time, most of the trainees had left, so Clem and I carried on as I was still in a very happy place. Our first sea day was coming to an end and what a day it had been. It was coming up to midnight and I was ready to turn in. The wardie was just getting interesting, though, as shoppies, dancers, and photogs all came in for a drink after their shifts were ending. Clem was friends with a lot of the musicians, so I began talking with them also, mostly about music and what they did. This was a period of great discovery and getting to know people. I left Clem to close down the wardroom and go to the nightclub, and I went to find my stateroom. When I got in, I discovered that we had inherited another roommate. Jane had joined us and was in bed with Steve, so it was now three boys and one girl. We still had our Aussie to come. Sebastian was already asleep and the lovers were chatting. I fell into my bunk and drifted off to the motion of the ocean.

# Chapter 8: Learning the Ropes

The next day was sea day two before we would hit our first port, St. Thomas. I awoke with a slight twinge in my head that soon washed away with a hot shower. I forgot Jane was in the room and I left the shower with a towel loosely wrapped around me. Steve reminded me there was a lady present. I felt like reminding him that I had not invited her and was not consulted about this extra roommate in our very small space. But then I remembered how tall he was compared to me and that I may need a similar favor one day, so I kept my mouth shut.

We were to meet at the training table restaurant for the first hour of the day and then work our schedules. After a quick breakfast in the mess, we got together for our lesson, but upon arrival, I could sense that Alison had an air of anger and upset about her that I had not previously sensed. Once we were all assembled, we received our first telling off. Her voice came across with disappointment and annoyance that her instructions had not been followed. The night before, Stef and Debbie decided to hit the disco on formal night in their own clothes—even worse Stef was wearing jeans. They had been spotted by the night manager and told them to return to their cabins. Luckily it was quite early on before the bulk of the senior officers and purser had arrived, so they were spared that embarrassment. We were now all officially grounded off passenger deck areas until further notice when we could be trusted to stick to the rules of the ship. Nice going,

Stef—one day at sea and we were already in trouble and banned from drinking in passenger areas.

With the telling off and sentencing out of the way, we got started on the first hour of the day's lessons from the WAVES manual. After that, we would be split into two groups and go to visit the various departments for two or three hours at a time to get an idea on what it was all about. I still felt guilty about what had happened the night before and that we had let our leader down, even though not all of us had been involved. I was determined to put extra effort in to ensure that I would show how keen I was to be a success in this role. Our visits of the day were to begin with the crew office to learn about what goes on there. We were dropped off by our teacher and left in the hands of crew purser. She was about the same age as Alison and looked no nonsense; she was, however, charming and seemed very good at her job. She explained the goings on in the crew office in great detail.

There were three roles in the crew office: senior assistant purser (the boss), assistant purser (looking after the daily paper work), and the JAP crew, who was an Italian lad with strong espresso breath and slight body odor. The office had window hours in the morning and afternoon where the AP and JAP served the crew with money exchange, safety deposits, general enquiries, and phone cards. There were 1,113 crew members onboard the ship and all had to be treated like they were internal customers. Each of the crew office team members explained their roles and daily duties. The Italian JAP was sent out for coffees so I joined him for a chat and to help carry. He explained that you carry a certain amount of respect if you work in the crew office because you have the best interests and welfare of crew members at heart; you also pay them their cash wages and look after their money in the crew safe. He explained that he was going to be working at sea until he made it to the top as a purser; he had good ambition, but terrible breath. Our morning in the crew office went quickly, and I had a decent grasp of what they did there by the time I left. It certainly would be a good escape from being around passengers, if I was given the opportunity to work in the crew office.

 Back to the mess for lunch. Now that it was sea day two, it was busy again with officers ordering off the menu quickly to get their afternoon hours of rest in. It was only my second full day and I already felt like I should be falling into that "afternoon nap" routine too. After lunch I went back to D320 to join the rest of the boys, and we decided to take our WAVES manuals out on deck to read them. We were due back in the dining room in the afternoon for lessons with Alison. Out on decks the sun was shining but the wind was present; there is something magical about being at sea and surrounded by water. The ship was swiftly cutting her way through the deep blue. Our destination was St. Thomas at 8:00 a.m. in the morning. All the outside passenger areas were very busy, and we could not locate a free quiet area to relax, so we opted back for the crew deck. It was quiet again with the exception of a few waiters in Speedos sunning themselves. We started to read our bulky ring binders in the afternoon sun, chatting about what we had experienced so far.

At 3:00 p.m., it was time to go and join our class for more instruction. We were told that Martin had landed in St. Thomas and would be joining us the next day. Alison also broke the news that after our three weeks' training onboard, we would be sent to various ships around the fleet. There was no guarantee whom we would be with, but there was the possibility of a few staying on the Grand also. The prospect of staying on this ship excited most of the group as she would be heading across the Atlantic to Europe in a months' time, and the cruising then would be highly exciting with amazing itineraries. Personally, I had no actual clue what the ship or any ship in the fleet were doing and was quite surprised and worried about everyone else's knowledge on the subject. At this stage I was very easygoing and would go wherever the company or the ship took me. I was just very grateful for the chance to even be there. This was just so much cooler than my previous life of running the hotel and being in the same place every day. I could see the worry for Jane and Steve at that announcement; their relationship's defining moment would be approaching at that three-week passing out parade.

The afternoon's lesson flew by with learning about the ships in the fleet and the history of the business and who did what in the ship's company. It was all very interesting and I did enjoy learning about it. It had been a very long time since I had to take an exam or study, and I was aware that I was out of practice. I had a sickly feeling in my belly and was very nervous already about failing the exam and being sent home. I was determined for that not to happen, so I decided to fully apply myself and learn the manual. The manual would go everywhere with me, and I would digest and pass with flying colors ... I hoped.

At the close of the teaching lesson, we were dismissed for the evening and would meet up again in the morning to see our arrival at our first port of call: St. Thomas. We would be helping with tour dispatch, getting the passengers off the ship on tour, and then some of us would go on tour and the remainder of us would have a few hours off and spend some time on the desk and see what the assistant night manager does. As we made our way back to our cabin, I was reflecting on the amazing change that I had made to my life and how happy I was already at this new set up. I really did not want to lose this chance for anything. This training course reminded me of the movie An Officer and a Gentleman during their basic training before "passing out and getting jets." I obviously played Richard Gere in my white uniform during that particular fantasy.

Back in the room, we made space for our new arrival, as we were already four in a four-berth cabin and about to become five. I sat on the bed and read through my manual for a few pages, and then I decided to go and try my laptop out at the business center. The business center was a small room with six computers for passengers' internet use. I had heard you could get connected with a laptop through a special cable. I eventually managed to find it on Deck 7, opposite the Mexican restaurant. Upon arrival I was met by the computer officer, a medium built and light-haired Canadian named Simon. The greeting was not exactly a polite one, and I certainly got no help whatsoever in my connection enquiry. I was told that the laptop connection was $15 per minute and not very reliable, the business center was for passenger use only, and then was suitably ignored for the remaining few minutes that I was awkwardly hanging around. I returned to the cabin with my tail between my legs after encountering my first bit of real negativity onboard.

I decided to go to the desk and sit with Grace and feed off her positivity for a while and learn more standard responses to the thousands of different questions that are thrown at the desk on a daily basis. The desk was quite busy with lots of questions about what to expect at the first port of call, the location of shops, walking distances, and general questions from people who had left their brains at home before they went on vacation. I am exactly the same though. When I am on holiday, I do not want to think, and many of the things that are happening are out of my comfort zone, so it is easy to be cynical about it and mock the stupid questions, but we all do it. That is why Grace and I were so good at the desk; we understood people and we both empathized with each stupid question on an individual basis, making every passenger feel like an individual and that their enquiry was of huge importance.

There was another English chap on the desk I was meeting for the first time. He was called Ross, and he was a very well-spoken and switched on lad. We got on well quickly; basically, we were from the same country and had that in common. Lisa was also working on the desk; she was tall, pretty, and Swiss, quietly spoken and gentle. It was a good strong team on Deck 6. The current desk task was to input the credit card details of all the passengers so that they would be all set for automatic check out and all the bills would be paid on the night of departure. Each JAP had a selection of letters, Grace had J through M, so I helped her input them into the computer system, which was just basic data input. Once all the cards were inputted, the Accounts SAP would apply for authority through GCS, Global Card services, and the owners of any cards that were declined would be contacted and asked to produce alternative methods of payment. This would mean that all our little ducks would be in a row for a smooth turnaround day, and everyone would be able to pay their onboard accounts so we would not have any surprises.

    Several hours on the desk passed quickly with work as well as getting to know the team members; a few senior officers noticed that I was putting in extra time. It was no hardship though; I was really enjoying learning about this new lifestyle and colleagues. But I was ready for a beer; as our shift ended, Grace and I walked to crew areas and headed to the wardroom for a beverage. I was getting to know this remarkable girl quite well in a very short space of time and liked everything about her. She was clever, funny, pretty, and her parents owned one of the biggest manufacturing companies in the United States. She also had a boyfriend, though, but not on this ship. From what I had heard, he was a bit of a legend in ship terms. He had just been promoted to the next level up from us, an AP and had done most of the crazy things you would have associated with ships. In his earlier JAP days, he and his cabin mate had one of the CRUISE credos posted on their cabin door. It stated "WE NEVER SAY NO," and apparently many a lady took them up on their generous offer. Grace had shared with me that he had gotten into the habit of watching porn while making love to her, which I believe did not please her very much. Why should he need those images when he was with her? That is the funny thing about ship life. You do get to know people a lot quicker than on land, and you build friendships and relationships at a very fast pace. This really suited me as I was a very social person and loved having lots of friends.

It was past 10:00 p.m., so the Wardroom was getting a little busier. Clem arrived, and we sat and talked and closed the bar again. The cold beers flowed as did the time. I really had a best friend onboard in Clem. We were both very comfortable in each other's company in remarkable circumstances on this massive cruise ship.

# Chapter 9: Tour Dispatch

The next day was our first port, St. Thomas. We had an early start as we were meeting in the Theatre to help the tours team dispatch the passengers that had purchased a shore excursion. There were over 1,000 passengers going on tour, and it took great organization and a level head to get the operation done smoothly and swiftly. The tour office had one SAP, one AP, and three JAP positions; tours were quite a niche job. Once you were in tours, you quite often stayed in tours, especially at AP and SAP levels. It was 6:30 a.m. and our job was to put different colored stickers on passengers and direct them to their seats before they were led off by the escort to get off the ship and onto the tour buses at the quayside. Steve, Debbie, Stef, and I greeted the first wave of passengers and stuck the correct sticker on them and showed them to their seats; it was simple, fast, and efficient. I was still a little delicate from the previous night but managed to charm every passenger I met. A lot of the passengers took it upon themselves to arrive early and throw a spanner in the smooth workings of the dispatch, so they had to stand around with nowhere to sit. Very soon the theatre was empty again, and we were waiting for the second wave of touring passengers. Once we had dispatched the last of the passengers, we would be joining a group and having a half day on tour to get a feel for what it was like to be a passenger on tour.

We had to race to our cabin and quickly change from our whites and then join our groups and escort them off the ship. Panic set into me as I had real trouble finding my own way around, let alone being in charge of a group of passengers and leading them down to the gangway and off the ship. This massive responsibility was weighing heavily on my shoulders. I asked Stef and the others if they had any concerns about getting lost, and they did not. Great—just me then. I felt very alone all of a sudden.

I went to change, and on the way to my cabin and on the way back, I ran the route to ensure I had at least some idea of where to go, but there were two gangways forward and midship, so I could get allocated to either. Back in the Theatre our groups were getting ready to leave, so I was put into position and stood next to my group of about 40 passengers and awaited which direction I was required to travel in. The JAP tour was on the microphone keeping everyone informed with timings. The moment came and I was instructed to take the group to forward gangway, which was the best option for me because it was the closest. I lead the way out of the theatre and my guests followed in confidence. Little did they know I was already going wrong and missed the staircase taking us down to Deck 6. The pressure must have gotten to me and I ended up amidships in the atrium walking past the desk to some strange looks from my peers. My fears had become a reality and I had gone wrong. I could hear the radios on the desk asking about the whereabouts of my group on the dockside and the theatre advised that it had been dispatched already. I had two choices, double back to the forward stairs and risk going even more wrong or take them down the midship gangway and claim stupidity. I decided on the latter but still kept the pretense up with my followers that all was under control and we were going in the right direction. I did have a bit of a sick feeling in my belly and felt my bottom wobble a bit once I appeared midship. At the gangway, all the passengers logged out one by one with their cruise cards, and we were met by the other JAP tours who seemed surprised that I had been sent to midship rather than forward, where the coach for the group was waiting. The consequence was us all walking half the length of the ship again in the morning Caribbean heat to reach our tour transport. It wasn't the biggest problem, but I was annoyed at myself for getting my one simple task messed up. I vowed to learn the layout of the 109,000-ton vessel.

 I coyly joined my group on the bus. Most of them were aware that I had gotten us lost. I now had to spend the rest of the morning in their company with them knowing of my potential stupidity. They were probably just relieved that I was just the escort and not the guide. Once the last guest embarked the coach our guide got on the bus and introduced herself. Before she could finish her welcome speech, an elderly woman stood up and asked if we could please wait for her husband as he was not onboard yet. I had zero hours experience in dealing with missing husbands and had a blank look on my face as all the passengers and guide looked at me for a decision on the next course of action. My worst fear had been realized. I had the attention of all the tour participants, and I did the only thing I could think of and spoke to the passenger asking about when the woman last saw her husband. She said that he "just popped to the toilet" as the tour was being dispatched from the ship, and she had not seen him since. I saw one of the tour team just on the dockside and jumped out of the coach and sought advice. He got on the radio and enquired if there was a gent looking lost wandering about who answered to the name of Mr. Rees. Time stood still for what seemed about ten minutes while the whole coach was looking at me, the trainee JAP, for answers. Eventually Mrs. Rees said that she could see her husband waving from the top of the gangway, but I had a feeling that something was amiss. He was not moving with much urgency toward the coach. As he got closer, he was waving his hands in the air and seemed to be shouting something. It was apparent that he had a serious toilet accident and was walking like a cowboy without his horse. I was panicked. I had not experienced D & V (aka "Dolly and Vera") since I was in the hotel in Eastbourne and we were hit with a winter vomiting bug—what a mess that was. I ran out of the coach and advised Mr. Rees that his wife was coming off now and the tour JAP alerted the public area supervisor and medical department for assistance. At least we kept him off the coach and away from the passengers. He would be looked after onboard. Not a great start to my first tour—getting lost and then having to leave Mr. and Mrs. Rees behind.

Finally, the tour set off from the pier. It was basically a scenic coach drive for those passengers that could not walk very far, not very exciting but better than being in an office. We saw Beacon Point, which offered views of the surrounding British Virgin Islands and the Skyline overlook where we saw the Charlotte Amalie coastline. We stopped at the St. Peter Estate, formerly a private hideaway of the famous. St. Peter Estate boasted wonderfully landscaped grounds and classic Caribbean architecture. The highlight for me was the rum punch refreshment before heading to mountain top located at 1,400 feet above sea level.

    By the time we returned it was time for lunch in the mess and we were blessed with a few hours free to study before starting back at 3:00 p.m. for lesson catch up and then meeting the assistant night manager at 6:00 p.m. Back in the cabin, the others had returned and we had a new arrival. Our stray JAP trainee Martin from Australia was in the room. He was a small-framed chap with a pale complexion; he looked frail enough to snap and as if he had not slept for three days. His eyes were bagged and bloodshot like someone who had been sleeping at airport terminals; he assured us that he had been trying to sleep at these terminals and had really struggled to get here, having suffered delays and flight drama. He spoke exactly like you would expect an Australian would, but seemed like he would jump out of his skin of you shouted "boo!" to him. I was lacking in certain confidences, but Martin was so far in his shell he was literally hibernating.

    We all chatted and Martin told us of his travels and that he had been on a ship training course before but had to go home for compassionate reasons. Even though he was late arriving on the scene, he already had a head start on the learning, which was good for him. Martin was granted the rest of the day off to sort his uniform out and recover for a fresh start the next day, while the rest of us went to watch St. Thomas sail away before meeting the assistant night manager at 6:00 p.m. The assistant night manager was the highest level of responsibility for a JAP on the ship. The shift started at 6:00 p.m. and was handed over any issues from the SAP on duty and then had to collect the chits/signed payment receipts from all revenue locations across the ship—mostly the bars, and there were plenty of them. Once all the chits for that route had been collected, the night manager would return to the back office and check them for irregularities and mistakes and wrongly posted items. If this was done correctly, fewer incorrect charges would be on the wrong stateroom accounts and fewer passengers would be at the desk disputing charges on the last days of the cruise. Passengers have to sign for anything onboard, so if there was a charge on an account, there should be a chit with a signature on it. All the chits were stored in date order in a cupboard until turnaround day and all the bills settled.

    The assistant night manager was Mike, a very tall, camp kiwi who had been in the job just over a week, so he was still getting used to it. First impressions showed that he seemed quite arrogant and a bit of a bully, I thought. He was in charge until the night manager came on duty at 11:00 p.m., so basically the power had already gone to his head already. Mike showed us what he did, and we did a round with him watching him pick up the bar chits from all the locations. It was certainly a job that would keep you fit with all the walking of the decks and bars. As assistant nights, you were a bit of a free spirit and your boss was the night manager, who in this case a very direct Brit, she seemed highly efficient and really knew her stuff. We stayed around until she came on duty, and then I went to meet Clem in the crew bar for a few beers. It had been a bit of a long day and the next day we were in St. Maarten with another early start.

    The crew bar was quiet. We talked and then I headed back to the cabin to find a full house, including Jane. I washed up and took my place on top bunk, and we all chatted for a while like we were on a camping trip. Martin was awake now but said he could still sleep for days. He had not gotten out of bed since his arrival, but the next day, he would have to be on the desk with the rest of us.

# Chapter 10: St. Maarten

The morning came too soon and we all took our turns in the small shower and washroom and getting changed. Jane kindly went back to the girl's room to get ready to give us gents a little bit more space and privacy. That morning we were split up again, and those who had not gone on tour the previous day went ashore, and the rest were on desk duty. Our start time was 7:30 a.m., so we had no time for breakfast; luckily, Grace was on duty so I could sit with her and make the most of her skills. That day, we were in St. Maarten, an island of the Dutch Achilles, it is half Dutch and half French. The ship tendered into the Dutch side where there were quaint streets and opportunities to buy lots of crap and eat in Indian, McDonald's, or local fare restaurants. It was small but seemed to be well geared up for visitors.

I had no clue of the concept of tendering, but I was about to learn. Basically, tendering is when there is nowhere for the ship to dock, so everyone has to get off the ship by way of smaller vessel or lifeboat. These are normally the ships craft or local shore side craft. A lot of the passengers knew as much about tendering as I did and asked the same questions that I asked first thing when I started my shift. How long does it take? Can I smoke, eat, go to the toilet, etc. on the tender? The desk was mainly busy with questions about the tendering process. The tour passengers got off first in the main and then independents passengers got a tender ticket from the explorers lounge and were called by color. It was a process that worked well and organized the passengers so chaos was not caused down by the gun port doors where the tenders were embarked.

We were on the desk until 11:00 a.m. and then we were allowed free time until 4:00 p.m., so I had lots of time to learn about the front desk, lost and found, floats, credit cards, and PIFs (Passenger Information Forms). We were never short of anything to do and we were learning the standard responses to all the questions passengers ask. But there were always unusual questions that never failed to amaze us. Like, do these stairs go up? what time is the midnight buffet? and when will it stop raining?

Martin and Stef were working on Deck 5 but finished at the same time that I did, so we planned to go ashore for a walk. Even though Martin had just arrived, he had a good amount of knowledge about the life onboard because he had already done half the training course. Stef, on the other hand, was clueless but sailed by on her charm and ample breasts. The morning shift flew by and before long we were meeting at the gangway to get on the tender to go ashore.

The majority of passengers had already gone ashore by this time, so getting a tender ashore was no problem. It was my first experience on a ship-to-shore tender. They were driven by the petty officers in the deck department that ran a continuous service throughout the day; the landing point was right next to a beach bar that had tables and chairs outside, and it seemed a lot of the crew members were settled in there already. It was all very colorful and kiosks sold cans of beer for a dollar, and both Stef and I took them up on that offer. Martin was still finding his mojo so he had a Coke for a dollar fifty. I liked it there already—a land where beer was cheaper than soft drinks. We walked around the main street in town that had many outlets selling local goods, electrical items, drinks, and services. As we walked past one of the colorful locals we heard, "Weed?" said in a slow deep Island accent and nothing else. We wisely kept on walking. The buildings were very colorful and of a colonial style and certainly gave the town a sense of character. Charming though it was, I could see that coming here every week for six months might not give me the motivation to leave the belly of the steel beast that brought me here in the first place.

  After an hour or so of wandering around, we stopped off at the bar by the tender point watching all the passengers getting back from tours and milling about while we had a drink. A lot of the crew seemed to be having a good time and ordering platters of food and cocktail refills; it made me smile to think this was how to spend free time. Drinking beer in the sun was my favorite pastime. I was a happy man, and it was still only my fourth day onboard this new life.

  Getting back onboard the air conditioned ship was very refreshing and it was like stepping into a fridge after being in the hot desert. Martin and I had time to rest in the cabin before our 3:00 p.m. learning session with Alison, so I lay on my bunk with my WAVES manual and dropped off for a short nap. After a shower and freshening up I head back into the dining room for the continuation of lessons. Debbie finally had her uniform on because it had arrived from the head office. Martin had finally awoken from his jet lag, and we were finally a unit of fully dressed Trainee JAPs. The learning had certainly stepped up a gear, and we were working our way through the WAVES manual with swift purpose. The goal was to finish the manual and learning about all aspects of ship life in good time to then spend the final few days revising and going through anything that we were not sure of in preparation for the exam.

Due to our time off that day, our lesson went onto 7:00 p.m., by which time we were ready for some food and went directly to the mess. There were always jugs of red and white wine available in the mess, mostly for the benefit of the Italian officers, but we dove into those with our meal. I ordered a surf and turf off the menu, which even though it was good, to my normal standards it appeared mass produced. It did the job though. After a few beers in the officers' mess, I met up with Clem. The album getting heavy rotation was still Californication by the Red Hot Chili Peppers and it was fast becoming the soundtrack to the cruise. It seemed that the ship's company was tired after another day in port, and it could be seen in the amount of early nights going on around the ship. Clem and I would stay up through it. I networked through the departments, buying drinks and meeting a mass of amazing personalities, each with stories and tales that could keep the average land-based dinner party amused for hours. Everyone had a different story behind what they were doing on this ship. They were all from different backgrounds and countries and cultures, and everyone was friendly. This was the sort of environment I thrived upon and I soaked it up. I always was the sort of person who wanted to be everyone's friend, and now I had the chance.

Day five was a visit to an Island called The Cays, which was a private beach managed by the cruise company, where some of the ship's catering facilities were transferred over from the ship, bar services, and barbeques. It was basically a day at the beach and it seemed a big workup for the crew due to the tendering, as all the drinks and food had to be transferred over before the passengers. It was a very early start for some. We were not going to get off that day, as we had a WAVES lesson and then desk time. After that, I had business center in the afternoon for a few hours, which I was not looking forward to after my initial meeting with the grumpy computer officer.

The island that hosted The Cays was part of the Bahamas; the crew did not tend to get off there due to the lack of things to do. You could not really get away from the passengers anywhere, so it was a big day for afternoon naps. There previously had been grumbles from passengers who were bitten by beach bugs, so there were wasn't much motivation to get off there. I thought I would do it at least once to say I had been there, but not that day. Instead, we all met in the restaurant for WAVES training with Alison, who did seem a little worse for wear from the first time. She claimed that it was just because she "ate late," but we all knew that look, and it was a hangover. She was slightly gentle with us. Nevertheless, she was still no less informative and knowledgeable answering all our relevant questions and all of Stef's irrelevant ones. Martin had the most information about ship life in his brain from the previous half course, so I sat next to him and pulled from his skills. Sebastian was as arrogant as ever, still trading off his father's name, but people, especially ship people, do not suffer fools gladly and will only tolerate a certain amount of name-dropping to open doors. It was raw talent and natural ability that was the real currency onboard. I had bags of that and seemed to get on with everyone, but Alison seemed like a closed book and revealed very little about herself.

    Debbie was enjoying looking like the rest of us now that she had her uniform. Claudia was a very clever lady, and even though she was quiet, she certainly contributed as much if not more than anyone. Jane and Steve both complemented each other well and it would certainly be a shame to see them split up, but those decisions were out of our hands. The eight of us—all very different and from different backgrounds—got on well, and I was certainly sure that these three weeks would be something I would remember forever. It was such a unique experience being on this massive ship with so many interesting people, and that was just the crew.

    Many of the crew members remained on the ship in this port so our little city was busy, especially at the mess from lunch. We sailed at 3:00 p.m. with all onboard at 2:30 p.m. We had an hour free after lunch, so once again, we went to the crew deck for a dip in the pool and to lie in the sun for a while with the sounds of the passengers on their pre booked wave runners buzzing in the background. I kept my WAVES manual with me to read as I was very aware of the fact my brain was out of practice at learning these days. I certainly had the drive not to fail the exam and have that embarrassment hanging over me, especially if everyone else were to pass.

My afternoon was to be spent in the business center learning what the JAP does there. I hoped that I would not encounter the computer officer who had an attitude of being unhelpful and grumpy. The JAP at the business center was Sophie, a moody Scottish girl who had done many contracts and not been promoted as of yet. She certainly had a chip on her shoulder about it. She was not bad looking, but not good looking, and she was very hard to communicate with. She was not at all easygoing, and the opposite of me, so the three hours we spent together were hard work. I had dated a Scottish girl back in the UK; she was nice but a bit crazy. I did have fun with her but she was not for me in the end because I did not really want a girlfriend. I just wanted to go out with my friends without having to report my actions to anyone. I did find the accent attractive though.

She explained her duties, while she did her best not to help passengers with their internet issues and was as difficult as possible. I found it a lot easier to be nice than to be difficult, and it is much more rewarding for both parties, but some people cannot see that. Nevertheless, I watched with interest and was certainly learning about the internet, something I had no real knowledge about beforehand. There were six computer workstations, one cable connection for laptops, and 2,300 passengers—so demand far outstripped supply and most of the computers were in use most of the time. Sophie managed to be her most rude when she had to inform people that their 15 minutes on the computer had expired. I was convinced there was a nicer way of talking to these people who had paid for a cruise. It was $7.50 for 15 minutes and when a passenger sat down, a note was taken on the chit receipt of the time in the bottom right hand corner of the PC. Then, they were rudely advised that time was up in thick Scottish accent, awkward but attractive.

  In my capacity to be able to get on with anyone, I did my best to enjoy the teachings of this JAP who had no clue about customer service, but I was glad when the time came to close up. Sophie rarely smiled and did not seem to have any drive or lust for life, so she was slightly taken back by my huge enthusiasm. It was certainly a hard few hours and at certain cringe worthy moments of poor service, I wished the ground would open up and swallow me, but it is difficult when you are in identical uniforms not to be associated. I would have just liked a T-shirt stating, "I am not with her."

  As the door locked on the small room with six computers in it, Sophie asked if I was going to the mess for dinner. I declined because I was drained from her negativity, so I went back to the cabin to catch up with the rest of the gang. Both Steve and Sebastian had been to the business center and were aware of how miserable Sophie was. We all decided she just needed to get laid and cheer up. It was a job none of us were willing to do; she was not ugly, but certainly not a looker. The girls came around to pick us up for dinner and told us that the crew disco was that night in the crew bar and we should all go and check it out. It started late though, so it was recommended that we eat and "rest up" first for an 11:00 p.m. start.

  We decided to have a later dinner and hung out together looking at our WAVES manual for a few hours in the cabin. Steve and Jane went for a walk and talk, making the most of each other's company in case the worst should happen. The next day would be the last sea day of our first cruise before docking back in Fort Lauderdale; the queues were already mounting at both front desks with passengers needing to check out their bills and complain about what they were being charged for as well as needing the gratuity envelopes to tip their waiters and stateroom stewards. The questionnaires had been delivered to the staterooms, so they were being filled in, which made up the score of the cruise that would gauge the guest satisfaction levels. We were due to spend most of the day on the desk shadowing, watching, and learning what goes on during this important day. But that was tomorrow, this night was our first crew disco night and we were going to have fun. After dinner, I met up with Clem in the wardroom for a few cold ones; it was the second formal night of the cruise and quite a few officers were eating out in one of the specialty restaurants as passenger demand would be less due to the lobster being served to the passengers in the dining room. It was about 10:00 p.m.

and the plan was the meet the rest of the JAP trainees in the cabins to go to the crew disco together; it felt good to dress in our own clothes and be going out.

    We went out to the crew bar together and would certainly be classed as "very fresh meat" ready to be eaten and taken by many of the players amongst the crew. The crew bar was a dark and dingy area at the best of times, but this evening it looked particularly bad. The actual bar part of the crew bar was in a separate section from the dance floor and main seating area and had sticky lino with seating for about 40 or so, with a jukebox and dartboard. It was connected to the disco and dance floor and seating area by two doors, one large with a bank of about twelve fruit machines along the wall. The dance floor and disco area had bench seating for several hundred and also sticky carpet. The bar was not very busy considering there were around 1,200 crew members, there was probably only about fifty people scattered about, making it seem very quiet. The DJ was playing loud electro music and not one person was dancing. It seemed we had been excited for nothing and our crew disco debut was a washout by 11:20 p.m. A few of the team decided to hit the hay due to an early start on the desk, a few of the other JAPs off-duty formed a bit of a posse. Stef, Sebastian and I decided to wait it out for improvement. There was a bit of a scene starting as midnight hit and more and more crew members appeared and the place filled up. For some reason, I was talking to grumpy Sophie from the business center, who with the aid of a few drinks, decided to confess that she thought I was "quite attractive" and decided to give me her cabin number. I thanked her for her kind offer but was horrified on the inside. There was no way I was going there. She went to bed, and I carried on drinking and talking to the team. Grace had arrived and we were getting into a good talk about ship life and relationships. I naively felt that I was in with a shout if I played my cards right, as we seemed to get on very well.

The night wore on, and I found myself at the my most "socially confused" since arriving onboard; time passed fast and the drinks flowed faster and I made the astonishingly bizarre decision to take Sophie up on her offer of going back to her cabin. A decision I would have never made in any sober state, but it just seemed the easiest option at this late stage of the night where I could not really talk properly anymore let alone perform my emergency duty if I had one. I stumbled out of the crew disco and started my search for her cabin on the tenth floor—a deck I had yet to visit. Upon arrival, I noted quite a few senior officers' cabins were around this area, so kept my noise level to a minimum. If I was quiet and subtle, no one need know about this indiscretion except me and miserable Sophie. I was going to do my best to cheer her up. I stumbled about various floors, mumbling to myself and arrived at cabin number 10023 and quietly knocked on the door. I was horrified to find Grace answer the door. Was this all a clever ploy to get me and Grace together on the quiet? No such luck. She was certainly not expecting me, and I had to quickly explain who I was looking for to get myself out of this hugely embarrassing jam. She explained that Sophie was in cabin 10032 across the hall and, like a big sister, she took me to the correct cabin, knocked on the door and dropped me off. Sophie smiled for the first time since we had met when she saw me at the door and dragged me in. I could hear Grace giggling to herself in the corridor as the door slammed shut. What had I let myself in for? It was apparent she had been asleep for the last two hours since she left the crew bar and I had been drinking. It made for a very awkward encounter, which I can probably honestly say that she had a lot more energy than I did. But the deed was done and I had broken my ship duck virgin status, with the most unlikely candidate.

# Chapter 11: Mad Morning

I awoke with a blind panic. It was dark because there was no porthole, and I had no idea where I was or what time it was. I could be late for my desk duties and be in line for a written warning or I could have been asleep for 15 minutes. I still felt the effects of the crew bar in my brain and in my mouth. I could not find the light switch and swiftly remembered that I was not in my own cabin and I was missing the presence of three other blokes. As I stumbled about looking for clothing, my jaded and spinning head was playing back the events of the night and it dawned on me where I was and what I had done. I managed to find my clothes before literally falling out into the corridor. It was morning, early but bright, and I was lost on floor 10. I exited out a door which I thought would take me into more familiar territory, but I was greeted by the bright early morning sea air and strong sea breeze. The door nearly swung back on me the wind was so strong. I was on the outside deck on Deck 10. My mind computed that it was sea day before Fort Lauderdale, but that was about it. I still felt seriously dizzy as I wandered lost along the floor 10 outside deck. I let myself back into another door and was in passenger areas, by more luck than judgment. I was doing what was known as the walk of shame, walking back to my own cabin in the previous night's disco clothes and still half cut. I eventually managed to find D320 after one of the longest walks I had ever been on. Sebastian and Steve were just finishing getting ready as they were on the 7:00 a.m. desk shift and gave me the "we all have an idea what you were up to last night" stare. I started work at 8:00 a.m. so opted to return to my bed for another half an hour. It was a wise choice. I sank into my top bunk duvet never wanting to leave. Martin asked if I was okay, and I answered in the affirmative. I said we could go for breakfast in 40 minutes if he wanted to. I shut my eyes for about 10 seconds and it was 40 minutes later and Martin was ready to go.

 I had to sort myself out. It was the busiest day of the cruise for us, and I would be on the desk all day with Grace. Even though we got on well, I knew she did not tolerate messing about at the desk, and she knew exactly what, and who, I had done the previous night. I already felt like I had made a massive glaring error. Even though there were 1,200 crew members onboard, it was a very small community and everyone knew everything else about everyone else. Martin had me ready by ten minutes to eight so we could afford a swift breakfast. In the mess I saw Steve and he was the first to bite, "Good morning!" he said in his strong, loud, and proud New Zealand accent. "Good night was it?" I nodded as I picked up my orange juice. He continued, "I heard rumors about last night mate—Scottish rumors."

 I hoped that the ground would open up and swallow me. Grace must have spilled the beans at the desk during the early morning shift. It was juicy gossip and hot off the press, so I could not be bitter. I was fair game. But just when I thought things could not get any worse, the Scottish rumor arrived for her breakfast before her shift at the business center. Now I really wanted to run, but as she was next to me in the buffet line, I greeted her with a cheery good morning and commented on how rough I was feeling after last night. She nodded a quiet good morning, got her breakfast, and sat next to us. I suddenly realized just how small the 109,000-ton floating village could be.

That was the end of the breakfast torture for me as Martin and I escaped to the desk. I arrived next to my "super-grass colleague" and set about the day's work. There was a very long line at both desks as the passengers made enquiries about their room accounts, demanding to see what they signed for. That is the time that you find out if the assistant night manager had been doing a good job checking the signed chits or not. It really made the difference between a smooth disembarkation and a difficult one, and it also saved the company money. Everyone was getting ready for passenger disembarkation the next day, which was organized by calling off the passengers in luggage color tag order depending on what onward arrangements they had. It was a very carefully coordinated operation organized by the AP position of "practica," or not in Italian—"passenger administration." It was a very busy time at the desk and it was all hands on deck as the phones never stopped ringing but were seldom answered due to the relentless lines at the desk. The benefit of being busy was that both my hangover and fatigue were soon forgotten and also the time flew by. Before I knew it, I was tucking into burger and chips in the mess before a few hours' break to study for the WAVES exam.

Back in D320, Martin was asleep again and Steve and Jane were chatting quietly while I sat on my bunk as the slight motion of the ocean relaxed me to sleep with my work. The afternoon shift came around swiftly and we had a back office debriefing with Alison on how we were getting on before going back to our posts on the desk. By then, I had worked out that my future would be on the desk because that is where most of the JAPs end up, unless you are singled out for one of the more special jobs like crew office, business center, or best of all, assistant night manager. I did not mind the desk. I was really good with passengers and enjoyed getting stuck into the problems. My only slight concern was the $15,000 float that we would be given and were required to balance every night.

The desk was the hub of the ship as far as most of the JAPs were concerned. The deck officers thought that of the bridge, the photogs of the gallery or lab, and the casino teams of their tables. Each department had their own central universe from which their onboard lives would gravitate.

On Deck 5, I met a JAP named Luka, who barely looked up from his computer as he was introduced and just said "I want my life back." He was coming to the end of his six-month contract. He was a bald, Italian pushing 40 and seemed really bitter. Ship life can get to people like that and when that time comes, it is time to leave. Some people become bitter and twisted, moaning at everything and everyone, stating that "things are not like they used to be," and in the end, the passengers suffer. Luka had received a written warning for being rude to an American passenger the previous cruise and from our introduction it seemed to give him no desire to buck his ideas up. I decided I would never get like that and vowed to leave this position if I ever became a menace to the team.

Back on Deck 6 and with Grace as my desk coach, I was getting the best training available. Every response was professional, qualified, and delivered with conviction and confidence. The passengers loved her and she enjoyed helping them out. All I had to do was learn the automated responses and deliver them in a similar vain. Before long I was feeling confident enough to start trying to help passengers but found it hard because I did not have a float and most of the enquiries involved some sort of cash transaction. I reverted back to being her shadow. The hustle and bustle of the day before turnaround sent the ship into a spin of activity. Everyone had a task to do, everyone knew their jobs, and it was a hive of motion. Below deck, the M1 corridor was being prepared for the thousands of pieces of luggage; roll cages were assembled by accommodation staff and the teams had begun clearing the long passenger hallways of baggage. It was a mammoth operation that required detailed organization and team work. It only seemed a short while earlier that the luggage was being loaded on for the start of the cruise and now it was getting ready to be unloaded again.

The desk and the JAPs were as busy as I had ever seen them. The whole department was in overdrive, helping passengers as they came with their issues and problems. Some had bought art during the excitement of the art auction and could not pay for it; there were passengers enthusiastically filling envelopes with cash for their room stewards and waiters, and there were people complaining about everything from rude bar stewards to the food in the Italian restaurant. If you were a neutral, it made outstandingly entertaining viewing, but we were not spectators, we were the targets and had to provide responses to keep the passengers at bay until they left the ship. Most passengers were paying their stateroom accounts with part cash and part card; all the stateroom accounts would be settled by their allocated credit card after the last bar closes tonight normally around 1:00 a.m. But most passengers would like to see their bills before the payment is processed so we would have to print them out.

    I was good at talking to people, and I seemed to be able to communicate with the Americans quite well. I just treated them with respect and genuinely did my best to ensure that I helped them as much as I could. Before I knew it, the shift was coming to a close, and we had a replacement, Ross, waiting to move into our position. That was a great help because we could leave the forty-five people in the queue at the desk without feeling too guilty and without being shouted at as someone was stepping into our space at the desk. The next step was to transfer our amount of money over the $15,000 floats over on the computer system and balance the float and stamps in the back office. Grace's float was very well organized and she carried out the process with outstanding efficiency. I did not really grasp what she was doing as she did it with haste and my mind was already on that first cold beer in the wardroom.

We walked down the stairs in the back office to Deck 5 and left the desk from there because it was less exposed to passengers. Grace instructed me to walk with purpose, look straight ahead, and not make eye contact with any of the many lost looking guests. It could open a can of worms and could hold us up. I obeyed, and before too long, we were safe "underground" in crew areas away from the hundreds of questions and passengers problems.

Grace and I had a swift dinner in the mess together and she jokingly asked if I was seeing Sophie again that night. She bid me good night and went straight off to her cabin to phone her man. I made my way back to D320 and managed to con Martin into coming for a beer with me in the wardroom. I still did not compute the fact that I should really stay in and study. It was a very quiet night in crew areas, especially after the previous night and with the busy day coming. I learned that the night before turnaround was not a big night for the pursers department. Martin and I sucked a few cold ones back and then retired to the cabin to rest and prepare for our first full turnaround day.

## Chapter 12: Turnaround Day

I awoke in pitch black again: "Note to self: must get used to no natural light." I was just relieved that I was in my own cabin this time and had no headaches except a slight twinge of fatigue from the week I had just experienced. We were all due on the desk at 7:00 a.m., which stung a little; we all took turns to get ready quickly and left in convoy to the back office to pair up with our more experienced full status JAPs. There was already a queue at the desk and the ship was minutes away from docking at Fort Lauderdale to say goodbye to all the passengers and pick up a new load.

Grace was not due into work until later, so I was without partner. I was told to shadow Ross with Sebastian. Ross was also very efficient and helped the passengers with great speed but with slightly less sincerity. He was British through and through and was slightly patronizing toward the more challenging questions the Americans would ask. Some JAPs had differing patience levels to others; I certainly was very patient. Sebastian and I crowded around Ross to help him in any way we could and to take in what was going on around us. Most of the questions were about passenger room accounts; some would queue for 20 minutes to pay the bill that already had been settled automatically by their credit cards. Others would get in the queue just because it was there and they expected to be getting off the ship at the end of it. Some would be checking when and how they would be disembarking the ship. They all had luggage label tags that they would have to show at the gangway upon disembarking.

The red luggage tags were normally the first ones off the ship, and they were mainly for people with early flights to catch. The AP admin position would organize the disembarkation and coordinate or make the announcements in the public areas to inform passengers they could get off and where the gangway was located. This process would continue until the ship was empty; meanwhile, below on Deck 4 the luggage was being transported and placed in either direct transfer to the airport or to a hotel or kept in a holding area for collection in the terminal building.

The queue at the desk never seemed to die down and the work was continuous. There was no breakfast break, but bacon and egg rolls and pastries were brought into the back office. The SAP accounts would be in control of the back of the house, having all departments, like photo manager and spa manager pay into him for the cruise one at a time, and passenger relations SAP would be in control of us desk jockeys. SAP Accounts would tell the JAPs one at a time to transfer as the passengers were getting off the ship and the queues were dropping off. Ross's turn came eventually and we watched with care as he counted his float to balance and placed the surplus amount, which should be the same as the amounts of transfer on the computer system, into an envelope and handed it to SAP Accounts. Each JAP would be left with $15,000 float again, which was a combination of stamps and cash and "trash."

Trash was everything that was not cash that we exchanged for cash with the passengers, like checks and credit card slips. Every time we accepted payment or cashed a check, there was a set process and boxes to complete on the credit card slips and back of the check as well as calling Global Card Services on the satellite phone for authorization. There was always a time delay of a few seconds when using the ship's phone and it took some getting used to; even the most experienced caller could end up talking over the person on the other end.

    The ship was being emptied of passengers quickly, and it showed, because the desk had no queues of passengers around it and the time had come to wrap up this cruise and prepare for a new one. The desk looked like a bomb site with rubbish and paperwork everywhere. The first purser walked past at that exact moment with pomp and grace and instructed us to get it sorted before the PSD saw it. We cleaned and packed up lost property, completed lists, and helped Ross with his float jobs. Sebastian was his normal arrogant self, being taught but thinking he knew it all already, but really, he had no idea. I identified to myself that he would be dangerous in this job, especially when dealing with a $15,000 float. The final announcements of the morning were being made and Alison came to pick us up to give us a tour of the different types of stateroom, while they were not occupied by passengers.

    She was making subtle enquiries regarding our morning performance and seemed quite pleased, so that made us all happy that we might be allowed to stay on for another cruise. The tour of staterooms began with her leading a trail of eight Trainee JAP ducklings through the now empty corridors of the ship. The room stewards were busy at their carts, tending to their sections as we passed in our week old white uniforms with half stripes. The first stop was a regular balcony room; we all squeezed into it and looked around the quite surprising tight space, but there were eight of us and Alison in it. I opened the sliding door and stepped onto the balcony into the moist humid Fort Lauderdale morning. It smelled like the dock it was, filling the nostrils with an unpleasant mix of fuel, food, and a light twinge of sewage.

    Even though the stateroom was a small space, it was bigger than our two inside rooms with four a piece and all our belongings in them. Our next stop was up a few decks to a mini suite. Debbie was already complaining about the amount of walking and stairs and wanting to know when we were going to eat, shortly followed by Martin, who even though he was as skinny as half a rake had a big appetite. Some people are motivated by food and others are motivated by beer. The ship was a whole different beast when it was empty and was like a shell that needed to be filled, a body with no heart. It was quite surreal to walk around in this quiet state. The mini suite was a vast improvement with a seating area and mini bar section as well as more precious floor space. These were serviced by the ship's butler service from this grade up. In total, there were approximately 200 different categories of room, many with very slight differences but they could be classed as an upgrade in the brochure.

Our final stop was to the suites and the grand suite. These were much grander and took us all by surprise with how much luxury was available onboard if you had the money. The grand suite was like an apartment with two balconies and two bathrooms, one adjacent to the master bedroom. It was currently retailing at $17,000 for this cruise and was always booked.

After our tour, it was half past eleven and embarkation began at high noon. There was a race against time to get the ship ready. It was a really amazing feat of organization to turnaround the ship's staterooms so quickly. We were granted a few hours off to have some lunch, go ashore, or make some phone calls. We all went to the mess together to eat the paltry offerings, and then we split. Some went to the cabin, others went for a walk, and I decided to have a look ashore and source a phone. It was a warm day in Fort Lauderdale and everyone dockside was busy. I had very little idea of where to go, so I followed a random crowd. They lead me into the terminal building and then out to the terminal car park with buses, cars, and taxis spread around an area the size of a concrete football field dropping people off and picking them up.

I followed the crowds to a bank of payphones and joined the queue in the midday sun. There were about twelve payphones and all were in use with crew calling home, mostly Filipino men. I had no idea who I was going to call or even what time it was in the UK, let alone how to dial the code. I waited in the nonmoving queue for about half an hour before deciding to give up and wander around aimlessly. I decided that it was more time effective to go ashore with a purpose each time rather than just explore independently. Time off was very tight and could not be wasted. I could have been having a rest or reading my WAVES manual rather than just wandering aimlessly and achieving nothing.

I was actually pleased to get back in the cool air conditioning and safety and security of the ship. I retired back to D320 to freshen up before the afternoon pre-cruise lesson and before desk shift began. Sebastian was snoring on top of his bed with his uniform and shoes on. Steve and Jane were kissing and talking under their bunk bed, and Martin was sat up reading on his bed. I rested for a short time before the lesson with Alison and then continued onto the desk for embarkation turnaround duties.

We spent an hour with Alison and she reminded us about what to expect at the desk during passenger embarkation: big queues, lost luggage, stateroom upgrade requests, dining room enquiries, and passengers asking for directions. It was always wise to carry two items with you at all times as a JAP: a copy of the ship's daily newspaper with guidance of what was happening where on that day on-board, and a map of the ship, which came in a foldable pocket form. I needed it for myself more than anything else because I was still very shaky on what deck I was on and where anything was. The other main tip was to stick with your JAP shadow and listen and learn. I was confident that I had the best shadow of them all, so I would follow that advice to the letter; others were not so lucky. Martin had the moody Italian Luka and Claudia had

Marco who was also coming to the end of his contract and did not care too much.

As we approached our respective desks, we could see and hear the queues and the loud American accents. My stomach was turning with anticipation, and fear of what was coming. At least we were not let loose on our own yet and still had the umbilical cord of an experienced JAP with us. I was starting on Deck 6. Every workstation was occupied with JAP and passengers queuing around the atrium. Grace was in the first position directly in the line of fire. I joined her as she was in mid-flow of explaining to a couple that, "Over 10,000 pieces of luggage are brought onboard today and it does take time to get them to everyone's staterooms." The guests wanted their bags right then so they could unpack and the luggage also had the husband's medication in it—nothing was ever simple. After a short discussion, the passengers were appeased and went off to one of the bars to calm down. Grace had explained that their bags would be with them soon and faked a call to the accommodation supervisor making enquiries. The next ten passengers were the same sort of enquiry, asking when their luggage would reach their rooms and every phone call was the same. Others asked about the possibility of a stateroom upgrade, with each JAP simply pointing at the signs on the desks advising that "the ship was sailing full and there were no alternative staterooms available."

Where the passengers were embarking through the gangways on Deck 5 and Deck 6 a member of the cruise staff would welcome them and the security teams would code their cruise cards and get them to pose for the security photo in the gangway camera. It was the same process that we went through with our key card on embarkation.

The first purser walked past the desk and took Sebastian, Stef, and me to one side and told us to stand on the gangway to greet the passengers as they embarked. This hour period was the most intense part of embarkation with most passengers getting on due to the arrival of several charter flights. With uniformed officers greeting the passengers, it gave the impression of a slick and professional ship indeed and may well help in the passengers' service questionnaires. I had no idea at the time, but it was a shrewd move by the well-heeled first purser.

I enjoyed that part of the day, and I was certainly at my cheeriest just being able to say "Welcome onboard!" to embarking passengers. They were mostly happy to see us and to be onboard after the rigors of check in and security. They had not yet reached their staterooms and discovered that it was too small and that their luggage was missing and that they were on the wrong sitting list for dinner—happy days all round. But my peace was not to last because it was soon time to get back on the desk and meet the very same passengers in a very different mood. Don't get me wrong. I am making it sound like it was all about complaints. There were many happy passengers too. It is just that when there are 2,400 passengers coming onboard there are a percentage of moaners and people with issues, and they all migrated to our desk.

Several hours passed on the desk and it flew by very quickly indeed; when you do not have a moment spare, time does fly. Before we knew it, the GES was being called again, and we took up our positions in the Theatre to watch the drills again. On the way back to the desk, we took a detour with Alison to check on the progress of the luggage distribution to give us an idea of what was involved. It was total chaos down on the M1; bags, suitcases, suit hangers, and sweaty accommodation assistants were everywhere you turned. Thousands of pieces of luggage were being sorted by deck and wheeled by roll cage into the respective lifts. It made me glad I chose the pursers department to work in, that's for sure. Our turnaround tour continued onto the gangway and terminal building to be shown how check-in finished off and was packed away at this late stage. The ship was still waiting for about 20 independents who had been delayed by a late flight. The person in charge told us that the chances of them making the ship for sailing in fifteen minutes were very slim. We were instructed to get back onboard promptly as the gangways were being prepared to be stripped down.

Before we knew it, we were back on the desk and it had quietened down a little due to many of the passengers taking their positions up on the top deck for sail away with Enya blasting out of the speakers. I remember that moment giving me goose bumps the previous week as we left on our first cruise and now we were entering our second week of training. We completed our last hour of work on the desk and then we were finished for the day.

We certainly felt finished for the day. The group was exhausted as we made our way to the officers' mess for dinner and then an early night. It was the first time in a week I did not go to the crew bar or wardroom.

# Chapter 13: Falling

All five of us awoke to the ringing of Martin's very unfriendly, loud alarm clock. It was truly one of the most unpleasant noises at any time of day, let alone the noise to take me from my distant slumber. It was a cross between a wartime siren and the scream of a child not getting its way, which is incidentally about as close as you can get to breaking the sound barrier. We all hated the alarm but it did the job. Jane got up and kissed Steve and went back to her room. Sebastian jumped up and dove into the bathroom selfishly before anyone else had the chance. Martin cursed as he realized that he set his alarm too early and went back to sleep, and I dozed while I waited for the bathroom. It was a strange situation all five of us in one tiny stateroom with all our belongings for six months, but for some strange reason, it kind of worked. We wanted to secure our roles as JAPs and get the dream of a perfect travel and work balance. Even though we had our moments over the last week, we did seem to get along quite well considering this was really a room for just two people.

It was sea day one of cruise two, and I started to see a pattern emerging from a distance. I had awoken the freshest since I joined, due to a great night's sleep and lack of crew bar or wardroom. We were all back in the dining room today to continue our lessons on learning the contents of the WAVES manual for the exam next cruise. I had breakfast of coffee and toast. In the classroom, we were waiting for Stef who had become rather friendly with the Welsh Safety Officer since inductions, and rumor had it she had been spending long periods of time in his cabin. She eventually showed up and we got lectured on the importance of being punctual on the desk and showing respect for our work colleagues—thanks to Stef for that. As we worked our way through the procedures of what to do in ship emergencies and reviewing what we had learned from our last few days shadowing, it was clear how far we had all come in just one cruise by being on the desk and learning the ropes from someone else with experience.

Stef managed to still press everyone's buttons by asking irrelevant questions and wasting our time. Our time was precious and in short supply as the pressure of the exam was looming; we did not want to get sent home for failing. Alison was her normal firm but fair self and started to dismiss some of Stef's more stupid points, as did the rest of us. As we went through the WAVES manual a page at a time, we made notes and did our best to take it all in using our varied methods of learning. For me, it was writing things down as they were told to us. I figured at least I was inputting the information on paper and had an outside chance of remembering it. It would be interesting to see how everyone would get on in the exam, as there were varied levels of intellect among us. I knew that as long as I studied, I would have a decent chance of passing, so my destiny was in my own hands. Martin knew more than all of us so he would sail through. Sebastian thought he knew more that all of us, so he might stumble during the actual written exam. Steve was a steady guy and with him and Jane learning together they would both be fine. Claudia was methodical and clever and would have no problems with the material, but Debbie was a bit slower and had a bit of a chip on her shoulder so could be in trouble. As for Stef, goodness knows how she would do, but I feared the worst.

It was the first formal night of the cruise and we were expected to be seen on decks during the cocktail parties again, but we were not permitted to attend the passengers disco due to our ban after the non-uniform episode from the previous cruise. The photogs were out and about at 3:00p.m. setting up their backdrops for the photographs. I bumped into Suzanne and Claire and did some more top-level flirting. There was certainly some kind of connection between the petite Suzanne and myself, and I certainly enjoyed talking to her. It was classic "I like you and you like me" flirting, and we just wanted to know more about each other and were hungry for information. She was easy to talk to, interesting, and seemed to be interested in what I had to say, which for me was a miracle in itself and seemed too good to be true.

We had a break after which we had to attend the pursers back office meeting, which I did not enjoy very much and was not looking forward to in the future. Attendees were given tasks to contribute to the discussion before the meeting and had to add substance, which was not something I felt I could do with any great effectiveness. The assistant night manager covered the desk at 5:45p.m., while the meeting went on and was hosted by the SAP PR and SAP Accounts. This meeting was focused on the CRUISE credo and how we use it on a daily basis—nonsense I know, but all JAPs had to sound enthused. I was still keen and wanted to impress the stripes. After the meeting, we had to help with inputting credit card details in the system with our shadows; our shifts finished around 8:00 p.m., and I was ready for a few beers after staying in for the first time the previous night. At the meeting I met fellow JAP Southampton supporter Tracey; she had just come off night shifts, so we got talking and decided to go a few rounds at the "pub" as she called it, better known as the wardroom. Tracey was a good drinking friend already it seemed. She listened well and spoke sense. She was tall, blonde, and funny, but not my type, so she was safe from being part of my journey of infatuations. There was only one on that list at the moment and she was South African and working hard at formal night taking photos while I was building new bridges. Tracey knew all the Brits, especially the bridge and engineers, and she introduced me to all of them. We became involved in their rounds at the bar, and I felt part of the Brit club that certainly felt like home.

    Most of the British officers were going out on decks to eat and have a drink in the passenger bars, but Clem had arrived after his evening hour of work in the atrium plucking his guitar and joined us for a few rounds. He got on with Tracey too, and we spent the night talking and exchanging stories and drinking with whoever drifted in and out of the wardie; we were like permanent fixtures for the night. I was on the cans of bud in a "fresh from the fridge" chilled half pint glass and they were going down smooth. Before we knew it, the bar was calling last orders, and a gaggle of dancers arrived thirsty after the show. We all ordered a few more each. The atmosphere was fun filled and Red Hot Chili Peppers came on for the encore. I finally hit the sack worse for wear after 1:00 a.m., but had a great night just talking to so many different people. I got on with them all, and everyone seemed to like me too. It was strange but it gave me a real sense of belonging.

It was sea day two of cruise two, and we were really stepping up the pace with the learning and powering through the WAVES manual learning about ship life and the role of the pursers department. Our department was all about administration and customer service. The deck and engine officers ran the ship, but the pursers ran the hotel. I had started the day with a well-earned hangover and was not elated when I saw the signs on the M1 of the crew disco that night. I had no interest in it at that moment, but by noon, I would probably be up for it again. It felt like I was back at school or college with every night a new opportunity to meet new people and especially new girls. What I did not know was that a lot of the ship hotties were spoken for and in a ship relationship, but what I did not know did not bother me. I was like a kid in a candy store and as far as I was concerned there were endless opportunities to meet interesting women, even if my motivations were for companionship and having a drink and a laugh. But for the time being the most important priority was to get through this exam and make the best possible impression on my peers. So far, it was going quite well. I am one of the most polite people, thanks to my parents. My dad always said that he would excuse everything in life except bad manners, which is something I took to heart.

The afternoon saw us in the classroom deep in discussion about desk duties and how the ranking system worked. I could feel a slight tension and urgency building as everyone was keen to pass and also very keen to know their fate and where they would end up at the completion of the three-week training course. In time, the question did accidently pop its way out again. Alison advised once again that our futures would not be disclosed until the exams had been taken and results distributed. I was slightly averse to change and could really do with staying on this ship, as I had met Clem and already built up strong relationships with many departments. I felt at home and comfortable on the Grand and it was the biggest and best in the fleet; for some reason I was proud to be part of that.

Class ended at 7:00 p.m. and I decided to hang out on the desk with Grace and keep learning from her. I really wanted to feel at home and confident with my desk duties and the best way forward was to get stuck in. The desk was not busy, so we talked about the WAVES manual, and she went through her float and balancing and trash procedures. Grace was missing her fella and was grateful for the company, I believe. I provided a suitable distraction, and she was certainly making me feel welcome. She finished at 9:00 p.m. and we went for dinner in the mess together joining a few of the other JAPs just finishing. After that, we went to the wardroom for a few drinks and met up with Sebastian, Steve, and Jane, who were just leaving to rest before the crew disco. After an hour or so, we said goodnight, and I went back to the stateroom to catch up with the rest of the guys and see if we were all going out together. From our previous crew disco experience, things did not really heat up until at least midnight, so it was important not to "go out and blow out" too early.

    I got changed at a leisurely pace and we all left for the crew bar just before midnight. It was already a lot better than last time and there were groups of different departments in the same area all chatting over the loud music. We based ourselves in the actual bar area where you could actually hold a conversation, and Clem was already there with some of the photo department, including Suzanne and Claire. I knew immediately where I would be based and sat next to Clem near the photog girls. Clem was getting on really well with Claire, so that left me and Suzanne to spend some overdue time having a really good talk and getting to know each other. She had a very soft, caring accent and seemed very gentle and kind. I already could tell she had a good heart and was certainly the sort of person I could be with. I could see that she also had eyes for me for some reason, and it seemed to fit. The time seemed to fly by and the drinks flowed as easily as the conversation. Before I knew it, I was being dragged to the dance floor by the rest of the trainee JAP team and was being berated for ignoring them all night. We had a good dance and I was just hoping that I had not lost my chance with Suzanne by leaving her to dance with my trainee team. I could just tell that we wanted to kiss each other.

I went back to the bar area for a refill and saw that Clem was now getting on even better with fellow JAP Claudia—very close indeed, smoking and talking. Claire and Suzanne had, as I feared, disappeared, and I decided to hit the dance floor again in despair, trying to find the woman I was getting on so well with. The dancing was fun though and the floor was packed with all departments, but mostly Filipino men having a great time. I loved it and was certainly having fun. It was just about to get better as Suzanne reappeared by my side, saying that she thought that she lost me. "My thoughts exactly," I muttered to myself. We danced together and were getting closer and closer until I could hold out no more, and I leaned forward and kissed her. It was magical and we just wanted to keep kissing and take it further. Until I realized that I was actually on a dance floor full of people. But it must have been going through both of our heads and the chemistry was intense as we left the crew bar hand in hand. She led me through the heavy door and up the stairs onto the crew pool deck. The warm evening Caribbean air hit us both and we continued to kiss as if we were the last people on earth. We laid down on one of the blue sun beds and really got to know each other very well indeed; it was an absolute experience. Not once did I think of the fact that we were making love outside on the crew deck and that it was an arresting offense in the United States, which was the law we were sailing under. Also, anyone could walk out at any time and catch us, but the biggest factor was the crew pool was overlooked by the imposing bridge and the officer of the watch could be sitting there enjoying the show with his binoculars or even worse not enjoying the show and on the phone to security to come and breathalyze us both and lock us the in the brig for indecent exposure. I finally looked up at the bridge and noted that we were just out of eyeshot. I have no idea if that was judgment on Suzanne's part or pure luck, but I was thinking the latter.

As we lay under the Caribbean night sky in each other's arms, it was an almost perfect moment, and most certainly one of the most memorable intimate experiences of my life to date. We eventually uncoiled from each other and made ourselves presentable for the walk back to the cabins. It was decided that we best retire to our own rooms even though I wanted to stay with her for the night. We kissed goodnight and made our way back to our homes under the early morning light.

I awoke quite fresh considering the lack of sleep and the amount I had drunk. It had been my first excellent disco night. I was obviously in a good mood but had a feeling that fatigue would be hitting me in a few hours. We were in St. Thomas for the second time in two weeks and were granted shore leave after a morning on the desk watching our mentors sell stamps and advise passengers on what to do with the day. Suzanne and Claire popped by to say hello at the desk and to invite me to go on a tour with the photo department the next day in St. Maarten for a few hours. I checked my schedule and it was clear for the required time so I accepted. I checked if Suzanne was okay with a kind of half cool reassuring Han Solo wink and smile; I hoped that she would realize that I was thinking of her. Steve was first with the taunts about the previous night, enquiring if "I was going to stop once I had completed all the ship's nationalities on every disco night."

    We had a few hours off and I wisely made the executive decision to rest so that I was fresh for the rest of the day's challenges. We would be in class that afternoon, and I needed to be on the ball. I retired to D320 and fell into bed noticing that Martin was already there in his bunk. That guy certainly likes his sleep; the jet lag must have worn off by then. I awoke with the normal confusion of having no idea where I was or what time it was due to the lack of natural light in the inside staterooms. Class began at 3:00 p.m., so I had time for a quick shower to freshen up and uniform on and then went off to school with my classmates. As I was walking, I did stop for a moment to take in that I was very fortunate to be here and these moments would not happen again, especially with having a course for three weeks to learn a new job at reasonable leisure. This could be the first and last time I did anything like that in my life. From talking to my fellow experienced JAPs, not even a quarter of them had the benefit of a training course and were just thrown in at the deep-end straight on the desk with a $15,000 float and very little guidance or training. We arrived at the dining room and sat with Alison going through the WAVES manual and completing the spot tests in preparation of our exam the next week. I vowed to myself that after the next day, I would just focus on studying to get the best possible result in the main exam and try to stop having so much fun. This was a difficult thing to vow when there was so much fun to be had: shows to watch, people to meet, parties to attend, restaurants to try, cocktails to test, and girls to talk to. But I would certainly do my best.

It was safe to say that all members of the training group were enjoying themselves and having the time of their lives, especially Stef who seemed to have had a quiet life up until then, but was certainly making up for it and having a ball. Claudia who was as quiet and clever as ever was soul searching, leaving her past behind in South Africa. She was very pretty and had everything going for her, and she was becoming a closer friend to me now due to her newfound friendship with my mate Clem. She was very softly spoken and caring and gave the impression of a very gentle, loving human being. I could certainly spend more time with her and get to know her better on a friendship level. I was not really getting to know the American Debbie very well due to the fact she did not drink or go out much, but we got on okay. As for Jane the Kiwi and other half of Steve and Jane, she was a fun girl, and we male trainees knew her well due to the fact that we were all living with her.

Out of all the boys, I was closest to Martin because he was quiet and a good listener. Sebastian was a walking social time bomb, and I was hoping that I would be nowhere near him when he became unstuck. Maybe I would have a chat with him and try to get him to change, but then again, maybe not. Steve was the tall and thoughtful Kiwi, and he adored Jane; everything he did seemed to have a process, focus, and purpose to it, and he would certainly do well in whatever venture he undertook. That approach was just a little too sensible for me, but it certainly worked well for him.

    The afternoon lesson and discussion session flew by, and it was time to go to the mess for dinner. We had sailed from St. Thomas and I had not even noticed, actually I had not even gotten off the ship that day, and I was not that bothered. Tomorrow was the photog crew tour in St. Maarten that I would be gate crashing being Suzanne's plus one; everything felt like a whirlwind. I made my way up to the wardroom to meet Clem for after dinner beverages. He was already there sat with Claudia, his newest biggest fan, staring into his blue eyes and hanging on his every word as I had done the previous cruise when he charmed me into being his new best friend. He was a natural nice guy, and you would have to really struggle not to like him for his calm, gentle, and soothing nature, not unlike Claudia's, actually.

    We all got on with the business of running up our bar tabs as much as we could in the time allotted. Claire and Suzanne arrived with a few of the other photogs including their manager, a well-built friendly Kiwi. I shook his hand and thanked him for allowing me to join them for the crew tour tomorrow. He explained that he had arranged it personally and it involved hiring out the two boats from around the world sailing race, and it would be an exciting day. I only really took in half of what he was going on about, but I nodded along with enthusiasm. The wardie was buzzing as the clock struck midnight and people were getting the message that Suzanne and I were becoming am item from the constant chatting and flirting and occasional touch and kiss. I actually knew very little about her, and she knew even less about me, as we had not really had that many conversations that did not involve the giving out of "I fancy you" signals. I made a note to myself to ask the general consensus on her sanity and track record; anyone that had been onboard for more than a few months must have had some sort of history or story attached to them that most of the drinking circle knew about.

    The wardroom bar closed, and I was thinking about turning in for the night, but the photogs had other ideas. There was an entertainment department corridor party going on and we were going to check it out. I was up for that, although should not have been, but duly followed around the corridors into parts of the ship I never even knew existed holding Suzanne's hand. Lo and behold, the party was in full swing with tables laid out with food and cocktails and cruise entertainment staff getting excited about someone leaving. I had no idea who or why, but happily joined in and took full advantage of the hospitality. It was really amazing that all this was going on while most of the ship passengers or crew had no clue what excitements went on below decks after hours. I eventually went back to Suzanne's cabin to kiss her goodnight, and I fell into my top bunk around 2:00 a.m. What a great night and what a fantastic date Suzanne was. We had talked and laughed and kissed and chatted to people as if we had been a couple for years, but really it was only 26 hours, and we had really not even talked about being a couple.

# Chapter 14: Sailing Free

The crew tour was meeting at the gangway at St. Maarten at 11:00 a.m., and we would be going out on two boats that were used in the Americas Cup. The sun was shining and it looked like it would be a good day. I was on desk duties with Grace working with a quite severe hangover, but I had an excited feeling from inside that kept me going. I felt I was really getting into this lifestyle and especially life on this vessel. I was really grinning on the outside and inside. The morning was smooth and involved giving directions, selling stamps, and answering stupid questions, which I still tackled with bounding enthusiasm. I was granted to leave ten minutes early to change for my tour. I ran back to D320 and threw on my shorts, T shirt, grabbed my sunglasses, security pass, and away I went.

There were about thirty crew members going on the tour and about ten of them were from the photography department; the rest were made up of shoppies, dancers, and a few other random departments that were lucky enough to be granted a few hours off. There were no Filipinos I noticed, which was strange since they made up the most of the crew numbers. Suzanne told me that most of them work a lot of hours during shore time and prefer to send money home to their families rather than spend it on themselves. It really hit me that many people were here for many different reasons, and not everyone was here for a jolly like I was.

Suzanne and Claire were giggling and advised me that I was an honorary photog for the day, and I was privileged with this title. Suzanne looked cute with a little head scarf on, not dissimilar to a bonnet; it was a hit, and she pulled a potential fashion disaster off. I did notice that she kept very close to me the whole while and almost to the point of me feeling like I needed space. It appeared that she was happy to have me as her boyfriend, even though I was not sure what I wanted yet. I was non-committal and undecided but was not letting that show at this sensitive stage of our relationship. She was a great girl. When she looked in my eyes, I could somehow tell that she wanted us to become a serious item. Maybe she waited long enough for it, who knows. I was not really used to such close forward contact at such an early stage in a relationship—only thirty-six hours in. But I guess this was my "welcome to ship relationships"; they move on average about 500 times faster than relationships on land do. You could find yourself living in the same cabin with someone you slept with a week ago and it was normal. If you consider that on land it could possibly be a year or even longer from the first date to actually moving in with someone. It was a whole different world with massively different ideals. I was not sure yet what was wrong or right.

I was taking the bait though and enjoying being part of a team and just following along with it all. We were escorted to the tour embarkation and safety briefing area. We were divided into two teams—USA vs. Australia—to recreate the final sail in the famous race. I was placed with the photogs and to my surprise our first challenge was a Miller beer can drinking relay race. I was still feeling a bit tired from the night before and was almost shocked to find myself drinking a beer as fast as I could before 11:00 a.m. on a tour organized by the ship. I was not going to complain; it was great fun and the relay was exciting. The losing participant would have to drink the can of Miller from a hole pierced in the side of the can, creating a tsunami of lager. In this case, the loser was a girl called Vanessa who could handle her drink as well as I could. The first leg of the challenges was won by our team. After a bit more fun with cans of Miller, we were briefed on our jobs. Each of us had a role to play in the sailing team. Each person had a job allocated for a certain part of the sailing vessel, from steering to pulling ropes at certain times to wincing. We even had a 'bar person' to keep the supply of cold beverages flowing. I was given the task of winding a pulley with both hands as fast as I would when instructed, also known as a primary grinder. It was cool that everyone had a purpose and would not be just sitting about and it certainly encouraged team building.

    Both yachts were stunning and in fantastic condition. We all set off to have some practice in our jobs before the actual race commenced. The sun was shining with enough wind to fill our sails to give a bit of speed and excitement. I had a cold beer in my hand, and I was surrounded by mostly beautiful, confident, and successful people. This had the feeling of another amazing day. I felt alive and happy as if opportunities were endless and anything was possible. Suzanne was looking and smiling at me while I enjoyed myself with my top off making the most of the sunshine. Before I knew it, the bar had to be packed away for the race and we were off chasing against our fellow shipmates in the USA boat. There was a safety marshal boat following us, which was also the referee/judge and would stay in touch as we sailed swiftly around St. Maarten bay.

The race was very close for the forty-five minutes it lasted; we were passing our competitors tacking every ten minutes or so, shouting fun abuse, and taunting each other before each crew member went back to being busy at their particular job to help ensure team success. My arms were aching from all of the work I had been doing, I dared not complain though as everyone was mucking in to try to win the race. Our onboard crew members did a great job of encouraging and motivating us, keeping us updated if we were falling behind or shouting praise if we were in the lead. It was all very exciting. They were excellent at their jobs, and I am sure the exact same thing was going on in the USA yacht also. The five-minute countdown had begun to finish the race, and we were told it was neck and neck; one last tack and taunt at our rivals, as we were speeding up and reaching a climax.

We were moving into the home stretch after our final maneuver, and the tension and excitement were building as the crew had whipped us all up into a frenzy of wanting to beat the USA team. The marshal boat would hold a flag up for the winning team as it was too close to call. As we crossed the finishing markers, we all looked intently at the flag and it was confirmed that we had won.

It seemed strange as the USA team also claimed that they had been victorious when we all met up on the quayside. We sailed back to the dock and were all presented with a souvenir shirt and were given the opportunity to tip the crew, which we all did. It was a truly brilliant morning. I was sat with Suzanne and Claire as we recalled the morning events over a beer at the bar by the tender docking area. I had to get back onboard, as we had class that afternoon, so I kissed Suzanne goodbye and jumped onto the next tender to re-board the ship. I had caught the sun and was feeling refreshed and happy. Every day since joining the ship had been a whirlwind, and I had not really had a chance to stop and think about what I was doing. I was just doing it to the best of my ability. I was just hoping I was doing it right; no one had told me otherwise so far.

Back onboard, I managed a power nap for half an hour and shower before walking into the class for another afternoon of concentration. I was still bursting with life from the enthralling morning and attacked the afternoon's Q & A session with vigor and enthusiasm. We were making waves through the WAVES training manual and would have another morning lesson the next day and then hit the desk again for more practical experience as we approached turnaround day again. I did remember my vow to myself to study and take in the manual a lot more from that day on and would do exactly that.

That evening we had a team JAP trainee dinner in the mess, which was a decent bonding session and a quick drink in the wardroom with Tracey and a few of the others. Clem joined for a while; he was spending a lot of time with Claudia, drinking coffee, smoking, and lots of talking. That seemed pretty much the opposite of what me and Suzanne were doing; we were in this strange trance of love without much communication. The evening wore on and I was tired and needed to rest and I think I needed some space also. I walked from the wardroom with Suzanne. She looked at me into my eyes, reassuring me that it would be all okay and subtly enquiring what was going on inside my head. I could not really give an answer, so I just held her. I was not really communicating properly for some reason. I knew I was happy and having a great time and had not really had a chance to catch my breath. What I wanted to say was let's just be friends for now, and see how it goes but I could tell that she wanted to be in a relationship with me. From the look in her eyes, she already was. I was part of a couple already, and I did kind of like it more than not. I just felt I may have jumped in too soon and not given myself a fair crack of the whip being single onboard. I was quite shallow but I was not an expert at relationships, that's for sure. I was just a chap who liked a laugh and was good fun to go for a drink with, I did not want to lead anyone on intentionally.

  I kissed Suzanne goodnight and collapsed in my bed with the thoughts of the day on my mind: Clem and Claudia, me and Suzanne, ship life. Where would I end up in the fleet? There was still the risk of being sent to Alaska and off this ship that had become my beloved home in just two weeks, I was sure of one thing: I was very happy on the Grand, and I would not want to leave and get transshipped. That would be the fate for at least six of the eight of us at the end of next cruise.

# Chapter 15: Costly error

I awoke in the darkness again totally disorientated. All the bunks were full; my new family was home safe and sound. I checked my watch by turning on the small side light; it was early but not far off from time to get up if I wanted breakfast. I decided to be the first in the bathroom for a change. I would take my WAVES manual and go get some food and study, I had to focus on learning as much as I could and passing the exam. There was still a chance that any of us could fail and be sent home. I wanted to stay so much it would be worth the sacrifice of a few early nights and extra study sessions. In the mess I had coffee, cereal, and toast and read up on my procedures and policies; there was so much to take in and the questions in the exam could cover anything.

Class began at 9:00 a.m. and Stef let us all down by being a half hour late. We started without her and Alison was not happy with her tardiness. I felt embarrassed for her, and Stef looked like she had a big night, with her hair all over the place and bags under her eyes from lack of sleep. The class continued and in between chapters of the manual we were debriefed on how the next few days and the next week would work. That afternoon, after our break, we would be back on the desk and then the same for the last sea day before turnaround. On turnaround day, we would do desk duties again, followed by a big treat of sail away from the bridge. The first sea day would be a tour of food and beverage facilities and, if we were lucky, an actual engine room visit, but that would depend on the mood and availability of the chief engineer. The remainder of the week we would be studying for our exam and going through any WAVES manual areas that needed to be covered again. The exam would be on Prince Cay's day, and the results and the news of which ship we would be assigned to would be revealed on the last sea day. We all had to mentally prepare to pack and transship because there was a big chance that some of us would be leaving. That would be an important day for us all.

The nerves and tension in the group were quite high due to the lack of stability in our lives for the next week or so. Claudia was worried because she'd become quite close with Clem. I met up with Clem for a drink that evening and he was more than concerned that he could be losing the two closest people in his life in the coming week, his hands were shaking more than normal. Steve and Jane were scared about being split up on different ships; there were no reassurances or hints of hope from Alison that they would be together. Sebastian, Debbie, and Stef were not that worried about staying on the Grand except for the itinerary of the upcoming Europe season. Martin just did not want to pack and move again; he was still getting over his flights and travelling from Australia. I got the impression that he did not like change much. It was amazing that we had become so familiar with each other over the past two weeks from being thrown into a quite intense environment and situation together.

The last sea day was upon us and I was back on the desk with Grace, ever reliable to give great service and a friendly chat to her fellow Americans. The queues at the desk were mammoth with everyone wanting the same requests and questions as the previous cruise: change for tipping, envelopes, a copy of their stateroom accounts, and various complaints. The ship was gearing up to disembark all these people and their luggage and welcome a new group of passengers in Miami. I was amazed that this ship and the other six ships of the company were sailing full every week. Where were all these people coming from and how could they all afford to cruise? I knew America was vast and had a lot of people living in it, but we were talking about a lot of money being spent on cruises and onboard once they got there. Grace told me that Americans work hard and normally only have one holiday a year, so they make the most of it and enjoy themselves. We had just passed the millennium and the future looked bright for the American economy; confidence was high and people owned their own homes more than ever with vast availability of mortgages and were spending well on their credit cards. They all seemed happy that they could meet the financial commitments and were not afraid of the debt; they embraced it as part of life in the new millennium.

    The phones were ringing off the hook, and we hardly ever picked them up due to the many impatient faces staring at us from the other side of the desk. I was starting to feel a bit more confident in my responses to passengers, and Grace was allowing me to use her float to give change. This was a big trust on her part because she was responsible for that $15,000. If I were to make a mistake, it was her that would receive the written warning. As passengers paid off their accounts in cash, check or alternative credit card, the amount tendered was added to the computer system under that JAP's sign on and that would be set against their balance of the float. I was still trying to get my head around it and was becoming nervous about taking my own float in a week's time—possibly on a different desk on another ship where I knew nobody and had to start from scratch with friendship and relationship building. That thought really scared me; I was in a comfort zone here after two weeks.

    The desk was very intense on Deck 6, and I certainly felt as if I had huge exposure to passengers and hoped that I was showing that I was worthy of a place to stay on the Grand. There were video cameras on the desk and our moves were being scrutinized by the watching SAPs in the back office down on Deck 5. The day was flying by with great speed and as a team, we seemed to be bonding and actually getting on with what we were there to do. At the end of every cruise, the passengers had to each fill in a questionnaire, and from the responses of those questionnaires scores were calculated from a formula on how the cruise was rated from a certain percentage. The desk was always a difficult one because there were a lot of passengers that complained, so they could mark the desk as poor even though it was the spa, bars, or shops that had upset them. They always communicated their grievances at the desk. At present, the average desk score on the Grand was 87%, but our PSD wanted to see them go to 90%.

Our shifts finished at 8:00 p.m. and we went for dinner and a few quiet scoops before another day before turnaround early night. Not everyone had an early night that day; some were on the later morning shift, and some crew members were disembarking the next day at the end of their contract so they were getting ready for a big party night. Most of the pursers department had to go to bed early due to how busy those days were. All except Stef, who decided to go out and party with the crew members leaving even though she had an early start the next morning.

We could see it in her eyes the next morning and also by the fact that we had to phone her to get her out of bed to her desk shift on Deck 5. Not the best impression during the beginning of our last week as trainees. I felt as fresh as a daisy and ready to take on the world—well at least the few hundred passengers I would encounter in the coming hours. It was 6:00 a.m. and in three hours' time the ship would be empty again ready for another cruise around the three port stops. At least Stef was tucked away down on Deck 5 and would be less exposed to passengers. Sebastian and Martin were on Deck 6 with me, and the others had a later shift.

Grace and I were now like an efficient little team working the crowd together and showing the highest work rate on the desk, closely followed by Ross and the lovely Swiss Lisa. Confidence was high and I was feeling a little cheeky with it too. I felt unstoppable as the hours flew by, and before I knew it, the queue was dropping off as the amount of passengers onboard became fewer and fewer. I had felt invincible until the horrible moment in the back office when we balanced Grace's float and found it to be $150 short. All of a sudden all the smart cheeky cool comments and great service I had supplied to the morning passengers dissipated into nothing. I was in disbelief and felt a massive fear as if I had let Grace down too. I could have made a mistake giving change or lost my concentration for a moment by being too confident. I had no idea when or what it was, but I was sure it had to be me. Grace's track record in keeping a balanced float was fantastic. Drained of all self-belief and previous happiness, I gave her my heartfelt apologies as she counted and re-counted. I told her that I would pay it back and would put it down to an expensive mistake. Grace was okay, but a bit annoyed with herself as she had allowed me to have free reign of her float. I just did not want her or anyone to think that I had stolen the money; that kind of a cloud is a hard one to shift and can cause permanent damage. If we went public, it would cause more damage than good for us both; policy and procedure says that we must report it and both get a written warning from the SAP Accounts. Neither wanted that, so Grace said that we would pay in half each and keep the matter to ourselves. I was more than happy with this arrangement and we both sneaked $75 each into her float. It was an expensive lesson to learn but an important one at such an early stage in my seagoing career. If I had someone with less kindness than Grace, it could have turned nasty with accusations. I had a close shave and vowed to learn from it and be more careful with cash handling.

That was the end of float sharing, but luckily it did not damage the relationship between Grace and I; she was such an even-tempered person and had made things easy for me. I left the desk after we finished packing up the lost property and cleaning the desk. I had arranged to meet Suzanne for a coffee and catch up; we had both been very busy over the past few days. We met in the Horizon Court, the 24-hour buffet on Deck 14, and sat outside and chatted about the last few days. Neither of us had our own cabin, so it was difficult to find anywhere for privacy. We were really starting to enjoy each other's company, and I was actually happy, but still at the same time not letting myself become too comfortable. It could well be our last week together. We decided to make the best of it and our leave our future to the hand of the gods in the Head office in LA. Suzanne and I went back to her cabin for a bit of a kiss and cuddle, and then I retired to D320 before the madness of embarking passengers.

I was on shift at the same time as Sebastian, so we got ready together and walked to the desk. Sebastian was already becoming bored with the routine, and from what I gathered, he just wanted to be promoted so he could boss people around. I did get on well with Sebastian, but I could hear the alarm bells to keep him at arm's length. I just felt that even though he came from good stock he could end up being a bit of a wrong 'un. Any trouble he would get in would be from stirring it up with the wrong people, and I needed to distance myself from that if I was going to be liked and to progress in this environment. He also was not very good with the passengers and was quite rude to them on occasion, which embarrassed me. It made me feel like I did not want to be on the same desk as him as I did not want to be tarnished with the same "poor customer service" brush.

Grace and I were on Deck 5 for a change, so it would be a little quieter. Sebastian was on Deck 6 and would be very busy. Every workstation was filled and as one JAP ended their shift, another would take their place. There were 14 JAPs in total filling the various full-time roles, and with an extra eight trainees, there were plenty of bodies to help all the passengers with their enquiries—or so you would have thought. The queues on both desks were long and the embarkation gangways were on both Deck 5 and Deck 6, so we were busier than I had first hoped. I noticed that Grace was not in as good a mood as she normally was. She told me that she was missing her man and really was considering trying to move to the same ship as him. Her boyfriend had been promoted and was starting his new contract on another ship. Grace had formulated a plan to join him and would be presenting it to the Passengers Services Director later that day. She figured that she would catch the PSD just as he was having his first glass of wine during sail away to optimize his good mood.

Alison called us all together after an hour on the desk saying that we would not be able to go to the bridge during sail away, but the Captain would let us visit the bridge during sea day one. We were disappointed but it was just postponed and not cancelled, so that was okay. I was secretly more disappointed with the fact that we had to carry on working instead of getting the distraction of a bonus bridge visit break.

It would soon be time for passenger GES and we would be shadowing our JAP to see what they did during drills, so we would have a better idea for the next week of the different jobs involved. Grace was a door checker and that would mean we would be standing in the Theatre advising passengers where to sit. In the event of an actual emergency occurring, we would be given a counter to click the correct amount of passengers through our allocated door and onto the lifeboat. I was a little overwhelmed and mystified with the many various duties of drills, so I nodded along and pretended to understand. The process of the GES seemed to run smoothly and all crew members knew what was expected of them; we were soon back on the desk for the last leg of turnaround day. Grace made her move into the PSD's office to present her appeal to be transshipped. I was selfishly quietly hoping that it would be declined just because she was such a very positive influence on my ship life and I had also become secretly attached to her. But I also wanted her to be happy, as she really deserved it for being such a special person, so I had to eliminate any such selfish undisclosed thoughts from my mind.

After about a half an hour and about fifteen missing baggage enquiries later, Grace reappeared by my side and had a half smile. She said that she would talk to me about it over a drink later, when we did not have seventy-five passengers in front of us all wanting to know where their luggage was located.

A natural reaction for some passengers just before we set sail would be to fly into a blind mad panic if their bags were not in their room, which I did not really blame them for. I would also be very nervous if the ship was sailing off and I had no idea if my personal effects were onboard or not. Our preferred procedure would be to keep sending them away until we sailed and they had dinner. If their bags had not appeared by then, we would fill out a lost luggage form and put it on the desk of the SAP PR for attention in the morning. With over 10,000 bags being distributed, it takes time; most of the passengers took this advice and thankfully their bags appeared and we did not see them again, but upon occasion there would be a problem. The problems happen when the JAPs take a gamble on the bags turning up later on, hedging on them not being lost, thus they put off the filling out of the form for as long as possible—sometimes too long. Passengers like to know that some action is being taken to locate their bags and that someone behind the scenes is searching high and low; the truth of the matter is that no one really takes any action until the next day unless there is a huge amount of bags, and then we will call in for help or await for the night manager. Calling in for help from SAP's during the gap between about seven and eleven is not really a smiled upon option, so the assistant night manager sometimes has to step in and talk to the passengers.

    Ross had gotten himself into that very situation this evening on the desk, and all we could really do was sit back and watch the show. This particular passenger had been persistent regarding their lack of bags being delivered and had been to the desk repeatedly since 3:00 p.m. worried about the situation. They had seen most of us and we had sent them away in the hopes that the luggage would arrive and that would be the last we would see of them. All the standard lines had been used up and I may have even advised them that it was "not really worth worrying about until we have sailed." In my defense, even at that point it is not really worth worrying about because so many bags are being delivered to the wrong rooms and are sometimes even lost in other passengers rooms until the next morning, when they realize they have an extra case. But this couple was now worried, tired, in need of a change of clothes, and most importantly, angry. They could have spoken to any of us at the desk, but bad luck for Ross; he was the one free when they reached the desk. It can be a lottery at times. We had sailed an hour ago and they were very angry, shouting, calling the team at the desk and the Cruise line incompetent, and they wanted to get off the ship. Ross needed to pull this one back a bit because they were getting out of control and loud. He decided that he would have to take action and try to help them locate the bags. He started with checking if any more cases were left for distribution down on Deck 4 with the accommodation teams. This resulted in no luck. The M1 was now back in full service as a motor way for bodies rather than roll cages filled with luggage. The next stage was the dreaded lost luggage form; these took an age to fill out as it was done by hand and involved asking lots of questions from near hysterical passengers. Ross filled it out with them for ten long minutes asking questions about their transfers and airlines and content of the bags. He advised that further searches would be carried out on the ship and in the coming hours and the report would be looked at by the night manager and SAP PR in the morning. These passengers were still not satisfied and wanted to know what they could wear now; they had no clean socks or underwear and nothing to wash with as all their toiletries were in the case.

Ross went out the back and had to get the assistant night manager to authorize giving out lost luggage kits, which had a basic wash bag and $50 onboard credit to go and buy some bits from the shops. This was only normally given out by SAP PR in the morning but these passengers were becoming more and more upset and even had been rude to Ross, who kept his cool well. That was as much as we could do for that evening; if their luggage was not onboard, they would have two long sea days without any clothes and one formal night to get through. The lost luggage form said they also took connecting flights, so the airline could have lost the bags. The follow up investigating phone calls and email enquiries would be made in the morning by the SAP. Ross, Grace, and I left the desk together and went to the mess for dinner after finishing our desk shifts, leaving a long line of passengers at the desk for our replacements to deal with. I asked Grace if she was going to balance her float, but she hardly touched it that day and would do it in the morning. After our meals, we went up to the wardie for a drink so I could hear of her plans.

As we both settled into our vodka and cranberry juice, she said that she stated to the PSD that she would like to request to transship where her partner had just started his contract as AP. She figured that there would be at least one or two of the trainees moving from the Grand to his ship, so why could she not replace one of them. They had no real requirements of requests to go anywhere. All of this was fair comment as she was basically using opportunity of the transshipping trainees to get off the Grand and join her man. The PSD liked Grace, as everyone did, and said he would do what he could for her; he would hate to lose her off the desk, but it was pointless having a really good performer unhappy and not giving 100%. I did not want to lose her either, but if she was leaving the Grand, it gave a greater chance for me to stay, as that was now my main goal and be with my good friend Clem and Suzanne.

Both Claire and Suzanne appeared for a drink during that hour and were soon joined by Clem and Claudia and a few of the other team, including Tracey. We had a great night drinking and talking as the hours flew by. Clem and I had realized that we had too many vodka cranberries again and we were putting the world to rights. We were also deciding who should stay on the Grand, and in our ideal social world, we decided it should be Claudia and me. It was amazing that we had both found someone special in the space of two weeks. I was a bit of a social butterfly and certainly spoke to loads of different people but always ended back in Suzanne's arms. We were both having fun and she was enjoying showing me the ways of the ship's social life, and I was lapping it up. She was a great hostess, and I was enjoying it very much. We did not have much space to spend quality time alone, but at this stage, it was not a problem, in my mind at least. The night had drawn to a close; it had been another long day and great social evening, which went against the norm on the night of turnaround. I walked back with Suzanne and we lay together on her top bunk for a few hours before I left to go back to my cabin.

# Chapter 16: Our Fate

The first day of the new cruise was upon us again, and it was possibly the beginning of our last week onboard. The tensions were beginning to show with the difficult changes on the way, as well as a career defining exam to study for. It seemed there was a lot at stake and the atmosphere in the first sea day classroom showed it. Everyone seemed to have a new sense of purpose and the morning class was busy with finishing off the WAVES manual. This would be followed by a full review to try to identify what areas needed to be concentrated on for each of the trainees.

After lunch, we were all taken on a full tour of the F&B stores and kitchens by the first purser F&B, who was a fellow Brit and talked and worked at 100 miles an hour. He whizzed us around dry stores holding about half a million dollars of champagne and caviar, the storerooms where all the drink was kept, as well as a totally amazing amount of clean fridges and freezers. The catering operation on the Grand was spectacular, and we were all taken aback as to what was involved. On a twelve-night cruise, passengers would be served 37,440 eggs, 400 lbs. of lobster, 78,000 lbs. of canapés, and 45,000 lbs. of game and poultry. Next came the kitchens: all tile and stainless steel was immaculate and all areas had constant attention from chefs and assistants in well laundered whites. It was how I imagined and hoped the behind-the-scenes of the ship's F&B facilities would look, and I was relieved. The tour ended in what was called the "bell box," which was the term for the catering area for room service. It was located on Deck 12 and was a self-contained operation in its own right. The team took orders for the room service menu and supplied the butler service with their needs. It was a hive of activity for such a small space.

We were given a half hour to go and get a cup of tea and then had to meet back up to continue the review of the manual in the study dining room. We continued for several hours going over things we really had very little clue on; we all were feeling a little tense and nervous regarding the upcoming exam. It was the first formal night of the cruise again, and we were all going to dress and meet for a few formal photos so that we had evidence of these days together. Martin and I snuck to the wardroom for a cold beer before we all met at 8:00 p.m. outside the Mexican restaurant. We chatted about what we were hoping to get out of the coming week, and we were both really getting quite desperate to stay on the Grand. We had decided that our subtle hint dropping about our preferences to stay on this ship needed to be stepped up a gear. I had mentioned to Alison that I was very keen to stay, so they could benefit from my outstanding customer service skills, and I believe that she did take my intentions seriously. But at the end of the day, she gave nothing away, not even a hint, even though she was pushed for information during class, especially by Stef, who was constantly asking.

The trainee JAPs were ready in full formal attire at the agreed time, except Stef. She was late again and now keeping us all standing around looking like lemons waiting for the photos. Alison was becoming annoyed and we were embarrassed on behalf of Stef who arrived ten minutes late. The timing for the meet was arranged by Alison, so it was in the middle of the two evening dinner sittings, so the queues were at their smallest for photos, which only served to fuel her annoyance of Stef's tardiness. Nevertheless, we had all finally assembled and were having a smart formal photo taken on a colorful backdrop. We all looked our best. One of Suzanne's friends from New Zealand was taking the shots and said we should have a fun one too, so we also had a photo of us all making faces. We were advised about meeting time in the morning for lessons and then went in different directions.

My direction took me for a little solo walk around the ship to do some people watching, seeing all the guests in their formal clobber looking very smart. I walked past the atrium where Clem was performing his set, and I sat and listened for a while to his soft classical guitar music. It was certainly calming as I enjoyed in particular his versions of Garcia pieces Les Ajoncs d'Or, Les Grandes Jaunes, and Coeur de la Rose. I felt blessed that I had become good friends to this very talented person. I walked past the photo gallery and threw Suzanne and Claire a smile and a kiss; they clearly admired me in my smart bow tie and white formal jacket with a half of a stripe on it. They were busy selling photos and putting them on display fresh from the lab, having been shot only an hour or so earlier. I found myself at the aft end of the ship in a show lounge where the cruise staff members were introducing the act. I watched for a while before disappearing through the crew only door that took me underground into the staff only quarters, my closest bar was the wardroom, and I found myself there with Tracey. We enjoyed a few cold beers and chatted about the upcoming European ports and how she had been to most of them before. An hour or so later, Clem wandered in cool as you like with his bow tie undone like a member of the rat pack. We continued to drink and talk until Suzanne and Claire popped in for a quick break from working in the lab. We had a quick kiss as I walked her back into the M1 and delivered her back to work as I re-joined the team in the bar to close down the night. It was a strange feeling. I had been having many late nights and drinking far too much, but I was on such a high from what was going on around me, I had not really had enough time to be tired or drunk or so hung-over I could not function. I did not really have much of an idea of what I expected from this ship life and if there was even going to be a bar for the crew onboard open every night, so what I had discovered and the way of life was a real treat and pleasant surprise. This experience had already surpassed my expectations.

    Sea day two was upon us, and we met for our morning lesson in our normal empty dining room, all present and correct in good time thanks to our leader's harsh words and stern looks to Stef the previous night. We were still going over the WAVES manual in earnest and ensuring we had understood all areas and were ready for the big exam. It was an open forum to ask questions and seek advice on what we had covered so far. We had all come a long way since we had joined just over two weeks earlier. I had made a Scottish error but was now semi loved up with a special South African photog. I had made great friends, especially Clem, and I had made the decision that this ship and ship life was the life for me. I had quietly become teacher's pet just behind Claudia, who was an exceptional student. I was getting on well by being polite and friendly to everyone I met, a credit to the CRUISE credo, even if I do say so myself. I had immersed myself into a new era and was not looking back.

The day passed with us learning more about what our next six months would hold and the information seemed to be sinking into us all. After the day's class, I took my manual and went to put in some extra desk time with Grace who was pleased to see me and told me that the transship idea had been approved. She would be moving after the next cruise before we headed off to the Mediterranean. Even though I was very happy for her, I was a little sad that she would be leaving. We had gotten on very well and she had helped me out a great deal with her patient teaching. In celebration we decided to go for a cocktail together in the Wheelhouse bar after our shift. I helped Ross and Lisa complete their PIFs (passenger information forms) in the system and then we were free. The Wheelhouse was full of leather sofas, big chairs, and nautical memorabilia; there was a big wheel and many model boats in glass cases being the centerpiece. Grace and I sat in large leather chair and her tiny frame was engulfed by the huge piece of furniture. The large sofa we left empty for Ross and Lisa who would be joining us shortly when their shifts finished. A bar steward appeared and we both had a good idea what we wanted even though the bar menu was vast with cocktails, beer, wine, and spirits presented in such a way it didn't really count as alcohol. We were both in the market for cosmopolitans as there really was no substitute for it being served in a James Bond style glass. The drinks arrived with a bowl of Bombay mix and we chinked our glasses together in toast of her escape from the Grand and to being reunited with her fella. I got the feeling that if she did not get to transship, there would be no relationship for her to go back to after her man's contract as an AP with his own cabin. Nothing I would mention to her about, but just a feeling I got from what she had told me about this very interesting boyfriend I had heard so much about. If I met him I am sure we would get along well.

Ross and Lisa arrived as we finished the first round. I was quietly hoping I would not get stung for the round of four drinks. At $6.95 plus 15% tip every time it could get expensive—not that I was tight, I just could do without it at the moment, as my bar bill was probably mounting up. We all ordered cosmos again and had separate checks to which I breathed a secret sign of relief. The company and the location were civilized with us drinking our overpriced cocktails from actual glasses as opposed to the normal crew bar plastic glass with a straw for our vodka and cranberry juice. It was a very pleasant end to another day at sea.

The next two port days of St. Thomas and St. Maarten flew by with more study and lessons than anything, as we all realized that we needed to pass this exam for the fun to continue. We could party all we wanted once we passed the exam but in the meantime it was heads in books. We were all nervous but getting along well and it would be a shame for this chapter in our lives to end, as it was fun being a trainee and on a course, especially in the cruise ship environment. I had spent minimal time with Suzanne during recent days, but the time we had spent together was intense and we both wanted to be together onboard. The alternative of me being transshipped was a big threat looming only three days away. Clem and Claudia had been spending a huge amount of time together and were like the coolest couple on the ship. They both faced the same fate as Suzanne and I If the decisions went against them with Claudia being transshipped, it was all very exciting and very scary.

    The night before the exam, Clem and I had a quick beer together in the wardroom before my early night. We chatted about the fun that we had and how our friendship had grown so strong in such a very short space of time. We were close friends and cared for each other even though it had only been three weeks. Living on a cruise ship does that to you though; your relationships develop at an accelerated pace due to the close proximity of the situation. It suited me fine as I never was one for messing about when it came to my friends; my male friends had been more important to me than girls for most of my life.

    All four of us roommates slept with our WAVES manuals that night as we tried to cram the last of the information under our wall bedside lights. I felt that I had learned more from the practical work at the front desk than I did from the actual lessons and the manual. Having the pressure of passengers in front of you causes the urgency to raise your game and forces you to know your stuff. I had learned about lost and damage forms, focus files, lost luggage reports, lost and found, lost children, stamps, and floats.

The exam was at 11:00 a.m. in the dining room, so we had the morning to study and ask any last minute questions of Alison, who seemed just as nervous as we were. I had a feeling that she knew of our future ships already from a look in her eye when Steve pushed her for information again. But she stated that she would reveal all that evening once the tests were marked.

Martin, Sebastian, and I went for breakfast in the Horizon Court as a treat. This eating location was a huge double-sided passenger buffet that stretched almost over half of Deck 14. It was 9:00a.m. and a lot of the passengers were trying to get ashore by tender, so we were allowed to use the facility as long as it was not too busy or abused. For all of the passenger areas, the general rule was that as long as you were not taking a seat/place that a passenger was waiting for you were okay. In today's case it was touch and go as the tables all looked packed, but we got our food in the buffet line and found some seats outside. I had gone for the disappointing American streaky bacon and crap link sausages with fried eggs. It was not at all like an English breakfast and was one of the few things I missed about the UK. But it was better than the officer's mess, so I would not moan out loud; we chatted about the day's exam and asked each other questions on areas we were unsure of. My prediction was that Martin was a fountain of knowledge and pass with flying colors, Sebastian would just scrape by, and I would be okay due to my extra desk time. Steve and Jane were doing some cramming of their own in the cabin, Stef was studying with the three-striped safety officer, and Claudia and Debbie were testing each other in the girl's cabin.

After our hearty breakfast, we continued our last minute studying with slight panic that the next few hours would provide the keys to our futures at sea. It was a very big day and we all needed to perform. The clock ticked by and before we knew it, the time was ten to 11:00 a.m., and we received our papers and settled down to exam conditions. We were on a table each so certainly not within paper glaring distance. Alison came around with the papers as Stef asked to go to the toilet, holding us all up another five minutes. On her return, the papers were distributed again and we were off and running. The test was a combination of questions and multiple guess. My past philosophy on the multiple choice was it started with a B, then A, back to B, then C, A, D, and so it continues, but I had studied so actually read the questions and focused. I still possess the bad habit of looking around me for my fellow examinees' reaction to their first few questions for my amusement, and they were all as I imagined. Sebastian had his head down and arm protecting his paper so no one would copy, probably like he did as a schoolboy at whatever posh expensive public school he blessed. Stef looked like she was in some daze from too much sex and needed to snap out of it. I felt like going up to her and snapping my fingers in front of her face and telling her to concentrate. Martin was flying through it, as was Claudia who was already turning onto the second page. Debbie looked like she was about to cry. I needed to get my act together, stop looking at everyone else, and get to work on it—so I did.

The two hours passed swiftly, and before we knew it, we were handing in our papers as we finished. Martin was first, followed by Claudia. Sebastian was next, then Steve and Jane together—not sure how that happened. Even Stef had submitted her work, until it was just me and Debbie left in the exam room. I was still going through all the questions double-checking that I had not made any glaring errors. Debbie seemed to be still working through it. We both stayed until we were told to leave and were forced to hand in our work. I was quite pleased and confident that I knew a lot of the material. I handed it in and left and met the others for a cup of tea in the promenade bar area. The fall out was mostly positive, and we thought we all at least passed, but no one was sure. No one would know until that evening and the results and our futures would be announced. We all felt relieved that the exam was over, and I certainly felt like a cocktail, but it was only 2:00 p.m. and we had to attend desk duties from 4:00 p.m. until 6:00 p.m., so that was out of the question. We all chose to go to the crew deck for some sun, fresh air, and a swim in the crew pool. We knew that Alison was currently marking our papers and were excited about hearing the results later. The pass mark was 80% and anyone below that would have to face retake if that option was offered as well as the embarrassment of not making the grade.

    The mood at the crew pool was relief but also trepidation due to the possible relocation of most of us to other ships. The past three weeks' training had been so much fun. We had all made friends and gotten used to the ship we had regarded as home. It had been revealed that at least two of us would be staying because two JAPs were ending their contracts in two days' time, and we would be ideal to replace them. One of those was Grace. We swam in the tiny pool, relaxed in the Jacuzzi, and laid under the sun for an hour before making our way back to our cabins to prepare to work on the desk and pack our cases. Whatever was going to happen, we would definitely be moving out of our current habitat in under two days' time.

    The desk time was busy again due to the next day being the sea day before turnaround and those wanting a sneak preview of their bills queued and waited for their printouts. Our minds were on the meeting with Alison in the crew bar at 6:30 p.m. She said we would all have a drink together and be given the results and our JAP contract details. After our desk time, I went to see Suzanne and have a hug before I got the news. Claudia and Clem were going to the crew bar together and Clem would hide around the corner in anticipation of the news. Six-thirty was upon us and it would be the most important meeting since my successful interview for this position. We all felt nervous and excited. The main players were Steve and Jane and Claudia and I, as we had the most to lose from the ship movement decisions. Alison calmly brought us all a drink, and we all sat together in the lounge area. I sucked on the straw of my vodka cranberry with intense concentration. The first part of the announcements would be the exam results and the second part would by our ship assignments. I felt sick as I may have to get used to finding my way around a whole new ship. I had been on the Grand for three weeks and still struggled to find our cabin without a map. I would have to say goodbye to Suzanne and Clem and start again relationships with onboard peers. I really could do without packing and moving and flying to another ship. I really wished to stay on the Grand. I certainly knew that Martin had enough travel on planes for one lifetime. We all had our reasons for wanting to stay and a big factor was the ship's deployment to the Mediterranean for fourteen-day cruising with overnights in Barcelona and Istanbul.

    Our leader took a sip of her drink and made the first part of the announcements. She declared with pride that everyone had passed the exam and congratulated us for the hard work we had put into the training. We all suddenly had smiles on our faces and you could feel the relief in the room. Stef asked who got the top marks. "Not you" was what some of us were thinking. Claudia had the highest score and we would receive our marks with our end of training course appraisals the next day. With another sip of her drink, we could tell she was building up to the second important announcement. The tension suddenly reappeared in the room as we were all listening intently to the words coming out of Alison's mouth. The next few words would decide our futures for the next six months or so. I just wanted to know now, as the pressure was killing us all. Alison took a deep breath and started. Claudia and Debbie would be joining the Sea Prince in Alaska on turnaround day. This was the first bombshell and I could see the horror in Claudia's eyes. We both panned around to where Clem was hiding to see his head drop in despair. That was a harsh start and did not bode well for Steve and Jane, who looked like they were about to explode with anticipation. Debbie was more than happy with this result as she had found a friend in Claudia, and I got the impression that she did not bond that quickly with people. Sebastian was next as he was told he was heading for the Ocean Prince. He did not show any great emotion, as he quickly worked out in his mind that The Ocean would also be cruising around Alaska. My odds of staying on the Grand were looking better by the minute.

Alison turned to Steve and Jane, who were now literally in pieces and cowering in the corner. They were holding each other's hands so tightly it looked like their circulation would be cut off. She told them that they would both be transshipping to the Sun Prince together. The whole room erupted in joy as we all went to congratulate them and share their moment. It was a great feeling, and we all felt relieved for them; they deserved it. Alison turned to the second teacher's pet, me, and said with pride that I would be staying on the Grand, and from my ecstatic reaction, she could see that it was well-received news. I was a very happy chap and would not be taken out of my comfort zone after all. Lazy I know, but I was happy here, and I would not have to start trying to find my way around a new ship and make new friends. It's the little things that make the big differences. The next news was even bigger; she said I would not be staying on the Grand alone, as both Martin and Stef would be staying with me. I turned and gave Stef a hug and shook Martin's hand. It seemed that I would be getting to know Martin a lot more after all.

Overall, with the exception of Claudia, we were all happy with the final decisions. Well, Sebastian was moaning already, Steve and Jane were made up, and it gave me a warm feeling that at least half of our wishes had been granted. Claudia was clearly upset and Clem was now giving her a hug. Clem was also very saddened. I tried to comfort him with the news that at least I was staying, but that seemed little substitute at this moment. I figured it wise for me to leave them to make their peace and farewell plans over the next day or so. Martin was now on his second bourbon and Coke. He was clearly in the mood for celebrating. He was really pleased he had no more moving or flights to take. He could finally settle down and get on with his contract. Alison was busy receiving congratulations and thanks from us all for the great job she had done as teacher, looking after us, and keeping us out of trouble—well, as much as she could. Stef could not believe her luck as we were heading for the Mediterranean, fourteen-day cruising and overnights in ports. The crew bar was picking up now, and I decided to phone Suzanne, who was at work in the gallery, and tell her the news. There was silence on the line as I passed on my news, and she said she was coming down to see me straight away. After a few minutes she appeared, dressed in her blue photo polo neck with tears in her eyes as she threw her arms around me. It seemed that she had been waiting for the news as much as I had been. She was so lovely but very sensitive, which made me slightly concerned as we had only known each other barely two weeks. I had the feeling that she possibly may not have had many shipboard relationships, which was refreshing, as a lot of the girls had history with several people onboard once you start digging. I had a rare gem.

But that was the thing about these shipboard relationships. They moved so quickly. I had asked a few of my peers in the past week if Suzanne had been seeing anyone before me and no one said they had seen her with a boyfriend since she had been onboard. So, she was unique, genuine, and pure, and one of the nicest people I had ever met. I would also have to handle her with care, as I was still new onboard and had the look and feeling of a kid in a candy store with pretty dancers, shoppies, and beauty therapists at every turn. So much to discover and enjoy, but I had already been grabbed and tagged, so I was feeling a certain pressure from that angle. I had just run away to sea to get out of one relationship, and I had walked straight back into another one. It was currently fun and exciting, but I knew that dust would soon settle and who knows where that would leave us. But for the time being I was happy to have this sobbing South African photographer in my arms. She was cute, popular and a little different, interesting and strange at the same time. She also really cared about me and that was something that I needed at that particular juncture of my life.

Suzanne went back to work in the photo gallery, giving me the opportunity to really relax and celebrate properly. We were all buzzing on our exam results and ship news and in the mood for a party, or sorrow drowning in Claudia and Clem's case. They had one day and two nights to try to make sense of what they had become or wanted to be. Clem was convinced that he had found "the one," and Claudia was equally fond of him. I knew that she was on a journey of discovery and it had just begun, and even though Clem was a special person, she would be disembarking in a day and had to concentrate on a new ship, job, and making new friends. The drinks in the crew bar flowed and as more departments joined in the party atmosphere, it gave the feeling of a good night as the disco fired up and about 100 Filipinos and Thai boys hit the dance floor. Crew discos were strange affairs as you never saw so many different nationalities bonded by music. A few hours passed and just as I was feeling slightly lonely in a drunken way, the photogs arrived like some sort of cavalry with Suzanne and Claire ready to top up the party spirits. We had a dance and drinks and Suzanne and I eventually ended up in each other's arms talking and laughing until the early hours.

# CHAPTER 17: CUTTING THE CORD

The next day certainly had the feeling of the morning after. A lot of the ship's company seemed to be a bit quieter for some reason. I had returned to the cabin very late and we all awoke with slightly sore heads, including Jane who disappeared off to the girl's room once we all started to surface. She and Steve were still very happy at yesterday's result of being able to stay together, they felt extreme relief. Martin and I were the first on duty, so we hit the shower one at a time and then walked to breakfast in the mess to get some half decent coffee to help with the waking up process. It was an 8:00 a.m. desk start and we made it on time even if a little rough around the edges; our "passing out" presentations were at 4:00 p.m., so we had plenty of time to recover. It was the last sea day before turnaround and the desk was busy with queuing passengers wanting their bills to check through. I was under the close supervision of Grace who was getting ready to transship the next day. Ironically, I would be her physical onboard replacement and would take over her float, folders, and manuals.

She was excited to be seeing her man, I was happy to be staying but sad she was leaving. She was a charming, delightful person and would be missed as a friend and also as the best JAP on the ship. I was quite convinced that the extra work and hours I put in on the desk, as well as the fact that I got on well with most crew members was a contributing factor to me staying on the Grand—invested time well spent. On the desk, I was very aware that the next day would be the cutting of the umbilical cord, and I would no longer be a trainee. I would be a fully-fledged junior assistant purser; my unique trainee pass to be "a bit clueless and lazy" had expired and it was time for the serious stuff. I had worked out that in this large floating village, as long as you did your job and kept your head down, there would be no bother, and you could go about your business quite peacefully. I was a small fish in a big pond and the enormity of the organization I now worked in was dawning on me. In my awareness of panic of no longer having a shadow after the next day, I was inspired to concentrate and really make the most of the teachings of Grace and those experienced JAPs around me. The desk was very busy on this last sea day, and I was trying to help as much as possible, but I did not have computer sign on or float, so I was only half helpful to the awaiting guests. In a way, I was looking forward to having my own float, computer, and seat, so I could take care of business myself and get my teeth stuck into the job properly. My head was still pounding from the celebrations of the night before, so I was only really firing on half a tank. After lunch, I retired to the cabin for a power nap to aid the recovery process before our meeting with the captain to receive our certificates and have our photos taken.

    We were instructed to meet on Deck 14 forward at 3:50 p.m. to get together for our presentations, which was the location of the captain's office and his large conference room that doubled up as an occasional site for officers' cocktail gatherings. I made my way up there with the boys who were all now feeling fresh and back to neat after resting for an hour or so. There was nothing worse than meeting the Commodore stinking of drink and looking like we had a big night. He had the power to simply have us breathalyzed and disembarked the next day. The 4:00 p.m. timing, allowing us to recover, could have been part of a plan to keep us all in employment. We all waited in the captain's lounge that consisted of a huge conference table with about a dozen chairs around it, a lounge area with leather sofas similar to the wardroom, an en suite, and a mini bar; it also had two large windows facing forward to the oncoming mighty ocean. I was nervous about meeting the Commodore and felt it was like meeting a celebrity. The only time I had met him before was during inductions where he advised us where to buy drugs in St. Thomas before reading the riot act to the new joiners and when he was being applauded by the passengers during the captain's welcome cocktail party. I wanted to make a good impression, that's for sure; he was a very tall, thin gentleman with a slow, well-spoken voice filled with sense and commands. He already had my respect and I was a big fan of anyone with such power and four gold stripes.

    He entered the room with the assistant photo manager who would document the moment; he said good afternoon, and we all responded promptly and clearly. Alison gave the Commodore a brief outline of what we had been doing for the last three weeks, and he spoke with each one of us individually about our assignments at sea. I liked the Commodore. He appeared to represent all I would want to see in a man of that standing, and I felt confident that we were going in the right direction with him at the helm. He did spend a bit more time talking with Sebastian because he knew his father, which was nice and obviously Sebastian lapped up the attention and extra time with the main man. We all sat down holding our certificates, and Chris the photog snapped away and that was it—our passing out parade was complete. The Commodore said a few more words in the direction of "good luck with your contract and do the company proud," and then we were ejected. I was due back on the desk for my last two hours shadowing Grace before we did the float handover and transfer, so it would be a busy few hours for me.

It was about 5:00 p.m. and the desk was peaking with passengers and the ship was buzzing with pre-turnaround day activity; everyone was busy running about getting reports prepared, finishing their cruise data, and balancing their floats. The ship was sailing on her way to Fort Lauderdale and powering through the water at about 23 knots. I took a quick look outside on the promenade of Deck 7 on my way back and again took in the enormity of what I was on and how this floating hotel journey was shaping my life. It was amazing, and I was really looking forward to the next six months. Grace was in fine spirits as it was the last couple of hours for her on before transshipping and meeting up with her love. We made a great team together on the desk, and the passengers certainly benefitted from our great customer service skills. She was busy taking manual payments, and I was answering the dumb questions about the following day's procedures and how they would be getting off the ship. All passengers had received a disembarking memo on how it would work, but no one really read it, so I would read it to whoever needed it translated from writing to the spoken word. I did sympathize slightly, as I was never any good at reading information while on holiday mode either. If I could ask some JAP on the desk what time I was getting off the ship and where I was meeting that's fine, so that empathic attitude helped.

It was 8:00 p.m. and we decided to have dinner before we did the transfer and float handover, as we needed a break after the last intense three hours of hundreds of passengers asking questions. So we headed for the mess. As we were leaving the office, we did have to walk past the queue in the atrium so before opening the door into passenger areas, she again instructed me to walk swiftly with purpose and not make eye contact with passengers in the queue as they would stop us if they see someone in uniform. It was a great tip as we hastily glided past about 80 passengers looking impatient. We were walking with purpose.

At dinner, we sat with Alison who was disembarking the next day as it was the end of her contract. I would miss her guidance and support and wise words, but she said she as looking forward to having a well-earned break. I suppose she was right, after a six-month contract as a busy SAP and then adding on another three weeks at the end of it, having to train up eight JAPs who were inexperienced. I had great respect for her and hoped that our paths would cross again in the future.

Grace and I made our way back to the back office and began the float transfer process; it was basically taking out the payments that you had received from passengers accounts and putting them in an envelope and doing the sums on the computer so that the amount would be transferred into the SAP's computer accounts balance and the actual envelope would be physically handed over in the morning when SAP Accounts started work.

Grace completed that procedure with me observing very attentively. I had to really concentrate. I was very aware I would be doing this on my own the next cruise and there were no books or training courses that could teach you how to handle money well. A mistake or momentary lapse in concentration could be costly, as I had learned. We both counted the float and then I counted the float on my own, and then we both signed a receipt and the $15,000 float was now mine. I took the keys, and we began to hand over books and papers. Grace was like a mother letting her child go off to school for the first time and could clearly see how nervous I was about being set free. She made it worse, but it was a nice feeling of being cared for. It could be worse though. I could be on a whole different ship taking my float off someone dodgy trying to rip me off. It did happen I had heard, with dishonest JAPs leaving their float a few hundred dollars short and hope that the handing over JAP would miscount, so I was lucky to have Grace who I trusted completely.

I was now in proud possession of a float and was well on my way to being a JAP. It was exciting and I put my float away in its locker and locked the door, checking it several times. It was getting late and the next day was my first turnaround day as a JAP, so it would be wise to get an early night. But I needed a beer so I headed to the wardroom for refreshment. It was very quiet there so I had one beer on my own and then went in search of Suzanne and Claire. They were both in their corridor with a few of the other photogs having a drink and a chat. Suzanne and I broke free for a glass of wine in a quiet corner. We both talked of our relief of me staying and I told her of my new $15,000 fortune. It was very nice to have someone onboard who cared and listened. The ship can be a lonely place, as I had experienced for about the last half an hour, and I did not like it so much. I craved company and attention and someone to talk to while I drank my evening quota. Clem was still with Claudia discussing how unfair life was. I just hoped he was getting laid after all of that effort, but he was deeper than that.

Suzanne was a very unique girl and did take some working out. She was devoted to us it seemed and I happily played along even though I really was unclear about any feelings I had. I really enjoyed her company, and she was fun, different, and a little unusual, so my attention was held.

I went back to the cabin after a kiss and a cuddle with Suzanne to find Sebastian and Steve both still packing and sorting out their lives to transship. Steve was very happy as he got to stay with Jane, so no dramas there. Sebastian was moaning and told us they should just make him computer officer and be done with it. That way he would have AP status, a pay raise, and his own cabin. But then you are stuck as Compo forever probably and no real advancement hopes. In my stupidity, I let him have a look at my laptop to advise me on why it was running so slowly. I wish I hadn't as it was running even slower after he managed to crash it and get it stuck. He claimed that it was not what he did and my laptop was too old. I ended up having to take the battery out of the back to retrieve it. Luckily my work was not lost, but my faith in Sebastian's computer skills were. The boys had finished packing and we opened a bottle of wine that had somehow appeared in our fridge for a farewell toast after spending an amazing three weeks of learning together. It had been a real journey already and really it was just the beginning. I was happy and excited about how my life had arrived at this point. Martin was also very content that he did not have to carry his luggage to another airport and had a crooked smirk on his face. We had become close due to being four, and sometimes five, in a small stateroom really designed only for two. Stef knocked on the door and asked if any of us were going to the crew bar for one last drink. We all attended for a last farewell toast. Claudia was there too, a little bleary-eyed, but no sign of Clem. I decided to run up to his room and just to check if he was okay, as his cabin was with the entertainment staff on Deck 6 and not a long walk from the crew bar. He sat in the corridor smoking and looking sad. I approached, sat beside and asked him how he was coping. The truth was he was not really coping that well. He was an artist and a sensitive and tortured soul, bless him. He had fallen for Claudia, and I think she had fallen for him, but their relationship's growth had ended by someone in an office in LA making a decision on what ship she would go to. It was harsh, but that was ship life. I had learned in a very short period that you had to move on and not dwell too much. I did try to put a positive spin on things and say it could have been worse; I could have also been going. This was of course true, but given the choice; I think he would have preferred to have kept Claudia. It was a road I did not want to explore, so I did not push any further. That would probably be the response I would have gotten. I gave him a hug and told him we would get together the next night for a beer and a chat in the wardroom. Clem needed a bit of time to sulk and be annoyed, but I was sure he would be okay.

    I joined the others in the late night crew bar and gave a passing hug to Claudia, who I would actually also miss; we got on well. The crew bar was about to close, so we stocked up on a few drinks and sat and chatted for a while amongst several groups of departments that did not have early morning duties, including casino and shoppies, drinking, talking, and playing darts.

# CHAPTER 18: CREW CABIN COMFORTS

The morning wakeup call alarm on the cabin phone stung through my skull as if my head had not even hit the pillow. Great. My first day as a real JAP armed with a $15,000 float, and I had my worst hangover since I had arrived onboard three weeks earlier. The good news was that I was not due on duty until 10:30; the bad news was that we had to be out of our passenger stateroom by 8:00 a.m. The transshippers had to be ready at 7:00 a.m. to meet the crew office team in the crew bar to receive their instructions. It soon became stressful, busy, and messy in our cabin with luggage, uniforms, and bodies with headaches trying to battle for the bathroom and get ready for the journey. Martin and I let Steve and Sebastian get sorted, and then we shook hands and said goodbye as they disappeared down the long corridor to begin their journeys to their new ships and assignments. Both Martin and I were relieved to have some peace and space and were looking forward to getting settled into our own permanent JAP cabin. We had to report to the crew area supervisor for our keys around 8:30 a.m., so we went to the mess for a coffee and a bite. We were happy to be sharing a cabin together as we got on well and knew each other's habits and ways, so we had the ease of not having to get to know a new cabin-mate or the uncertainty of getting a weird one—at least that unknown element had been eliminated.

The JAPs all had to share same-sex cabins and they were located on Deck 4 and Deck 10 with en suite, a fridge, carpet throughout, and a room steward that tended to our needs. It would be great to have somewhere to call home and make our own, with our belongings and just be settled. We arrived at the crew area supervisor's office to pick up our new cabin keys—Deck 4 or Deck 10, we were wondering? But soon the alarm bells started to ring that all was not quite right with our new room allocation, when the crew area supervisor had to bleep the first purser. He looked at us as he spoke quietly on the phone and instead of handing us the normal key cards for the rooms we were given actual old fashioned metal keys and told our room number was 2114. Martin and I looked at each other as if some terrible mistake had been made and went to hand the keys back and complain, as if we were checking into a hotel, but we were abruptly told that is where we had to stay for this cruise due to room shortages. Instead of the technology of room key cards, we were given an actual key and were heading for the depths of Deck 2—not a great start. We were both scared.

Our hopes of feeling at home and settled in had been shattered, as well as my plans of inviting Suzanne round for a romantic evening when Martin was working. Deck 2 was very close to the engine room and where the community of Filipinos lived, not that I had anything against them. They were polite and nice in the name of cruise in passenger areas, but it could be a whole different story on their own turf, especially with two new recruits who knew very little about ship life. I was a lot more confident than Martin was that everything would be okay, who looked paralyzed with fear since the words "Deck 2" entered his ears; he looked even whiter and more ill than normal. I had faith that the Deck 2 community would greet us and we would be welcomed like we were entering a new tribe.

We were promptly ejected from the crew area supervisor's office with our luggage and keys and no sense of direction. We eventually found a hidden dark stairwell that led down and took the route to Deck 3. This was still not somewhere anyone would like to live, but then we had to go down another deck to the depths of Deck 2. This was more like the Bronx, and a very different underground world. It seemed like there were gangs hanging around outside cabins and an actual "hood." Of course, this was all in our imagination, but it was possible. The main differences on Deck 2 were the smell in the corridors, the uncomfortable heat, no carpets, no fridges, and smaller cabins that had a permanent strange aroma.

We eventually found our room with its red door located right next to the bins; we opened it and were greeted with the grunt of a shocked looking Filipino chap in jeans and T-Shirt who said he was "cleaning". He promptly left and we could see just how much cleaning had been done—not a lot. Martin said he was probably looking for anything left by the previous tenants. I was less cynical and tried to look on the bright side—it would only be for one cruise. We started to unpack. I was only taking out the essentials as this was only a very temporary arrangement, I was hoping. All of a sudden, our passenger cabin sleeping four for the last three weeks appeared to be a luxury. We had already showered that morning, so we did not have to use those facilities yet, and we put our uniforms on and decided to get some clean air before our shifts. All of a sudden the glamorous ship life had turned into prison life. I was quickly unsettled, and not having a very comfortable abode did not help. Martin and I wandered around the top outside decks taking in Fort Lauderdale around us. It was hot and we did not hang about for long. My thoughts were with the others transshipping to their new adventures, and for the first time since being onboard, I was wishing I was doing that.

    I arrived in good time for my first official shift on the desk, took out my float, and carried the large metal box up to Deck 6. I took my place third along the line, next to Ross and Luca. It was very quiet on the desk as we were waiting for the next cruise of passengers to embark; we were tasked with cleaning. Ross was in charge of lost and found, so he had to document all items on a spread sheet and box them up for landing with the hotel secretary. He stated that there was nothing worth holding onto this cruise, but claimed that his current digital camera was an ex lost and found item. I watched Ross log the items, which ranged from hairbrushes and clothing to jewelry and water wings. Ross was using another computer program called Microsoft Word to list the items; he said Word and Excel were used a lot onboard.

    The first purser walked past in a hurry in his normal straight-backed, efficient manner advising us that the first passengers were about to embark. It was now just after midday. They soon arrived and before I knew it, I was dealing with my first ever passenger. I felt like giving them a prize like the 100,000 person to shop at a supermarket, but I kept the significance of their visit to my counter to myself, especially as they were after an upgrade. I had my response ready and it flowed like I had being saying it for years. "I am sorry but the ship is sailing full." If they were really pushy, I would put their names down on a dispatch sheet for the attention of the first purser in the morning once everyone had settled. But they were okay with my answer and left as happy as they had arrived—my first satisfied customer I thought, that was easy. But it would get harder.

    The hours passed and I could see no end to the queue. I was constantly trying to get the amount of guests in the queue down because I did not want anyone to be waiting too long. It was affecting my karma and service levels, and Ross could see that, and he took me into the back office for a quick coffee and a chat. There was a small coffee station at the top of the stairs on top of the cabinet that held some locked floats, standing room only. Ross told me to calm down, keep my cool, and deal with one passenger at a time; the others would have to wait. I needed to focus only on the one in front of me and not let my mind wander off to the amount of people waiting. They would have to wait; it was as simple as that. He was right. I was trying to be superman and not succeeding at all. I was compromising the service to my passengers that I was facing by rushing through them.

I returned to the desk with my new attitude of giving the passengers in front of me the total of my attention and full concentration and not even looking at the others waiting. This seemed to work and was now what I would always do. There would be no point in doing lots of jobs quickly and badly. I was better off doing fewer well. My first shift was a success. I was giving passengers the correct information, and I had not even had to open my float. The first shift of turnaround day finished at 4:00p.m. which was a strange time because it was past lunch time but too early for dinner. I braved it back down to Deck 2 for a bit of peace as Martin was on the desk. Deck 2 was as unpleasant as I remembered and just looked like the whole place needed a good clean. The cabin was small, smelled of the last residents' old socks that had not been changed for a seven month contract, and I felt like getting a tub of disinfectant and scrubbing it or getting a flame thrower and torching it. I decided to try to forget my troubles and close my eyes for an hour. I had to set my manual alarm clock as the cabins did not even have phones. I lay on top of the scratchy sheets and blanket and did not decide to venture beneath the sheets yet as. I was nowhere near tired or drunk enough.

 I awoke refreshed enough but not brave enough to have a shower, so I put my whites back on and went up to the mess for some food before the evening shift began, which was from 7:00 p.m. until 10:00 p.m. I ate some chicken in the mess and then went to the photo gallery to locate Suzanne who had been ashore today with the photogs for lunch and shopping. Her face lit up when she saw me approaching and it gave me a glimmer of happiness on this difficult day. She said she had a break coming up, so I waited for her, and we went for a walk and chat. I suggested we had a romantic stroll to my new cabin. She was in for a shock as she was probably expecting a clean cabin with carpet, champagne in the fridge and not resembling a crime scene. I led her down to Deck 3 where some photog cabins were, so she was not too shocked, but it was quite a surprise when I said we had to go down another flight of stairs. Suzanne thought we were off to the engine room. I showed her our new cabin, and she was even shocked at why we had been sent down here.

"What's that smell?" she asked.

I had not pinned the actual source of it yet, but it seemed to be present all over Deck 2 and not just in our room. It was probably the most unromantic place on the ship, but we decided to make the most of our alone time and decided to get naked. We both showered afterwards and the cabin was now christened on its first day of ownership, not that I mentioned that proud achievement to Suzanne. I just felt we needed to wash after our bodies had touched the sheets that I was dubious about. She was due back at the photo gallery, and I was due back on the desk, so our quick meeting had been fun but was over. She got strange looks from some of my fellow Deck 2 residents as we left my cabin, as if women were forbidden. I had not seen any signs on the wall, so I carried on with my business of getting us out of Deck 2 and Deck 3 with our lives intact.

The evening shift on the desk seemed to glide by, possibly due to my late afternoon delight. I still did not have to break into my float, and I was dealing with just one passenger at a time and not trying to help them all at once. The desk was busy. We had sailed several hours earlier, the phones were ringing off the hook, and the queue at the desk was still long. There were a lot of luggage enquiries and questions about the location of the Da Vinci Dining Room that was located just opposite the desk. I turned around to see what Grace was up to and saw an empty space by my side, remembering that she had transshipped that day. I missed her already and wondered how she was getting on. That thought lasted just a few seconds as I had my next customer standing in front of me wanting to change his cabin because it was too small. Yeah, I know the feeling I felt like saying.

All the spaces at the desk were full of JAPs helping passengers in distress. The phones rang but were never answered because we always had someone in front of us, and they got the attention because they actually managed to drag themselves from their staterooms down to the desk, which counted for something. I asked Ross if he ever answered the phone, and he said no. Lisa said she was too busy, and Vanessa tried sometimes but it was not always possible. I decided to give it a try and answer a phone call in between front facing passengers. I quickly picked up and got an American gentleman wanting room service. I transferred him and then helped the next passenger. It was not so bad; I had helped an extra person. I boasted about this to the guys and said that if we class ourselves as a floating hotel, how would you feel if you were staying in a hotel and the reception never answered? As the words came out of my mouth, I realized that it was still my first day as a JAP and I should wind my neck in, so I did, and just kept trying to cut the phone traffic down in between passengers. This was until I took a particular phone call, maybe my tenth. The passenger sounded like a little old lady in distress. With a wobble of panic in her frail voice she stated that she was locked in her cabin and could not find her way out. I calmed her down, as she feared that she had missed her dinner trying to find her way out. I assured her that she could be fed at any time, and we would send someone to help her if the door was jammed shut. She said there was no door jammed shut, so I asked her why she had not tried to use the cabin door to exit the cabin. She said there were only two doors in the room: one of the doors opened out to the bathroom and the other door had a sign on it saying "Do not disturb." At that point, I decided that it was not the best idea to answer the phone anymore. I had tried to be a hero and revolutionize the way we worked on my first day and ended up doing a U-turn.

    The shift ended at 10:00 p.m., and it had been a long day. All I really wanted to do was go back to my cabin and watch TV and relax—not something I would be doing this cruise. So, I went to hunt down Clem for a beer to see how he was coping with his first day without Claudia. He was sulking and smoking outside his cabin door again. I gave him a hug and said all would be okay. It could be worse; he could live on Deck 2. I dragged him into the crew bar for a few vodka and cranberries to cry into. Clem was cool but also sensitive, and I could see that it would take time for him to get "back to neat." Suzanne and Claire joined us for a beverage until I eventually felt drunk enough to go back to my cabin and not be too affected by the smell and fear.

# Chapter 19: Off to the Mediterranean

The next morning, the first sea day was upon us, and Martin and I awoke at the same time and took turns getting ready for our desk shifts. I could not wait to get out of Deck 2. No offence to those who lived there, but there was something about it that made me want to go home. It could have been the lack of home comforts and mini bar, or that it made me want to constantly shower off, but not in my cabin shower. It also made me happy to be in the passengers' areas, something that is not really encouraged in your uniform as you are exposed to questions and complaints. It was a busy morning on the desk as all the JAPs had to input credit card details for every passenger who had been filled out during check in. This was done in between the many questions from the new passengers that had very little clue about the whereabouts of anything. The funny thing what that they were asking me—the man who was the worst at giving directions. I was getting better due to being able to copy the others' instructions, but I was still quite clueless, even finding Deck 2 was a fluke each time for me. My shift partners were bubbly kiwi Vanessa, Martin, and lovely Lisa. Down on Deck 5 was moaning Luka and his fellow moaning Italian friend Ivano. Deck 5 was always a lot quieter because it was a bit more hidden, so I am guessing that is where they sent the dead wood at the end of their contracts. I was fresh and had a good attitude and genuinely wanted to serve the passengers my best so they could have a happy and fun cruise. I found it a lot easier to be nice than to be miserable.

    Lunchtime arrived and the mess was packed with officers and entertainment staff getting their burgers and chips before a few hours' afternoon nap to recharge before the evening. I had a break after that and would have loved to chill out and relax in my cabin, but I hated it there. Instead, I went for a little walk about. The ship was busy. The first sea day of the cruise is always busy. Clem was playing his guitar in the atrium and for the most part being ignored, but I liked it a lot and a few others were enjoying his plucking. Clem played classical guitar, so he did not strum conventionally, but there was real beauty and art in what he did. It took years of practice to get to the level of skill that he was at; the man was an artist.

    I went outside Deck 7 on the outer promenade area to look at the amazing ocean. The ship was cutting through it beautifully, and I took in the wonderful sea air and natural surroundings. I stayed for a half an hour before I could no longer delay going to my Deck 2 pit. I walked past the photo gallery and got a loving wink and a smile from Suzanne as I passed. Martin was already resting in our cabin when I got there, so I lay on my bunk and dropped off. Martin's horrible alarm went off an hour and a half later and woke us both with a start. I was still not used to the nap culture and the lack of natural light. We both prepared for our shifts. We had a meeting at 6:00 p.m. with the SAP PR, who was going to give us a briefing about what to expect in the Mediterranean. Back on the desk, we continued to process our credit card details as the passengers became acclimatized to the ship as their first full sea day came to an end.

Just before 6:00 p.m., the assistant night manager came onto the desk to take over so we could have our meeting. We all went to the PSD's office for the meeting because there were so many of us. It was strange to have most of us in the same room together; it only really happens at meetings and Christmas I was told. There was SAP crew, PR, accounts and hotel services, as well as the APs and all 14 JAPs, except the JAP night desk and assistant night managers. It took SAP PR about five minutes to get us all to quiet down; she was not the loudest or most forceful of ladies it seemed. The structure of the meeting was a general meeting, and then the desk JAPs would stay after to get the lowdown on the Mediterranean. SAP PR hosted the meeting and went through the agenda items and issues, including complaints from passenger questionnaires, problems from the last cruise, and system updates. Martin and I were welcomed to the team and words of respect were paid to Grace in her absence about how her experience and skills would be missed, especially in the coming months. The blue "You made the difference" cards were read out, and we were all given a telling off for the desk scores from the passenger questionnaires being 86% and needing to be at least in the 90s. It was announced that the next meeting would be a focus on CRUISE principles, and we would have to all bring in ideas on how we can improve customer service and desk efficiency. It was at that point that I was really not enjoying myself: "Contributions were expected from everyone." I hated that, and I did not have much to say at the best of times. I like to keep myself to myself and lay just below the radar. I did not know much about CRUISE either, even though I had just done a three-week training course on it. It could be worse we could have been asked to do a presentation. Even so I was already stressing about it, even though it was still a whole cruise away.

    The main meeting was adjourned and the desk JAPs stayed behind with SAP PR, and we stated talking about the Mediterranean. Again, I was not ready or prepared to have to make a constructive contribution but she asked us what we knew about the Mediterranean and the ports we were going to visit. I was clueless as I had not even looked at the itinerary. I just knew that we were in the Caribbean, it was hot, and I only had two real port names to remember. Luckily, Tracy had done the Mediterranean before and stepped in to save the day. She knew the lot and was a fountain of knowledge on where we were going and the typical questions that were asked by passengers. I had already decided that she was going to be my new best desk friend, and we were already drinking buddies. There were some things I should have known, such as that Civitavecchia was the port gateway to Rome and that Livorno was the port for Pisa and Florence, but these facts had escaped me. It was also announced that we would be selling the currencies for the different countries from our floats, so we needed to be at the top of our games when it came to the conversions. That was something else I was afraid of—not only speaking at the next meeting, but I now feared the Mediterranean and money. Our current SAP PR had a knack of putting a negative spin on most things I had discovered, she also never really smiled much. But the meeting served its purpose, and I left it 100% more knowledgeable about where we were headed, then when we started, even if it filled me with a sense of dread.

We went back to the desk mostly excited about the new places we were going to discover. The nicer of the two Lukas was particularly excited about going to Venice because it was his home, and he would see his family. He invited Ross and me to have dinner with his family, which was nice, but I think he had also invited the entire team of JAPs. After this last cruise in the Caribbean, we would be crossing the Atlantic Ocean for a full six days at sea to Ponta Del Garda and then onto Barcelona to start our first Mediterranean cruise and embark new passengers. Some passengers would be on for the crossing and the first Mediterranean cruise too, so they would be with us for a while. It was best not to upset anyone because you would be stuck at sea with them for over a week, and possibly a whole cruise after that.

The rest of the first sea day ended on the desk, and I met Clem for a few beers in the wardroom. I had received my Rota so I had my hours set out for the cruise. It seemed okay, and I was happy to have a schedule so I could plan my days more effectively. I was working an average of seven hours a day and all split shifts. The day before turnaround was eight hours, but that could change depending on the needs of the passengers and the results of the end of cruise scores. I was happy to have a plan and conform to the work schedule and felt comforted by the security of routine. The beers flowed with Clem, and Suzanne joined us with Claire. Clem was still depressed about Claudia but I had not given my ex-trainees a second thought as it had been such a busy day. Clem only did between one and two hours' work a day, so he had more time to think about things and become disheartened. We tried to cheer him up by pouring beer down his throat, and for the most part it was effective. We excitedly spoke of the Mediterranean, and Clem was stoked about that. I walked Suzanne back to her cabin after the bar shut and then staggered back to the rotten Deck 2. Martin was already snoring, and I managed to keep my movements to a minimum as I sank below the scratchy blanket and questionable sheets.

# Chapter 20: Close call

The next sea day was steadier at the desk as our passengers had found their feet and the JAPs finished off our credit cards and PIFs. It was going to be formal night and the ship had the normal busy buzz about it, which I still enjoyed. I had been on Deck 5 with Ross, and we had some good talks getting to know each other. He was classically British and very proud. I loved that about him as it was not something I saw as much in the younger generation. He spoke well and liked to look at the ladies, but it seemed a lot of women found his approach too polite. I was polite but Ross had the natural British accent to really back it up. Stef came down to escape Deck 6 for ten minutes and asked if we fancied swapping desks with her.

"Not a chance, Stef." This was my first JAP shift on Deck 5 and I was enjoying the fact that passengers had to seek it out. Stef was hung over again and looked it. She was probably busy giving passengers incorrect information of some kind rather than asking or looking it up.

I kept with my normal routine of lunch, cabin avoidance, and rest for an hour before the evening shift, and then beers in the evening with Clem. I planned to get off the ship with Martin in the morning at St. Thomas for some fast food. He liked Wendy's burger bar, so that was the plan. Martin was motivated by food a lot, even though he was thinner than I was. Tomorrow we had the opportunity to eat out together with our similar shift patterns.

It was a hot day in St. Thomas, and even though I had a hangover most mornings, the early shifts meant that it had dissipated by mid-morning and I was ready for a nap or fast food followed by a nap. That day, it would be the latter. Martin and I coped with a few hours on the desk answering the regular questions and selling a few stamps before it was time to go ashore. By 11:00a.m., the ship was just about empty and even a lot of the crew were off visiting the supermarket to stock up on essential snacks and goodies before the six days at sea after Fort Lauderdale. It amused me that even with all the food on the ship, the crew craved what they did not have. The non-officer status crew had to get extra because the crew mess food was not the greatest, and they did not have deck privileges to eat in the restaurants or Horizon Court. At least as junior officers we had the deck privileges and the ability to order off the passenger menu in the officers' mess. The mid-morning St. Thomas heat hit as we left our air conditioned ship. I had never really experienced the need for air conditioning before as much as I did on the ship, and it was literally like a breath of fresh air. The jaunt would not take us far, as the Wendy's restaurant was only a ten-minute walk from the dock. There were a lot of the crew there and Martin and I ordered burgers and chips. I was amazed when it arrived because it was a square burger on a bun. I had never had a square burger before and it was strange. The meal and walk were over in a flash, and we took a stroll around the local area before being overcome with the heat. We were in need of a rest.

    The next day would be our last at St. Maarten, and I had a very early shift start of 7:00 a.m. Then I had most of the day off before returning for the afternoon shift at 5:00 p.m. I had no plans to go ashore on a tender and was looking at a lazy day sunbathing on deck and reading my book. I was on Deck 6 with Ross, Lisa, and Luka, and it was a busy morning. Ross and I were packing our floats away, and I asked what he was up to that day. He was generally a man with a plan and told me he would be visiting the Island of Anguilla, which was a British Virgin Island a ferry ride from the French side of St. Maarten. That sounded very exciting, and I asked who he was going with. He said he was going on his own. I asked if he fancied some company and we agreed to meet at the tender embarkation area in ten minutes. I felt honored that Ross would allow me to spend the day with him, and even though it sounded like a long day, it was more exciting than sitting around reading. I swiftly ran down to Deck 2 and changed into shorts and a T-shirt, grabbed my ship ID pass and some cash, and headed to the tender area, which was on Deck 4 not too far away. Ross was already there and we managed to get on the next tender, which took about fifteen minutes to travel to the dockside near that bar where many of the crew favored to have a drink and snacks.

    From there, Ross hailed a taxi and instructed the driver to take us to the French side of the island through the beautiful scenery. The drive was about a half an hour and we arrived at the French side of St. Maarten. From there, we waited for a water taxi to take us across to Anguilla. On the water taxi were couples on their holiday and honeymoons with cases, eagerly going across for a romantic break. There were also people going to work and delivering goods. The boat took about a half hour again, and we had to take note carefully of the return ferry times as our ship sailed at 4:00p.m., and we had to ensure we had lots of time to complete each return leg of the adventure. Ross seemed to have it all under control, and I trusted him as he had never missed the ship before and I was sure that he was not going to start now.

    We arrived on Anguilla and walked around. Ross found a sign that told of the island's British roots. I took his photo in front of the sign because he was trying to visit all of the British Virgin Islands and wanted specific evidence of the trip: a photo and a souvenir shot glass. There wasn't much to do in the port area, but Ross spotted a car rental sign and decided to check it out. We went inside to see about renting a car for a few hours. We had to apply for a local driving license and were granted one straightaway, to my horror and amusement. No driving skills or test was involved. We just emptied our wallets into the hands of the car rental owner and were the proud owners of a car for a few hours. We had to wait about fifteen minutes for delivery—it was probably his wife's car—but regardless, we were mobile and ready to explore. Ross drove and I enjoyed the scenery. It was a great feeling to be driving on a road on solid ground. We were still residents of the ship but had been granted liberation for a few hours, to experience something normal.

We stopped at a beach that the car rental owner had recommended, locked the car, and went for a walk. The beach was the most stunning beach I had ever seen in my life. It was like paradise on a picture postcard. The sand was a bright white and the sea was a perfect clear blue. Overcome with excitement about the beach, we sat down on the sand and took it all in. There was a smattering of couples and a few families around, but there was plenty of space with about ten meters between each group. Just along from where we were sitting was a hotel, a beach bar, and much else. We paddled and enjoyed the sun, and I thought how nice it would have been to share this with Suzanne instead of Ross, but I was still thankful to experience it at all. Just a month earlier, I had been in my old life and job in rainy England.

After about two hours, which felt like only ten minutes, we decided it was time to make our way back to re-join our floating home. We needed to access a car ride, a ferry ride, a taxi ride, and a tender ride—upon reflection a few too many trips, given that the ship wouldn't normally wait for passengers, let alone crew members with a total amount of one stripe between them. I wasn't sure what would happen if we were late or missed the ship. It was in Ross's hands and I trusted him to time it right.

I shouted across the beach to him, 'What time does the ferry leave back to St. Maarten?' He shrugged, and I then realized that he was not really in control as much as I had hoped.

I already felt like we were late. My body thrummed with nervous energy, and I suddenly felt like I needed to go to the toilet urgently, but there was no time for that. I alerted Ross of my concerns and we headed straight for the car. We had about two hours before the ship would sail, so there would be no room for error in our return journey.

Ross drove back and I read the map—the pressure was on not to get us lost. Even though the island basically had just one road, it would be my bad sense of direction and map reading that could take us the wrong way around it. I remained calm and concentrated and it paid off. I was confident we were on the right track and we both recognized things we had seen earlier on our journey to the beach. I was happy for the first time in a half an hour because we seemed to be back on track. Until, of course, Ross stopped the car and announced that we needed to pop into the shops to collect his souvenir shot glass of Anguilla. To this day, I know I should have put my foot down and vetoed that ridiculous idea. But I trusted that he would hurry; he knew how desperately short on time we were. After what felt like an age had passed, I began beeping the horn. I was becoming increasingly stressed and agitated. Eventually, he appeared and we set off in an angry silence toward the dock to return the car. However, no one was there and we both ended up running about like headless chickens trying to give the stupid car back. Eventually, we left the keys in the car and ran for the ferry—only to find that it was already pulling away.

We had missed it.

This couldn't be happening. My first week as a JAP, and I would be missing the ship at our second port of call? It did not bode well for my sea-going career. It could have sparked a very swift end to it, in fact. I stood at the end of the pier watching the ferry make its way to St. Maarten without us, standing beside a man I had trusted too much. I was annoyed beyond words—and scared. What would the Commodore do? Would I be stripped of my job and dignity? Sent back to England with my tail between my legs? The next ferry was at 3:45 p.m., which was about the time we had to be aboard and the time that the last tender left the quayside. We were doomed. I was not known for losing my cool very often, but I was moving toward a meltdown. The beautiful island was turning into a private hell for me; the walls were closing in. I had to get a grip and think of a plan. Ross was one step ahead of me, though. We checked how much money we had between us to see if we could charter a boat to take us over. We had a total of $35 left, but we also needed that money to pay for the taxi ride back to the ship. We were snookered. We ran around the area looking for a boat owner to take pity on us and take us across for $20. We offered to pay an extra $100 in the post, but no one was buying it. We even tried to give away our watches, and I was giving away Ross's shot glass, but nothing was working. The hour dragged by. Between arguing and laying blame, we finally found ourselves boarding the ferry and doing our best to convince the boat driver to leave as soon as possible. This driver, however, was working on "Caribbean mean time." He was in no hurry, which added to our stress levels. The boat eventually left and made its way through the once-admired scenery. Ross and I willed the boat to go faster, but it was not working. After what seemed like an age, we made it to St. Maarten. As soon as we docked, we ran as fast as our legs could carry us to the nearest taxi and in our most pathetic and desperate out of breath voices asked the taxi driver to "drive as fast as he could" to the port area. Thankfully, the taxi driver took our challenge—especially after we threw all of our money at him—and he sped off at a pace that finally suited us. Ross looked at his watch and made a face that looked like he had just shit his pants. The ship was sailing in three minutes by his watch, and there was no way we would make it. Nonetheless, we could not give up hope. In my head, I prayed for a miracle—my first prayer in quite a while. The tension in the taxi was intense; both Ross and I were too scared to mention anything, and the driver was speeding through the countryside like a racing driver.

    I broke the silence by asking what would happen if we arrived and the ship had sailed. Ross said that our passports would be landed by crew office to the port agent, and he would arrange flights to the next port so we could re-join the ship. There, we would face the consequences and the bill for flights and hotel accommodations for the night. Depending on whether the Commodore and company wanted to make an example of us or not, we might be sent home. I felt sick. I had blown my chance at the lifestyle I wanted by doing the one thing I should never do—miss the ship.

    The golden rule had been broken.

All credit to the taxi driver as we were nearing the port town. He had done well and halved the time that we had taken to get across the island earlier that day. We climbed the top of the hill and started the descent into the port area with our first glimpses of the bay, which we were now expecting the see the ship sailing away, but by some miracle Ross thought that he could see that she was still at anchor. He jumped out of his seat excitedly as he could see a tender leaving the ship and heading toward the land.

"It's still there! It's still there!" he screamed. "There is an outgoing tender, so we may have a chance!" The driver accelerated through the small town just dodging the locals and holiday makers finally reaching the security gate where we would get out. We thanked the driver again and told him that his driving could have saved our jobs and about $500 each. We sprinted through the security area flashing our Laminex passes. The tender landing area was in sight and there was a queue of about 20 passengers and the shore excursions manager with them.

"One of the tours must have run late," said Ross, "and that's the reason for the late sail."

Bill the security officer spotted us and gave us a look of a man who knew how late we were. He nodded at Ross and said that one of the tours came back late and that was the reason they had not sailed a half hour earlier. We both looked shameful and Bill flashed us our passports and said that we were very lucky indeed. Our passports had been landed and his next job was to pass them over to the port agent. We got on the last tender with the remaining passengers, the security officer, and the shore excursions manager. I had never felt so relieved and blessed. Ross and I looked at each other and gave an exhausted sign of relief and sat in peace for the tender ride, sitting in our own sweat and smell of fear.

Back onboard I expected to see our heads of department and the purser at the gangway with prepared written warnings in hand, but there was nothing and no one, to our relief. Ross and I parted company as I headed down to Deck 2, basking myself in the air conditioning. It was the first and probably last time I was happy to see my cabin on Deck 2. I had ten minutes to get freshened up and back on the desk, so I showered, got my uniform on, and ran up to my desk shift.

Ross was also on duty with me so we spent the whole time telling our colleagues of our adventures ashore that day. I looked around and was so grateful that this lifestyle had not been taken away from me for making a stupid mistake and missing the ship. I would never take such a chance again and would be my own organizer of trips so I was in control of my own destiny, rather than trusting someone else. But I had been a follower and I had to remember that I asked Ross to join him and not the other way around. I was the tourist. The four-hour shift flew by and I was totally exhausted but ready for a beer to catch up with Clem and Suzanne to recall my adventures. They were already in the wardroom, which was unusually busy, but then I was told that there was a leaver's pour-out and free drinks and snacks were being offered. We took full advantage and enjoyed the evening to the fullest, and we talked and even had a dance to the music on the CD player. Past midnight my eyes stopped working, so I had to drag myself down to Deck 4 with Suzanne for a kiss and a cuddle in her cabin. Her cabin was located on Deck 4 forward next to the laundry, and her top bunk was right next to where the anchor goes down, I was told. Claire was still out and about so we drifted off to sleep in each other's arms on her top bunk. It was a lot nicer than being on Deck 2.

# CHAPTER 21: CROSSING OVER

I was awoken by the sound of what must have been the anchor speeding past my head. I could literally feel the vibrations through the bulkhead as it sped down at what seemed an incredible speed. I jumped up with a start and realized that I was in Suzanne's tiny cabin on deck four. Claire was in the bunk below us and Suzanne was still in my arms. The noise of the anchor was unbearably loud, and both the girls said that it was the norm and they were grateful we only tendered on two days of the cruise. Suzanne grabbed her vitamins and headache tablets and could not find any bottled water to wash them down with, so she opened a can of Miller Lite. She only took two sips for her pills, but I was impressed at her ability to drink some beer at what must have been 5:30 a.m., but if it was me, I would have not been able to resist drinking the whole can. So, I took it from her and glugged the remainder of the can. I then kissed her and said goodbye to Claire and went back to Deck 2 to get the remainder of the night's sleep before a busy day started. Martin was sound asleep as I entered the cabin, completing my second walk of shame. Blokes could get away with it a lot more than girls can; I had no smeared make up or high heels to carry, just wearing track suit bottoms, T-shirt, and flip flops.

I sank into my horrible bed and drifted off to sleep feeling quite relaxed even though the space of my cabin was not a relaxing place. I woke up a few hours later to the sound of Martin in the shower and knew I had an hour after him to start work, so I was not in any hurry.

It was Prince Cays day, and I had no plans to get off. I had a shift from 10:00 a.m., so I couldn't have even if I wanted to, which I didn't. The desk normally became busy an hour before we sailed and my shift was finishing just about then, so I would be missing the start of the action. The next day was the last sea day before our final Fort Lauderdale day, and then the almighty crossing, which I was actually looking forward to. Martin excitedly grabbed me while I was getting my float and broke the news that at the end of this cruise we were moving out from Deck 2 into new abode. This news did cheer me up and we both went to see SAP PR for the details. Martin was moving up to the dizzy heights of Deck 10, while I was only moving up two decks to deck 4. I was going to be sharing with Ross, which was great news. He was fun, sensible, British, polite, and had good personal hygiene, even though I would not be going on one of his land adventures again. I was happy with the result and it immediately put me in a better mood with something to look forward to—finally goodbye Deck 2.

The end of the cruise came around swiftly with the busy sea day making me stronger with my float and handling passengers with greater confidence. The queue at the desk was constant, but I was no longer trying to rush. I was giving good, fast, and efficient service. Before we knew it, I was balancing my float at midnight transferring my balance to SAP Accounts, and I had managed to not lose loads of money, which was a relief. It did take me two hours to get the computer to work and do the procedure correctly, and I did have to call on the help of my new roomie Ross, but we got there in the end. At ten to one, we put my float away and ran to the wardroom to order up a few beers to relax. It was quite busy with those not having to get up in the morning making the most and a few of the leavers enjoying their last taste of very cheap bar prices. The way the night before turnaround shifts worked was that if you finished late and transferred in the night, you were not on duty in the morning of turnaround as you had no float, and you came on duty to greet the incoming passengers. I needed a few hours off in the morning as I had the job of moving house for the last time, moving up to deck 4 so that our cabin on Deck 2 could be incinerated.

    I awoke in the cabin on Deck 2 for the last time with a slight twinge in my head due to the six late rushed beers the previous night, but one thing was clear—I could not wait to get out of that room. Martin had already packed and was waiting for his new room on Deck 10 to become empty with the leaving JAP disembarking. I showered and completed the last of my packing and moved my things up two decks to my new home. Ross was at the door to greet me and helped with my things, at the same time advising I would be on the top bunk. My new cabin was just off the main walkway of the M1 down from the crew office, the first one through the door in the corridor of about a line of five cabins. I was unsure of whom my neighbors were, but I was sure I would find out in time. The cabin was massive and Ross explained that it was probably the biggest JAP cabin in the way of floor space. For me it was luxury to have carpet, a fridge, a TV that worked, decent bed sheets, and a shower that did not smell. I was happy and started to unpack my things and get settled. Ross was allowing me to have certain drawer space, and I got the feeling he was doing me a favor sometimes, but I did not care. I had a permanent home for the first time in four very long cruises. It was very exciting and Ross was a great bloke to share with. He was very British, with the backbone of the nation on his shoulders. He was very proud of his country and knew all about most things British. He enjoyed visiting the British Virgin Islands just because they were British. He spoke very well and had a great deal of knowledge about the cruise company and the ships themselves. He retained detail about them that would go in my head and exit almost immediately, like the tonnage of most of the fleet and how many passengers they carried. Ross was the salt of the earth but possibly seemed a little awkward with the ladies, but I did not even think that was his agenda. He was more about experiences, cruising, and visiting places, where I was about chatting up girls and drinking as much beer as I possibly could in the time allotted. He was not completely shallow like me. I had a feeling that we would make a good combination, and I already considered him a friend. I wasn't sure if he did the same for me, but it would come I was sure. He seemed slightly intrigued with my confidence, but being the rookie, I needed guidance. Most importantly we were both Brits and had to stick together.

    I spent the next hour or so housekeeping like a proud mother of my new property and had finished unpacking. I donned the whites and made my way to the desk for turnaround day and embarkation to start. I was in a good mood and far more settled than the last cruise when I had no nice cabin to return to and dreaded going to bed or shower. My attitude reflected this, and I was feeling ready to take on the world and help as many hapless passengers as the ship could throw at me. This was a cruise with a difference. We were on our way to the Mediterranean, so these passengers would be spending the next six days at sea and beyond in our company. It was important to make a good first impression because we wanted to be friends with this lot. Many of them were staying on for the first Mediterranean cruise too, so they would be around for a while. Embarkation was smooth and did not seem as intense or as busy as normal. A lot of the crew members had gone ashore to get their last taste of land for a while, and many had gone to stock up on junk food and chips to see them through the upcoming Atlantic crossing.

    While serving one passenger with details of the way the baggage works onboard, it hit me that if they did not get their luggage onboard today, they would be without it for probably over a week, which would be no fun at all. You could see that thought in the eyes of some of the passengers who filled out reports and felt that the airline had mislaid their bags. There was a sense of panic and worry. Ross told me to just let it go because there was nothing we could do about it—just treat it like a normal cruise. It was mostly the airlines' fault for lost baggage anyway, not us or even the cruise line. The cruise line gave out $50 onboard credit per day to help them out, but we did not have to; it was a good will gesture, so we were doing our bit. There was one couple that was not happy at all with not having their bags and blamed me, the cruise company, and the airlines. I had no choice but to get the SAP PR to have a chat with them because they no longer would listen to someone with just a half a stripe. The two full stripes of the SAP PR would normally do the trick and the passengers would accept what they were being told.

    The pace on the desk stepped up a gear and it got a lot busier the closer we got to setting sail. The queue was stretching around the atrium and a lot of them seemed to be panicking about their luggage. I didn't blame them as I would hate to spend six sea days in the clothes I had been travelling in all day with no toiletries. A new girl appeared on the desk named Katie. She was short, Canadian, and very cute. I loved her accent and she seemed very ship-wise; it was apparent that this was not her first contract. One of the great things and sometimes sad things about this job was the turnaround of new crew members coming and going frequently, but that did make it quite exciting. There were reports that gave out rotations of who was getting off and joining, but I had not yet learned how to read them or where to find them. Besides, I liked the fact that all of a sudden you would have a cute Canadian appear on the desk with you. We were all too busy to get to know Katie properly at this stage, but I was looking forward to doing so in the future. She seemed to be close friends with lovely Lisa; as they had sailed together before.

I looked up from my computer to see the angry shouting couple from before at my workstation demanding to see SAP PR again to discuss the progress that had been made on their luggage search. I was pretty sure that there had been no progress made, but these people scared me a little, so I went to get SAP PR. I stood beside her in a sort of nodding support role as back up, unsure if that was right or not. When they found out their bags had not yet been located, they demanded to get off the ship. I had not heard that one before. Getting off the ship would be a problem because we had been sailing for about ten minutes, and we were not going to turn back. The pair did not even realize that we had left the dockside and looked on in horror as SAP pointed out that the ship was sailing. It was apparent that they had been in the bar most of the afternoon and their judgment was seriously impaired by multiple cocktails. The SAP PR had to take them away and calm them down, and I did not see them again after that. Maybe she pushed them off the side of the ship.

It was dinnertime and I was relieved to finally be off the desk; it had been a long hard shift, but we were off and running and on our way across the Atlantic heading toward the Mediterranean. For some reason it did give me a pleasant sense of security knowing that everyone would be on the ship together for the next week or so and could not get off. I was quite often feeling that I had a sense of missing out on what other people were up to when they went ashore, and I was happy that they were all here on the ship where I could "keep an eye" on them. I would not be missing out on anything. I had the feeling that others were probably having a better time than me during their time ashore, knowing what to do and where to go. During sea days everyone had their jobs to do and would go about their routines in this floating village, it gave me a warm fuzzy feeling that we would all be in the same place and have similar agendas. I really liked the sea days with everyone stuck on the ship, and now I had a weeks' worth of them to enjoy.

It was our first sea day and we all had our Rota's for the week. I was on good form with my new home and room-mate Ross and set working hours, so I knew what I was doing and could plan things. The passengers seemed to have settled down nicely and all was okay on the desk. We had another meeting that night, and I remembered that we had to contribute about CRUISE values, which scared the life out of me. I did not really have anything of great value to say at this point and was still unsure about my confidence in front of others during meetings. My game plan was to be low key and stand at the back and hopefully slip under the radar. I met up with Suzanne for a cup of tea in the afternoon break, and we had a good talk. We both seemed okay and happy with our direction I thought, but I still felt very non-committal. It was a personal selfish thought that I would keep to myself, but there was just something missing for me—I had become addicted to the chase. Once the chase was over, the magic, buzz, and electricity seemed to fade very quickly for me. It was nothing personal to Suzanne, it was just I was not a "one woman man" yet. I seemed to play the part of that role quite well up to now. I know I am shallow and I'm not proud of it, but it was the way I was.

My afternoon shift started at 4:00 p.m., so I had two hours to prepare something of substance to add at this stupid meeting. It hit me ten minutes into my shift that I would just ask my colleagues their thoughts and then just copy and slightly amend their ideas. Luckily for me, my master plan worked well and I managed to hide at the back of the office during the meeting and several other more outspoken JAPs stole the limelight with their ideas that would probably never go any further than the back office anyway. The meeting was helpful to get all the JAPs together and have Katie introduced into the fold. Katie had requested to come to the Grand because she was seeing a shoppie called Craig, who was a mega confident American. Unfortunately Craig had apparently been sleeping around with anyone who was willing or able during Katie's absence. Katie had not found out about this yet but those fireworks were in waiting. No one was sure how much or little she knew, but her roommate and best friend Rowena would probably have to be the one that spilled the beans. That's what best friends were for. The annoying meeting was over within the hour, and it was apparent that I still did not like meetings, especially the weekly type that required input and feedback.

# Chapter 22: Atlantic Sea Days

The sea days passed pleasantly, and I was enjoying the crossing on the whole. I liked being on the ocean and especially staring out to sea from Deck 6 forward. It was the very bow of the ship where the tip of the ship's nose was, and you could stand there fulfilling your Titanic fantasies. I had not as yet invited anyone to share these moments with me. It was something quite private to me, and I enjoyed the peace, isolation and serenity of it all. I was someone who was very happy in my own company. As long as I had a barperson to talk to or even a fridge full of beers and a TV, I was easily pleased. Back in the UK hotel days, I would often sit in my room watching movies or videos of episodes of friends filling myself up with lager and then falling asleep on the bed. It was quite caveman-like, but I had the gift of being able to relax and I embraced that gift to the fullest. I could switch off and forget the stresses of the day from the bottom of a can of beer. I was a big fan of the drink Stella Artois. It was my favorite drink, and I had been without it for nearly a month. I was not worried because I had fine substitutes, but I knew that there would be a perfect moment when I found a pint or can of Stella somewhere on my adventures.

Every night in the wardroom there would be some sort of celebration or party featuring free drinks for a set period of time. I had now established my main crew of drinking friends and included Tracey, my fellow Brit JAP who was as much of a beer monster as I was, and she also had incredible knowledge about ships and the Mediterranean as she had done five contracts. She was very calm and softly spoken and understood pub culture, something that was lost in many other users of the wardroom who came from other countries. Clem was my best friend and he also got on well with Tracey. We drank as much as possible in the bar without really ever getting very drunk; it was strange and great. We drank with the British engineers early, then the entertainment staff, shoppies, and dancers later on; different departments would arrive at different times and we would be there for the duration. The photogs also played a large part in my life. I was half aware that I was putting having fun and my busy social agenda ahead of spending any quality time with Suzanne. We would drink and talk together and have a kiss and a cuddle on the way back to each other's cabins at the end of the night, but not much else. I was not really aware of what else I was supposed to be doing. I was very new to this ship life and protocol; I worked hard but also played hard. I had a really positive "can-do" attitude at the desk and in the office, and I believed that I was fulfilling my potential. I was having far too much fun every night and had the shameful attitude that if Suzanne wanted to be with me, she would show up and drink with the crowd, which she did not seem to mind. Upon reflection, I was a proper popular selfish prick. But there was a scene growing in the wardroom every night and more and more like-minded drinkers were jumping onboard. When the wardroom closed at 1:00 a.m., revelers would go back to a cabin party, stay in the wardroom with their own drinks, get changed and go to the passenger disco, try their luck in the crew bar, or go to bed. I normally did the last one; even though I seemed in the heart of all the party times at the wardroom, I would collapse at 1:00 a.m. I knew I had responsibilities and duties to perform the next day.

Clem would normally get involved with his fellow musicians talking about music, instruments, and performance. I would try to join in but it was way out of my depth, and even though I tried to understand, it was a struggle. Clem was a bit of a fan of the passenger disco on occasion, but I was not, so he would quite often saunter up there at the end of the night. Clem was getting on well with Suzanne's roommate Claire, from New Zealand, which was cool; it was helping with the healing process after Claudia. Even though it hurts being left behind, things move on quickly on cruise ships, and if you wallow in your own sorrow and feel sorry for yourself too much, it could spell disaster. Clem must have identified this; he was a sensitive soul and just needed to cheer up and move on.

The routines of the Atlantic crossing were simple: do some desk hours, have lunch and a nap or fresh air or lay out if sunny, few more hours on the desk, and then it would be playtime and cocktail hour. We had two disco nights in the crew bar, and we normally attended these late after drinking in the wardroom. The second disco night was just fantastic. It was as if most of the ship had turned out and the dance floor was packed and everyone seemed to be getting on really well. I had never seen so many males on a dance floor at once. I remember at one point dancing with Suzanne and Clem and Claire and knowing most of the people on the dance floor—not something you will get in any disco or club on land. It was important to stop and look around every so often to take in how much fun and how amazing it all was. It was very easy to forget who you were and what you had done in your life previously. During the disco, I had a flash of madness about me and grabbed Suzanne by the hand and took her down to her cabin. We were kissing most of the way there and did not make it to her tiny cabin on Deck 4, but ended up in the laundry room a few doors before it, increasing our knowledge of each other on the folded down ironing board. Not sure what got into me, but I felt like Superman that night for some reason. Must have been the drink and party atmosphere. If we had been caught, we both would have been in serious trouble—possibly breathalyzed and the sent home in the next port.

    I awoke in my cabin in pitch darkness, totally disorientated, confused, slightly drunk, and in a semi-state of panic. I could not find the light switch and found myself crawling around the cabin floor lost. This was ludicrous, but I was actually scared and lost in the darkness of my own cabin. I found myself looking for the bulkhead wall and following it around like a blinded person. After what seemed like the dark ages, I eventually located the bathroom door after falling over the small cabin table. I pulled myself from my knees and found the bathroom light switch that was on the outside wall. I turned it on and bathed in the glory of light and the ability to see. I felt huge relief and finally stopped panicking. That was certainly not cool; I really missed natural light and windows.

# Chapter 23: Shift changes

The week passed fast, and before we knew it, we were due to hit land in Ponta Del Garda. Most of the crew was tired of the sea days, but I loved them and was sorry when we had to stop. I guess I was very new and very fresh. I still had a good attitude, and had seen a lot of potentially good workers become stale over a week because they were nearing the end of their contracts. The work on the desk was okay, and the passengers seemed to have enjoyed the crossing and not moaned too much—well not at me anyway. A few of the guys were really sick of seeing the same faces day in and day out, but I was fine with it and enjoyed being trapped at sea. It was cozy. There had been days when the sea had reminded us that we were at its mercy and probably for two days we had Atlantic rollers, which increased the sale of Dramamine and ginger in the shops. If the weather was turning, we would have a message appear on our computer screens telling us to ensure we had such things in our floats to sell to the passengers once the shops were closed. If a passenger or crewmember was really suffering, and a few did, they would have to visit the medical center for a shot. Rowena, the hotel secretary and Katie's cabin mate, suffered badly, and we did not see her for a few days. On the whole, I had really enjoyed the crossing and would happily do it all the time. But land beckoned and I joined the others as we got up early to spot the shores of Ponta Del Garda. It was as if we were some sort of cruise ship version of Christopher Columbus discovering new land for the first time.

I spent the morning on the desk trying to convince passengers that I knew what I was talking about in giving information about this new port. We had some basic port info, but no great detail; everyone seemed keen to get some land and once my shift ended at 11:00 a.m., Tracey and I decided to venture ashore and have a walk around. It was a sunny day, and I was happy that I was back on land. I did not realize that I still slightly felt the motion of the ocean when I was walking. We only had a couple of hours off so we did some exploring. We experienced the strangest local phenomenon in the town square. There were local townspeople crawling around on their hands and knees dressed in traditional costumes. It really was a most unusual sight, and we were advised that they were crawling into the chapel by way of giving thanks, as what they had been praying for had come to pass.

Back onboard, we were preparing to set sail for another sea day before we went onto our next destination; things were going great and I was very happy, but all of a sudden things were about to be changed completely and my social life would be turned upside down.

We were about to arrive at our first Mediterranean cruise turnaround, and I had been advised that I would be starting as night JAP for the next two cruises. I must admit I felt most put out by this, and for several hours, I felt it like a boot in the balls. In my eyes, I was one of the strongest on the desk, and it seemed like madness to restrict the passengers' service by putting me on nights. I thought it was like having a Ferrari and leaving it in the garage and never driving it. Just not good sense at all. Nevertheless, I had no choice and had to just get on with it. The shift pattern was from 11:00 p.m. until 8:00 a.m. Even though I did have genuine concern for the onboard service the passengers would be missing out on with me in the sidelines, the biggest worry I had was how this change would affect my rocking social life. Who would look after Clem? What would Suzanne do? The takings in the wardroom would fall and I would not even be able to continue with my quest to try and chat up the dancers, my favorite hobby. These were all very superficial and selfish worries. Clem would be fine and so would everything else. I was just worried about missing something, being forgotten, and falling into obscurity. The change would happen the night before turnaround, and I would be installed for nearly four weeks, which was about two cruises.

    I went into a massive sulk, and Tracey took me to one side and explained to me that it was part of the Rota and everyone had to take their turn, so I was not being picked on in any way. She also explained that I would have every day off to explore the ports and could enjoy boozy lunches with that extra glass of wine where most had to stop after just the one bottle. She also said I would be tucked out of the way and it was a good little number if the night team was fun. The incumbent night manager, was finishing her contract and would be leaving in a few days' time and would be replaced by a new night manager, Sandy, who was a lot of fun I was told. That was a relief as the current night manager, scared the life out of me; she spoke very matter-of-factly and seemed very efficient. She took no nonsense; she was ex naval. I had seen her tell Ross off before for wearing the wrong uniform jacket, and Ross made the mistake of arguing with her. She won hands down. At this point, Ross interjected with my pep talk from Tracey to add that I would be missing the first overnights in Barcelona, which would be a huge night out for everyone. I thanked him for that and even though I felt better from Tracey's chat, I felt that I was not best suited for nights. I would be out of my comfort zone, and I was just getting settled into a fantastic routine of work, drinking, and friends—just my luck that the rotations SAP decided to mess it all up for me. Any protests would fall on deaf ears, and I would just have to get on with it.

I went to break the news of my withdrawal from the social scene to my peers. Clem was asleep in his cabin, but I needed to break the news that that night would be our last drink together for nearly two cruises. He appeared from behind the door of his cabin, his hair messed up and disorientated and in need of caffeine and nicotine. I said in a concerning manner, "Dude, we got to talk."

A look of fear came over his face as his mind wondered about what on earth could be that important to discuss by waking him up—what could have possibly happened in the last few hours since we were sharing a laugh and a few drinks together? He took it quite well. It was probably a relief compared to the alternatives working through his mind. He was sad but, "At least you weren't breathalyzed or being transshipped dude," was his response. He had already lost Claudia and he would have probably gone into meltdown if I was also off.

One down and one to go. Suzanne was next. I went to the gallery and they said she was on a break, I caught up with her also in her cabin having a nap. What was it with all the naps today? It seemed the only one that was doing any work, but that's nothing new, I thought to myself. The one thing in the pursers department I would have to get used to, would be always getting up early and working at times and on days when other departments were off or sleeping. It was something I would have to embrace, especially if I was going to continue socializing with other departments, such as musicians and photographers, who were notorious night owls. That is why departments often stick together, due to the convenience of going through similar stuff during the day and keeping quite similar hours. I woke Suzanne up by knocking on her door and she eventually came to the door after I said it was me. She was pleased to see me, be it night or day, bless her, and hurried me inside in a cute way looking as if I had just taken her out of hibernation in a burrow. I sat her down and broke my news to her; she took it even better than Clem who took it better than I expected him to. She was probably just happy that I was not breaking any worse news to her. Also, I realized that it took me out of the evening social scene that was getting in the way of me spending quality time with her. She just smiled and said it would be all okay and just genuinely seemed concerned for me, saying that I would "make it and pull through," as if I had some sort of illness. It could have been that I was coming across as just a little moany and in need of pity and attention.

That night, we all went out for my send off. Upon reflection, even though I was throwing my toys out of the pram a bit, it would all be over in two cruises, and I could go back to my happy desk routine. Or so I thought.

I had to sleep for a few hours during the day, as my first night shift started at 11:00 p.m. It was the night before turnaround, and it was still busy. I was handing over from Sara who had been the night JAP for several months. She had wanted to avoid a certain person during the day shifts, and her plan had worked. She was a night owl and had enjoyed it but was disembarking on turnaround day because her contract had ended. I had that evening with her to find my feet because we had to help the night manager get all the passenger folios printed out. Sara was American, in her early thirties, spoke at great speed, and really knew her stuff; she had done five contracts as a JAP and was overdue a promotion to AP. It was so overdue that her half stripes on her shoulders had become severely discolored.

Mike, the assistant night manager, was mincing about collecting the bar chits and checking them at greater urgency than normal due to fact that the night manager would shut the computer system down just after midnight and run end of day and end of cruise. Any incorrect charges could not be rectified after that time. Mike seemed a bit stuck up and seemed to treat other JAPs like he had already been promoted to AP. He had a way of telling people off that really rubbed them the wrong way, as I would discover all too soon. Sara took me down to the back office to meet both the night managers. Who were very busy doing handover, so they only had time for a very quick hello and went back to their notes and guidelines to shutting down the system. I already hated nights, everyone seemed so busy. Sara was the only one I liked, and she was leaving the next day. I wondered what my friends were doing in the wardroom whilst I was stuck on the desk.

The first hour whizzed past like a flash. I was serving passengers as normal on the desk, but by about half-past twelve, the queues at the desk had dissipated and it was just Sara, me, and a list of night-time jobs to do, including tidying and cleaning. Sara was helping Mike with the chits, and I was tidying the desk when both night managers came and announced that they would shortly be shutting the system down. We had to sign out of our computers and then load the printers with folio paper for the bills that we were printing. We would be using the printers on Deck 5 and Deck 6 and phoning the night manager when a particular batch had completed printing. The night manager would release the next print job to a particular printer. It was of paramount importance that the printers were working properly and that the night manager input the correct printer codes into the computer system. A lot could go wrong; the whole system had frozen in the past and then the computer officer would have to be called to sort the problem out. But we had a wealth of experience with us that evening with two night managers, two desk

JAPs, and an assistant night manager who was stuck up his own ass.

I had to admit that I enjoyed the folio printing and the hustle of reporting in and then ensuring that the stacks of bills were in the correct pile for the cabins. I was on Deck 5 so only had three printers to manage and Sara was on Deck 6 with six printers. Every person on the ship had a folio printed out, so the process took a few hours. I had several panic attacks when I kept running out of paper, and one of my printers kept jamming. I had to abort one of my printers so I was down to just two. The night mangers kindly blamed me for its problems, and after nearly two hours of running about from printer to phone and up and down the stairs to Deck 6, we had all the folios printed and neatly stacked in front of us. The two managers came up to me and instructed me to start delivering them. I was horrified that it was the job of the night JAP to deliver the bill to each of the 2,600 passengers. I was given a stack on Deck 5 to start with and I ran to each cabin carefully and quietly placing each A4 enveloped folio into the mailbox outside each door. My first stack took me about twenty minutes and only covered about a half of a quarter of one side of Deck 5. I went back to the front desk for the next load. This was going to take me all night. I was already exhausted and deprived of sleep, so the prospect of visiting almost every stateroom filled me with dread. When I returned, both night managers and the assistant night manager were smiling. As I reached the desk I could see the room service team taking the rest of the boxes of folios away to be delivered. I felt a sigh of relief but also slight annoyance that I had been the subject of a joke—like the trainee apprentice that is sent out to suppliers for a tin of tartan paint and a long weight. "Very funny," I said in my least sarcastic voice. Sara jumped to her own defense saying that she did not encourage such larks but still found it funny. I did too, after a cup of crap coffee.

That was the most stressful and important of the jobs of the cruise for the night team—to get the folios printed and delivered without incident and for the night manager to shut the system down and bring it back up again after running the end of cruise. We had successfully done that, so it was a good night all in all. The time was now 4:00 a.m. and Sara went to bed to get ready for going home in the morning. Mike the assistant night manager went off too, as his jobs were done and his shift could end. I was left all alone on the desk, totally exhausted from not really being in the night shift pattern yet. I did not see anyone for about an hour except the public area cleaner hovering up with a device that I can only describe similar to a Ghostbusters backpack. I saw my first passengers at 5:10 a.m., and I was joined by SAP Accounts and a fellow desk JAP at 5:30 a.m. By 6:00 a.m., the desk could not have been a more different place. Almost every JAP desk was filled, and we started to see passengers queue at the desk with their freshly printed bills in hand. The night manager was joined by SAP PR to start chasing up the passengers who had not yet paid, and the next thing I knew, we were docked alongside and my shift was ending. I made a hasty exit for my bed, tucked away from the impending turnaround chaos.

# Chapter 24: My name is Luca

After I had been on nights for several days, my system and body were used to the routine. I did miss the parties and drinking with my friends, but it was time for me to stop being bitter and just get on with it and make the best of the situation. The outgoing night manager had disembarked, I was officially installed as the night JAP, and so our team was now settled. It did not take too long for my night peers to realize that I was not just your run-of-the-mill average JAP. I had something constructive to offer and we started getting on well. Mike had stopped being a camp bully, and we all decided to go out for lunch together in Livorno.

    We decided to meet at 11:00 a.m., so that we could all get a bit of a nap in first and Mike could get some straight sleep. We were at the gangway at the set time ready for lunch and some Italian wine. We had made the executive decision to travel to Luca because it sounded a bit more off the beaten track and an adventure. Sandy and I met at the gangway together and were joined by Mike who did look like he had just woken up from a very deep sleep, bless him. I was a little nervous and shaky after my experience with Ross of nearly missing the ship, so I had generally gone with the rule that I would not normally let the ship out of my sight. But I was going out with the night manager and her assistant, so what could go wrong? After taking the shuttle bus to Livorno, we walked to the train station to travel to Luca. We all got our tickets and boarded the busy train with many Italians. As we sped through the stunning countryside, I once again reflected on how my life had changed so much in such a short time. Who would have thought a month ago that I would be here doing these exciting things? I was on my best behavior with my two colleagues; they had more ship experience than me. Both outranked me and had the potential to make my life difficult if they chose to, so I was my normal polite self.

    We got off the train at our stop and explored the charming town of Luca before finding a bar for a pre-lunch drink. I had been told that Sarah was a lot of fun and also had a nickname of "Lush," but I did not really know what it meant. I just was told she knew how to enjoy herself. She was in her early thirties, had curly short brown hair, and was from the south of England. She had a good body, but not overstated. The bar had outside tables and chairs, so we got settled and ordered a bottle of Italian white. I also had a beer to quench the thirst as I could drink white wine like water if I had not had the buffer of a few beers first to quench my thirst. It was a very pleasant moment in the sun in Italy drinking wine with my boss. The wine did not last long and before I knew it we were on our second bottle. I was getting quite hungry at this stage, and we decided to ask our bartender for a recommendation for a restaurant for lunch. He told us that next door was the best in town with fantastic pasta and seafood, so we took up his recommendation.

    We were not disappointed. The meal and wine were fantastic and served on perfectly ironed white linen table clothes with matching napkins, a sign of a quality restaurant. With Sandy's influence, we even ended up ordering dessert and a bottle of dessert wine, which I pretended to enjoy but it was not really my thing. It was a touch of class. It was not a cheap lunch by any stretch of the imagination and my Liras were running low after that, but it was worth every penny to taste normality and Italy a little off the beaten path. I was feeling more than a little tired at this point, and it may have been the four bottles of wine we had consumed and need for sleep, but I was ready for the journey back to the ship, which I now remember to have been on a train. Sandy's bubbly nature was really showing and she certainly was fun and the catalyst of our drinking speeds. I could see her cheeks getting quite blushed and she seemed to be getting naughtier and more mischievous as the wine flowed and time passed. Even though at first I was feeling safe under her umbrella, doubts were now entering my head as she spoke of a new plan to go for cocktails in the town of Livorno. This plan of hers was a bad idea. It had disaster and "miss the ship" all over it, even though I was still slightly paranoid after my last adventure ashore. Mike needed to try to get at least a few hours rest before his shift, and I needed to just close my eyes and rest in my peaceful air conditioned cabin. I thought that in her capacity as AP, Sandy would have been very aware of time and our duties. I had a worrying feeling that she could get wrapped up with locals drinking wine and join a barn dance or something and actually forget that she even works on a ship. I was not keen for that sort of action and had to get Mike to side with me to talk her into getting closer to the ship. Back in Livorno, we decided to have a drink at the station of all places, and there I made my speech about needing to get some rest. We were within shuttle distance of the ship, so I had relaxed a lot more. Mike and Sandy were in deep discussion about how Mike was now ready to be promoted to AP. I did agree but also felt I was also ready, even though Mike had done five contracts and I had done one month. After another bottle of wine, I managed to pile them onto the shuttle bus to drive through Livorno and back to the industrial port area. We made it. We had a great lunch and a day of discovery and were certainly socially confused from the amount of wine that had passed our lips. We said farewell to Mike, who had to be on duty in two hours. Sandy and I took the elevator up to deck 10 where her cabin was, as I had agreed to have another glass of wine with her. As the lift was rising, I decided that no good could come of me drinking wine in my new boss's cabin after we had a skin full already, so I bravely announced that I would go back to my cabin for a sleep before the night shift. This went against most of my natural instincts, but Sandy was already marked as 'D for Dangerous' in my head, even though she was great fun, I could see me getting into trouble somehow on the horizon. Sandy gave me a knowing nod and we leaned into each other and gave a pleasant kiss goodbye on each cheek, Italian style.

  Back on Deck 4, I sunk into my bed on the top bunk and decided that I would not be going out for lunch with the night manager every day. It would be the end of my liver as I knew it. She was fun and we had a laugh, but I would maybe do it once a cruise. As I fell into a deep slumber, my closing thoughts were with Suzanne and the fact that I had not spent much time with her for a few days.

After what had seemed like about ten minutes of sleep, the phone rang. I had to drag myself down from the top bunk and was wondering who could be disturbing me when everyone knew I was on night duty. As I picked up the phone, my heart sank as it was my alarm call. The time was 10:30p.m. and I had twenty-five minutes to get showered and on the desk ready to relieve my colleagues so they could go and party. After what seemed an age of fumbling around looking for an ironed shirt and getting myself straightened out, I made it just in time. I looked and felt rough but at least my shift would end in nine hours' time, and I could go back to bed. Mike came to say hello shortly after I arrived, and he looked as bad as me. Sandy finally rolled in at midnight and was quite quiet. We all had a feeling that this night team was pretty special and more fun times would be on the horizon.

Before I knew it, we were headed back toward Barcelona and every crew member anyone was talking about what their plans would be for the big overnight there. I had got used to the night shift patterns and team, and was quite happy after my initial wobbles. But I was certainly starting to feel left out and jealous of all of my colleagues' evening entertainment plans. Some were going for some traditional paella and sangria on the waterfront. Others were planning a meal and the club. Ross, Martin, and Katie and a lot of the JAPs were all going out in force the hit the bars and clubs and that would probably have been the group that I would have tagged along with. I smiled and wished them a good night through my gritted teeth as they came by the desk to say goodnight at 11:00 p.m. Most of the ship's company had gone out, as well as most of the passengers, even though it was turnaround day the next day. I was sure that there would be a few sore heads and at least I was not spending all of my money on expensive drinks. I tried to justify to myself. The night shift was actually quite entertaining and I could see crewmembers and passengers stumbling in at various times throughout the night and morning. At 6:00 a.m., Ross, Martin, and Katie came up to the desk while I was busy cleaning. I was shocked that they were just getting in now because their shifts started in half an hour. They all seemed trollied and had a ten-hour shift ahead of them in the terminal assisting with check-in. They told me that they all had an amazing night and were dancing on tables in bars and took full advantage of the scantily dressed girls selling them mobile shots. Each of them spent over $100, but they told me that it was well worth it. They went back to their cabins to shower and get ready for work, and I decided to administer my own variety of justice when I finished my shift and paid them all a visit in the terminal building to check on their progress. I saw Katie first and she looked green and not as full of energy and enthusiasm as earlier. She just nodded at me as she was helping set up the terminal building laptops. I caught a glimpse of Martin and his eyes were bright red as if he had been crying for a week and had some sort of bloodshot Halloween eye makeup on them. I could not see Ross but heard that he had been in the terminal toilets for the last forty minutes. I made it clear to them that I had now finished my nightshift and was off to my cabin to lie on my bed, drink a few beers, relax down, watch some movies, and fall asleep. I wished them all an enjoyable shift and went on my way. Even though I felt I had the upper hand now, it did sound like I had missed a legendry night.

My two cruises on nights came to an end swiftly, and even though I was protesting about it to begin with, I had grown to like the routine, the work colleagues, the sleepy sea days and long boozy lunches. The time was approaching for me to re-enter the social scene and get my drinking friends back. I was looking forward to a few nights out.

# Chapter 25: Lonesome Lisbon

I was off nights, back on the desk and the cruise was going well, even better news was that tonight would be crew disco. Things were moving in the right direction in all aspects of my shipboard life, or so I thought. I was back on days, my shift had just finished, and I was ready to party. It was my first disco after nights and it was time to let my hair down with my friends. I swung past Suzanne on the photo gallery to let her know of my plans, starting in my cabin for a few sharpeners and then onto wardie with Clem and then to the disco for a dance and get together with all the rest of the like-minded crew. Clem was still getting along rather well with Suzanne's roommate Claire, and that suited us all. It put Clem in a good mood and kept us all together in a close group. Claire was engaged to be married but was one of the most open, up front and honest speaking women I had met. She told us what was going on in her head and was as confused as the rest of us. A cruise ship is not the ideal place for a newly engaged girl, especially if her fiancé was back at home in New Zealand. I was not sure of the extent of Clem and Claire's friendship, but just noticed that they were close and shared a lot of time talking, sometimes that was all you needed onboard—someone to listen.

Clem was already on form in the bar surrounded by musicians swapping stories and the wardie was busy. It seemed that a lot of people were in the mood for a decent night out. I dove in headfirst getting involved and was soon part of the scene, laughing and drinking. Before I knew it, the photogs had descended upon us and were all onboard the crew disco express. We all loudly made our way along the M1 corridor at midnight, onto the crew bar for some bad disco music and to dance with a floor filled of many different nationalities. There were so many people to talk to if you were that socially inclined, and I was. I had a genuine interest in most people's stories and lives at sea. My brain was like a social sponge and wanted to soak up as much as possible. The evening flew by and before I knew it, I was on the dance floor with Suzanne swaying and singing to Aerosmith's rock anthem "Don't want to miss a thing." I felt grateful to have her, but also still had eyes in the back of my head trying to learn who was with whom in the dancers department. The shoppies and spa girls also seemed to be of interest to me; they were mostly hot girls. I was as shallow as ever, but still on first contract intelligence levels—basically a walking hard-on. At that particular moment, I was very happy with Suzanne. We were a popular couple and suited each other, just enjoying ourselves. Well that was my take on the relationship. What I did not realize was that I had to remind myself that I had a very sensitive, creative, gentle girl with me. I was in for a shock about an hour later.

    As we walked back to her cabin Suzanne started one of those conversations that would only ever go one way in my narrow-minded vision at the end of a night in the bar. Suzanne made it clear in a very subtle, tender, and kind way to me that we were not spending enough time together as a couple and especially not in bed. I think her exact words were that she was "not expecting to make love every night but every now and then would be nice." Looking back, I am sure that she meant for this to start a grown-up discussion about where we were heading and review what we could be doing better. But at the end of the night, after we had been drinking heavily in a crew disco was not an ideal time for that particular conversation. Instead it turned into a very short argument, which resulted in me storming out of the cabin, slamming the door, and pretty much ending the relationship there and then. Now, I could have really handled it all a lot better, but I took it as a direct insult to my sexual performance and it was messing with my manhood. Pathetic as it sounds, I was a slightly drunk, man of pride and felt like I was being insulted. I went back to my cabin and lay in bed upset, but I probably fell asleep a bit too soon, considering the relationship drama that had just occurred.

    I awoke feeling empty, alone and very hungover. We were in Lisbon and I was due on the desk at 8:00 a.m., just as we were docking. I felt confused and dizzy but went on with helping passengers as much as possible and probably still doing a reasonable job. During my shift, I was sent out to the gangway to help passengers find their tour bus. The photographers were shooting Lisbon gangway shots to all disembarking passengers. I noticed Suzanne sat in the shade with a few of the other photogs; she had a little lost baby bird in her hands. All I could really muster was to give her a nod of acknowledgement. One of the less trustworthy male entertainment staff went up to Suzanne with a wry smile and asked if she wanted him to look after the little bird for her. Suzanne returned the offer for help with a very suspicious looking, "no," as if to say, "If I gave you this lost baby bird, I fear that I could not guarantee its safety." My heart sank as I returned to the desk. Would you believe that on this massive ship of 1,200 crew members and over 2,400 passengers, of all the people I had to bump into first, on the morning after a relationship ending argument was that very girl. Just my luck. I was feeling blue but soldiered on at the desk as best as I could for the remainder of my shift.

During my break, it seemed that everyone had already made their plans and gone ashore, so I seemed to be left on my own to wander around Lisbon. I walked around aimlessly and did not enjoy my time ashore one bit. I felt alone and unhappy as I had upset my best friend onboard. I had stupidly and effectively ended the relationship. I was a stubborn person and would happily suffer in silence—not always the most sensible course of action but that's just the way I am. Back at the ship, I returned to my cabin and lay on my top bunk reflecting on the previous 24 hours. I christened this port," Shitty Lisbon," as it had been a shitty 24 hours that I would not forget for a long time. It probably would be better named "Lonely Lisbon."

The days passed by and I managed to avoid Suzanne and just get on with my job and spend some time with Clem, who was clearly campaigning for us to get back together, as were most people, including Stef who did not want to see her ex trainee chum and fellow South African in relationship meltdown. But we were not in meltdown. We were just broken up, and as far as I could tell it was over. Neither of us seemed to have approached each other, even though deep down we both probably wanted to. The cruise moved on, and the ports flew by. Monte Carlo was stunning, a real treat during which I actually spent the day with Stef and took lots of photos and we had fun walking around the sunny streets. During sail away, I took a walk around Deck 7 promenade and saw Katie the cute Canadian with her roommate having what seemed a heart to heart. It looked like she had found out about her wayward boyfriend. Her ultra-confident love rat American shoppie had been sleeping with half the ship during her leave. She was dressed in traditional breakup clothing: tracksuit bottoms with no socks and trainers. I walked past and just said hello politely and went on my way; she looked even cuter in a vulnerable sort of way.

Over the coming days, I was doing a few shifts on the desk and started to get on well with Katie. She had a very sharp sense of humor and had us in stitches. She had cute short bobbed brown hair, was not that tall and had an amazing personality. Her accent made her very attractive and interesting, and I was drawn to her. Things were very quiet on the Suzanne front, and I was feeling excited schoolboy butterflies whenever I saw Katie. I would actually look forward to my shift on the desk when I knew that she would be on duty with me. It was official. I had a crush. With that crush came the normal ritual of trying to impress her with my popularity, equally sharp sense of humor, British charm, and general showing off. It was half working and that was probably because she was feeling slightly ill at ease from her recent breakup. I was cashing in on her fragile emotional state, but I had just experienced a break up of my own. Things move on very quickly in ship relationships, and even though it had only been a few days since Lonely Lisbon, it was important not to dwell on these things too much. I was now looking to move on and possibly start a new relationship.

After nearly a week of me jumping through hoops, juggling balls, and being in the right place at the right time, I finally made a breakthrough with Katie. Even though it sounds like I was being desperate and semi-stalking her, I was clever and cool enough to make her think I was not a stalker and still managed to keep her at a distance—far enough to ensure she felt that she was approaching me at some instances. This was my sad idea of a winning strategy. We were in a cabin party on Deck 10 having a drink with a few JAPs, and toward the end of the evening, I felt a hand touch my knee and slip into my hand. I looked into Katie's eyes trying to be cool and she asked me politely, "Is this okay?" I nodded approvingly and no one else in the room even noticed what we were doing. I felt very excited on the inside, like the cat that got the cream, but I was very aware that I would have to approach with caution. She had just had her heart broken and she needed trust in her life. I was very fresh out of a relationship, and I had not really officially ended it with Suzanne. I had just stopped communicating with her since our late night post-disco argument. That evening, after the cabin drinks I walked Katie back to her cabin, and I kissed her goodnight very gently. I left it there and said good night and went to bed massively excited about this new development in my love life. As I lay in my top bunk, I considered how amazing the feeling was when I felt Katie's hand touch mine. It felt like electricity and I was very pleased with myself for getting a goodnight kiss out of it, but I did want more.

The next morning, I was working on Deck 5 and Katie came on duty with me. I was fantastically excited and was chatting like we were already a couple and as I was attempting to firm up some plans to see her again in a social environment. After about ten minutes, I realized that the conversation was a one-way street and Katie was not in any way excited about me. All of a sudden I got it, and it hit me like a freight train. Last night was a fluke and I benefitted from her feeling lonely, tired, vulnerable, and a little drunk. Bugger. There I was, making all these plans in my head for us both, and in reality, I was really just making them for me. I asked if she was okay, and she said all was fine. "Let's do our jobs and we can talk later about other things."

That was cold. I had gone from loving working on the desk with her to hating it and wanting the earth to swallow me up in about two minutes flat. The relationship that I had created in my head was classed to her as "other things." This was far worse than I had imagined. I was annoyed, embarrassed, and upset for exposing my feelings at such an early stage where she remained cool and distanced. I had been played at my own game, and I don't even think she did it intentionally. She was just saying what was coming naturally. I was just along for the ride and cursed myself for not keeping up the cool aloof image. I tried to take my mind off things by completing the front desk stationery order that I had recently been put in charge of. In my eyes it was a hugely important job and I was completing an inventory while at the desk, but this involved me popping into the back office to check on stock levels, so I did not over-order our stationery needs.

The problem was that in my absence from the front desk, we got caught unawares and it was getting busy. Katie had to fend off the barrage of passengers while I was in the back office counting pens. As I reappeared she said in a tone to be obeyed, "Can you not do that later?"

I agreed that I would continue it later. So now had I not only been snubbed by the woman I kissed the night before and had such high hopes for a relationship, but I had also been "told off" at work too. Could things on this shift get any worse? I just wanted to go back to bed and forget the whole thing, and I certainly did not want to do any more shifts with her in my current mind-set. My manliness had been messed with and even though only the two of us knew about it, it was one too many.

Eventually the longest shift in the world ended, and I did exactly as I had promised myself. I went back to bed to protect myself under the covers. I was starting to really miss the certainty of being with Suzanne. I had gone from being adored to adoring and being ignored, and I was starting to feel bad for how I had treated Suzanne. I was now getting a dose of the same medicine. Karma came around really quickly. I rested and drifted into a deep sleep.

# Chapter 26: Canadian Progress

The days passed and I was keeping a low profile after not making the grade with Katie. I was having a bite of lunch in the mess with her cabin mate, who mentioned that Katie did actually really like me but was not in a very healthy place after being cheated on. This did perk me up as she had obviously been talking about me to her best friend, and the news was positive. This gave my ego a much needed boost, but I would approach with caution because Katie was not stable. Her cabin mate said that they were going out for formal night, so they would be on decks, in passenger areas. She suggested that Ross and I meet them both for a drink. I agreed on behalf of myself and Ross in a flash, but I was warned that this was "just a drink and night out as friends." Neither Katie nor she was after a boyfriend. I said that it would be fine. I thought to myself that Ross would jump at the chance to go out with the girls, because even though he was a charming, quite good-looking, well-mannered typical proud Brit, he did not seem to have a great deal of success with the ladies. In Ross's defense, it probably was not on his agenda that much, but if a date was laid on a plate, he would not pass it up, especially if Katie was there. I knew he had a soft spot for her.

Ross had told me in past conversations that Katie was beautiful and most guys would certainly like to be seen with her. On top of that, she was a lot of fun and interesting. It seemed I was talking myself into pursuing her again, and I cannot blame myself. I never stopped fancying her, and her pushing me away had only increased my yearning. With our shifts completed, Ross and I went back to our cabins to get our formal kit on. While getting ready, I popped along to the crew bar to get a six-pack of take-away Corona beers to get us in the spirit of things. Upon arrival at the bar, I bumped into Suzanne and Claire who were sharing a bottle of wine and involved deep in chat. I was in good spirits so said a cheery hello and Claire did most of the talking. It was okay, but slightly awkward. I was still regretting not sitting down with Suzanne and having a good chat to her to let her know that I was the source of the problems and not her. Suzanne looked cute in a sad way, and I was feeling quite bad for her. She looked like she was still upset. I was still upset, but I had an unofficial date that night, so was slightly upbeat. I grabbed my beers and made a dash for it back to the cabin. The girls did say that they would also be out and about that night. That was the last thing I wanted—to be caught out on decks later, especially with Katie.

We met the girls in the wardroom for a few drinks to start off with and then moved up into passenger areas. Our first stop was the Wheelhouse bar, where the drinks were flowing and both Ross and I were on flying form. Katie was being responsive to me. I could see it in her eyes that I may have bored her into submission, and I could be on a winner again. Ross was oblivious to any signals that Katie was giving me and carried on charming both ladies. The evening ended in the passenger disco, and we had a bit of a dance. The chemistry between Katie and I was reaching fever pitch. I think we both could not wait to kiss each other again. It was more than likely the amount of cocktails we had drunk, but I did not care. It seemed like it was back on. Granted, there was still a massive amount of awkwardness about the whole situation, but I was excited, having fun, and enjoying the chase. We all decided to call it a night, but as we descended down the escalator walkway slope to the elevators, I could see Suzanne and Claire on their way up. The difficult moment had arrived. We looked like two couples on their way home after a great night out, and it had been. We all stopped to exchange greetings for a moment but the elevator could not come soon enough for me. Katie and Suzanne did not really say very much, and I just wanted to get out of there before anything happened. I was feeling shallow after making it look like I had moved on so quickly from being with Suzanne. The lift finally arrived and Katie's cabin mate added a semi-sarcastic, "Goodbye photogs," as the door closed. I felt quite sad even though I was not guilty of anything. The romance had evaporated from the evening sharply, and we walked back to our cabins and said goodnight. I could see it in Katie's face that she wanted to kiss me, but we remained apart and went our separate ways for the evening. As I lay on my top bunk with a very happy and slightly drunk Ross on the bottom bunk, I reflected to myself that in the long term it could have been for the best how the evening ended. Katie was probably not really after me.

    A few days passed and everything seemed to calm down. I had not seen Suzanne or spent much time with Katie, but I was enjoying my work on the desk and spending a bit of time with both Ross and Clem. Clem was as cool as ever, but was in a bit of a quandary; Claire had thrown some signals at him and he was unsure what the best course of action would be. She was engaged back home and it was not the sort of thing Clem was into really. But they did get on very well, and there was a spark. We spent several hours talking it all through and drinking a few beers. Clem did question me about the "cute Canadian" that he had noticed I had been spending quite a bit of time with. I gave Clem the brief outline and said I was "a bit torn with guilt" because of Suzanne. Clem just said that Suzanne was "an amazingly sensitive, artistic, and lovely girl." I of course agreed. Suzanne was someone I did want in my life. But then after a long pause a cheeky smile came on Clem's face, as he stated, "But that Canadian sure is cute." I breathed a sigh of relief. Thank goodness Clem was human and not just hell-bent on doing the right thing, or even worse guilting me into doing the right thing. He was a great guy and a good friend—something that was very important to have on the cruise ships. It can be very lonely and it was a pleasure to have someone to turn to. Seeing Clem among a crowded room gives me security that I have someone to sit with and talk to that actually cares and listens, it gave me a feeling that I belonged.

    That cruise we had two new Canadian girls join the team. They were both brand new to sea and started working on the desk without the benefit of a training course like Martin and Stef and I had. I would have really struggled to have had the baptism of fire being put straight in front of passengers with a float, so I thought myself very lucky. Both the Canadian girls, seemed bubbly and fun but had also lost their luggage on their way to Europe. They only had their travelling clothes and uniforms. They both would shadow the more experienced JAPs for a week, but I seemed to get on well with them both and they asked me a lot of questions.

I was working on Deck 5, helping the passengers and doing a good job of ignoring the phones when Ross made the unusual gesture of picking up one of the calls as it was a "longer ring" external call. Quite often that means it's the head office in LA. As he spoke, he turned to look at me and said to the caller "hold for a moment, I will just get him." Ross said to me, "Toby, it is your mum." I was in shock for a moment. I was far removed from home life at this moment and even though I stayed in semi-regular contact on turnaround days and the occasional letter, it was certainly out of the ordinary to receive a call on the ship's costly satellite phone. There must be a problem. Nine out of ten unexpected calls to the ship from a family member meant one thing: a death in the family. I said to Ross that I would take the call in the back office, and he transferred it through. I approached the ringing phone with my mind as in a million different places: Who died? Would I be able to go home? I had butterflies and felt sick as I picked up the receiver and said hello. It was my mum true enough, and we made our greetings and acclimatized ourselves to the several second time delay on the ship's satellite phone. Mum asked if I was okay and why I had spent over four thousand pounds on my credit card in the last seven days. The time delay on my end was longer than the natural delay as I took in what she said. At least no one was dead, but it seemed I was four thousand pounds down. I told her I had only tried to use my credit card in the 7-11 at Fort Lauderdale, and it was refused, but the balance should still be zero. I thanked my mum for the information and said that I would look into what had happened. I immediately called the credit card company and they said that the money had been spent over the last week across different states and mail order companies, including mobile phones and car rental companies. I explained that I had been on a cruise ship and had not spent anything since trying to use it at the 7-11 quite some time ago. They said that they would look into it and would shut the account down for the time being.

 Later that cruise, during a desk shift, Katie's cabin mate the hotel secretary, walked past the desk and passed out green crew comment cards for us to fill out and said, "Let's try and get DJ Viviano employee of the month." So, we filled out the crew comment cards writing nice things about the cool DJ, who had been present in the funky and hip New York scene during the 70s. I was amazed that she could do that, and did wonder how much influence it would have on the decisions of the CRUISE committee who decided on EOM.

 Deck 5 was quiet and we were in Monte Carlo that day. Katie was on the early shift with me and asked if Ross and I fancied going to explore the town of Ez with her and Mike, the assistant night manager. I was onboard in a flash, and we all planned to meet at the gangway at 10:00 a.m. sharp. We took the tender ashore together and it was a hot day, so I wore my summer festival hat, which Katie kept taking off my head and putting on hers. She seemed happy to be in my company, and we were having fun. We took the train to Ez, which was a small, stunning village not far from Monte Carlo. There was a rumor that Bono had a house there, so I was spending some time in the streets looking for the sort of house that he would own, but with no luck. I did try shouting his name out a few times but realized I was being a bit too noisy in this peaceful sleepy French Village, so gave it up. We walked around the town, took photos, and found a nice place for lunch that did not look like it would break the bank. Ross was doing his best to impress Katie, which did not bode well for either of us, but I knew that the "insider deal" was done and she was making the sort of subtle advances and comments to me that felt like it meant that our next step could be between the sheets.

Lunch was a simple affair with some local rose wine, and our thoughts then turned to heading back to our ship. Katie was a great organizer and got us all choreographed for interesting and different photos, with some with us lying flat on the ground around local monuments and fun poses. On the train ride home Katie sat next to me and we secretly held hands for a time; it was a strangely erotic experience for such a simple act. I think it was the naughtiness and undercover excitement of it all that made it so hot. I was excited that our relationship was back on track and that it seemed all positive. We made it back to the ship and sneaked a kiss in her room before her cabin mate came off her shift. We were both in bodily agreement that our relationship was ready for the next level, but the burning question was when and how? I still had guilt issues and she had trust issues, so it did suit me that we were not going public with this coupling as of yet.

The next evening we found our moment. Ross was rotated on a few late shifts, and I would have the cabin to myself for a couple of hours after the wardroom. Sure enough, after a few drinks together we found ourselves getting naked in my cabin. It seemed a long overdue experience and we were having fun. But whilst in action on my top bunk, which is no easy feat considering the space limitations. I heard the key in the cabin door and to my shock, Ross had popped back to use the toilet. He made a very quick exit when he caught a glimpse of my bottom and someone behind it. I was lucky that Katie was facing away from the door which kept her identity undisclosed. Ross apologized and fumbled and stumbled out of the door in true Hugh Grant style, almost causing himself a mischief as he left at such haste. I was confident that he was none the wiser that I was with Katie. Our first sexual encounter was hilarious, but strangely erotic and certainly a turn on. We both giggled in our postcoital state. She got her clothes and left quite swiftly after that, which suited me as I could have the top bunk to myself and get some half decent sleep. I know it was selfish, shallow, and a bit cold, but it did suit us both and was practical.

A few days passed and things were still strangely awkward between Katie and I, even though we had moved on to the next level by become very familiar with each other on my top bunk. Neither of us could really put our finger on it, but we both knew that something was amiss. All appeared OK on the surface but neither of us could be naturally relaxed around the other, this stinted our attempts to grow our friendship, and everything seemed such an effort. We were not relaxed or laid back or shared our feelings; neither of us communicated our thoughts and instinct can just tell when it's not clicking as it should. We were both keeping it off the conversation agenda to protect ourselves because if we did have "that conversation," it would probably be the end of us.

That night there was a party held in our corridor of all places, basically all those involved hosted drinks in their cabins, and we moved from one cabin party to another. It was like an air hostess party with each cabin having a theme, but without the actual bother and hassle of dressing up the cabin in this instance, just plying each other with drinks. Katie and I were getting more and more playful as the evening progressed and a few people were beginning to notice. My next-door neighbor the Lovely Lisa from Sweden had donated her cabin key to Katie to use the bathroom during the party in the corridor. And when nature called, I followed Katie into Lisa's cabin. One thing led to another and we ended up becoming intimate on Lisa's bed. This breach of "cabin key trust" could be an upsetting act for the owner of the bed, but Lisa had told us that she was spending most nights with her new boyfriend, the air conditioning officer, and the cabin was barely used. In our defense the room hardly looked lived in at all. Katie and I took full advantage of this fact and "bumped uglies" on Lisa's unused bed for a half an hour.

Then, we went back to the corridor party. We were both horny and drunk, so our inhibitions had been thrown out the window. I can remember hastily making the bed by just pulling the top sheet and blanket over the messed up bed and thinking that was enough. But in my drunken state, I did not realize that it was not nearly enough. I did not give our actions a second thought until the next day, when I wished I had changed the sheets, made the bed properly and redecorated the room. But by then it was too late, the damage had been done.

    I appeared at the desk for the morning shift feeling more than slightly hung over but equipped enough to handle our esteemed passengers. I was feeling confidently half drunk, but I quickly sobered up once I heard the conversation on the desk. On duty, we had a full complement and Lisa was holding court with all the JAPs, including Ross, and telling them how someone had got into her cabin last night and had sex on her bed. I was in total and complete fear of what was actually being said; actually, I thought I was dreaming but I had heard Ross repeat it back in a very loud clear perfect British accent, "Someone had sex on your bed?" in the most disgusted tone you can imagine. I was very confused as everyone was in total horror at what had happened to poor, quiet, loveable, popular Lisa. I felt my bottom rumble, as if I was in extreme trouble. What did I do? What could I do? Was she going to report the crime to the purser? Would I be found out? I was feeling very dizzy all of a sudden as I realized what I had done had an actual effect on a really nice persons comfort and violated trust. My confused paranoid mind could picture her getting the crew area supervisor changing the sheets and getting them DNA tested. I thought fast. I would confidently tell my peers now what had happened and get it out in the open and let them fire at me what they would. That way, at least the mystery would be solved and everyone would stop talking about it and just judge me for the disgraceful morally bankrupt human being that I was. Oh my goodness and I would have to explain to Katie that I had confessed on her behalf. I needed to consult her about this, but she was still in her bed, I had no time.

    I decided to tell all, but could not get the words out of my mouth. It just would not happen for some reason. I was just scared of what the immediate fall-out would be and I was not equipped to deal with it, in my current state. So I just stood there and listened or tried to shut out all the speculation and hoped that it would go away. I looked at Lisa but I just could not tell if she knew or not. Was she doing all this to teach me a lesson and test if I had the balls to speak out and confess my sins? I had a feeling that she knew it was me and wanted me to apologize to her, but again, I could not say anything or was not willing to take the gamble. We eventually got busy with passengers and everyone shut up about it, thank goodness. It had been one of the most embarrassingly difficult mornings of my ship life so far.

# CHAPTER 27: RECONCILIATION

Even though Katie and I had been getting on okay in certain aspects, we were still not public, and it was proving to be a challenge to naturally chat or relax in each other's company without some sort of strange pretention. We were just not clicking, it could have been due to all the secrecy and sneaking around we had done. I guess we were lovers and not friends—well not even lovers, more like secret shaggers. I will not deny that it was not great at moments, but I missed the friendship that I shared with Suzanne.

I had decided not to worry about it and just go with the flow. What would be would be, and I would stop trying to make such an effort trying to get a girlfriend. So I did just that and concentrated on working the desk and looking after the passengers. I was seeing some results and I was getting respect onboard as someone who did a good job. I had a caring attitude and way about me that, even though on the inside I may not be all that worried about a noisy cabin, lost luggage, or a passenger not having a bow tie or formal shirt for the evening, on the outside I made it seem like it was the most important thing in the world to me. I started to get some really positive praise and comments, as well as the blue "You made the difference" comment cards. I was still having a very active social life and chasing the occasional female lead, but to no avail. Clem and I were very popular with our peers in the wardroom and certainly immersed ourselves in the spirit of things.

Our new Canadian JAP's luggage had finally arrived, and one of the girls, who seemed shy and quiet upon arrival on the ship, was turning out to be very popular with the male officers. She was soaking up the attention and operating a "free love" policy it seemed. Amazing how ship life brings out different sides of people and releases confidence in people that may have not been there before.

The interesting, and slightly annoying, thing about life in the pursers department was that nothing stayed the same for very long; officers were joining and leaving constantly due to contracts ending. With new leadership came new and different values and styles, and the trick to survive all this change was to be adaptable. Several such changes came about within a few weeks of each other; the first was that I was told by SAP Hotel Services that I would be taking over the running of the business center at the end of next cruise and that Ross would be going on night desk JAP duties. As per normal, I was moaning about the changes. I had been happy back on the desk. I had a nice routine. I liked my colleagues and even Katie and I were getting on again with the occasional nude encounter. Ross was still under the assumption that I was getting back with Suzanne, especially after his unfortunate entry into his cabin at that inopportune intimate moment.

I did not like change, and I was being taken away from what I knew and liked and what I was good at. My new supervisor would be the grumpy computer officer who had not taken to me at all and seemed to be very cold and no fun whatsoever. Also I would have to take over from the miserable Scottish girl who was my first onboard sexual encounter, so the whole situation had awkward written all over it. But just because my potential new boss disliked me and I had shagged the current business center officer, was no grounds for me to put in an official request to reconsider the decision. I was going to have to cope with the cards that had been dealt me.

Ross seemed to think that this new job was a good thing; the basic desire of most JAPs was to get off the desk and not have to face complaining passengers every day. But I loved the desk and the Americans seemed to like my way of dealing with them. Ross said that he had asked to go on nights, so that he could spend some real time experiencing the highlights of these amazing ports we were visiting. He told me his plan was to go on tour every day as an escort so that he would not have to pay for anything. It was a good plan, but sometimes on tour you do have to adhere to a set itinerary and herd people around and be herded around. I would just be tempted to stop in a bar and sit there for the rest of the day doing my own thing, but Ross was not that superficial and genuinely had an interest in the places we visited, our agendas differed slightly.

Moving to the business center was strange, but I would give it my best shot even though I was scared. I had absolutely no knowledge of computers and did not even have an email account. I had half a cruise to get to grips with my new job, so I would have to concentrate hard. Sophie, the moody Scot I was taking over from, was getting promoted to AP after doing five contracts. Most thought that that the fact she had completed five contracts was the only reason she was getting promoted; she did not exactly set the world alight with her personality and charisma. We did get on okay, and she said we would start handover the next morning. As I left the atrium to go and tell Clem my news, I walked past a photo of DJ Viviano in the employee of the month frame. So he did get it then—amazing.

Employee of the month was chosen by the CRUISE committee, which was comprised of representatives of heads of department from all the officer departments. This included the first officer, photo, and shop manager, first purser. The monthly meeting was chaired by the purser, and during this meeting, they would discuss all matters CRUISE and vote on the employee of the month nominees. The hotel secretary (Hot Sec) took the minutes of the meeting and made all the preparations—thus, her giving us the heads up on DJ Viviano and taking her own personal campaign to finish the job. I was on the desk on Deck 6 helping passengers and the first officer Chris came up to me and asked if I had "lent my formal shirt and bow tie to a passenger."

I was taken back that someone as important as the first officer knew my name and would even talk to me. I was honored and retorted with a humble, "Yes, sir."

He gave me a smile and said, "Well done. That's very good of you."

An hour or so later Hot Sec came up to me and gave me the nod that I was in line for a nomination as EOM. I was very excited at this revelation. I had barely been on board three months and was considered for such an honor. The ship had over 1,100 crew members and little old me was in line for a mention. I had been in the front line of the passengers for months serving them on the desk and had received quite a few positive comments and green cards, so I was aware that I was moving in the right direction, but I was shocked that my efforts would be recognized at this early stage of my career.

At that point, I decided to campaign for myself and beef up my chances by getting some of my peers to fill out some green cards for me. Most of them did without question and when I found myself cheekily asking a few of the APs, I realized that I might be taking it a bit too far. I gave it up and decided, "What would be would be." But if you have a good mix of passenger blue comment cards and crew green comment cards, you would not be far off the mark, so I had given myself as good a shot as anyone thanks to the insider information. Hot Sec was keen to have a JAP as EOM; it had been a while, so she was on side to steer me in the right direction. She told me that the final CRUISE committee meeting would be in a week or so as the month end approached so the final decisions would be made then. I did have butterflies in my stomach, thinking that I would actually be in line. I have to admit I wanted the accolade to return home with after my first contract.

For now, my thoughts were on the business center handover and learning about the routine and processes of its daily running. I spent most of my spare time learning the job as I would not be granted much handover time due to being needed on the front desk. There was an element of pressure and time was a bit tight, so I just got on with it. The business center was located on Deck 7 forward in between the wedding chapel and the port side entrance of the main theatre. If you were not looking for it, you would miss it. It had a very subtle sign over a corner marble counter that sat opposite a door that opened into a small room with six chairs and workstations. There were two outside facing windows and a small notice board that held updated daily news and sports results.

    I went up to see how the afternoon shift worked as the opening hours were from 8:00 a.m. until noon and then from 3:00 p.m. until 7:00 p.m. This varied depending on if it was a sea day or not. On a sea day, we were open from 9:00 a.m. until 6:00 p.m. and the computer officer would relieve you for an hour's lunch break. Sophie was explaining the hours and duties to me and moaning about them at the same time. I tried to put a positive spin on things by congratulating her on her promotion and asking if she was looking forward to starting work in the crew office as AP. She almost cheered up for a moment saying that it was "as good a place as any to start." I had very different ideas about my approach to passengers and attitude, but for now, I would take her knowledge and grab the few pearls of wisdom on how to post charges and run the administrative side of things. From what I could tell, it was a decent enough job, and once I got into a routine and acclimatized to the grumpy computer officer, it would be fine. I was just very weary of ensuring that I got all the details correct from Sophie as I knew next to nothing. I took Sophie for a drink in the crew bar after our first completed shift together. It was clear that what happened between us at the beginning of my contract was a one-night thing, and I respected her for not pushing the issue any more. We did get on quite well with a familiarity that did not stray into weirdness too much.

In the crew bar as Sophie and I were toasting her promotion and my new role, Stef popped over and said that there was someone who wanted to talk to me. I walked over to a table in the corner and Suzanne sat there looking beautifully vulnerable and cute. I felt a bit sick and scared as it was the first time I had spoken to her since we had the stupid post-crew fight and a lot had happened since then, especially with Katie. But I felt that I had taken my relationship with Katie as far as it could go. Katie and I had occasional encounters but nothing soulful, and after the depth of the level of relationship attention I had received from Suzanne, it was just an adequate substitute. After a few moments of pleasantries and being polite, we got down to the nitty-gritty and Suzanne just came out with the question straight and direct, "Do you want to get back together?"

It was as simple as that, her just asking me one question brought us back together as swiftly as we broke up. I had no idea of how much or little she knew about what I had been up to while we were on our break, but I would keep that to myself. I would have to deal with Katie another time, but for the moment, it was all about me and Suzanne being a couple again. We had a little kiss in the crew bar and she had to scuttle off to work her gallery shift. But she had her man back and I was back in familiar territory. I wasn't too sure what I was going through or doing, but I certainly felt stronger with her at my side for support. I looked at Stef and she assured me that I had done the right thing and that Suzanne had been miserable since we had broken up. It was really sad to see such a lovely person go through heartache. She had been the bigger person and asked the question. I had no doubt that if she had not been the bigger person, I would have probably never spoken to her again properly. I had this weird stubborn streak about me that just does not want to budge if I get my teeth in something, for better or worse.

Clem and Claire arrived and joined the party. I told them the news of me and Suzanne getting back together again, and they were obviously elated. We would be the happy family we were before. Martin and Ross poured in and I got them bourbon and Cokes and the evening flowed well, Ross was celebrating his last night before he embarked on his night shifts and his tours quest to see all of the Mediterranean highlights on the tour escort bandwagon. Clem and I talked and he asked me how I figured on handling Katie because as of that moment, I actually had two girlfriends onboard, which was more true than not, I feared. I really needed to get to Katie before the news that I was back with Suzanne filtered its way through the ship's gossip systems. I would tell her the next day and hope that it would not be too late. I had no real solid plans to see either girl in the next sixteen hours, so that would be my strategy. I continued the evening celebrations keeping all things "Katie" at the back of my head, but knowing I needed to tell her. I owed her that much to try to prove that I was not just an indecisive idiotic love rat, which I probably was.

    I spent the next day finishing off my desk duties and continuing to hand over with Sophie and still feeling quite scared about the daunting task of helping Americans with the internet when I had no real knowledge of it myself. Sophie started me off by opening my very own email account with Yahoo, which opened the lines of communication with me and the rest of the planet via our computers. I had to admit I was impressed and even though it was a shaky start, I could see how easy it all was. Sophie also told me that she very rarely allowed crew to use the center even though officers were allowed to. She had fallen out with most of the officers over usage, and they just went to the crew internet café. I quietly vowed to myself to turn that around over time, as my goal was to be popular as well as to get the job done. I understood the importance of onboard networking from drinking in the wardroom and socializing with all departments.

    Earlier in the day, I had arranged with Katie to meet for a sail away cocktail, which she accepted. That would be when I would end our time together as two people who occasionally slept together and did not communicate properly. At 5:00 p.m., I met Katie on top deck and I got us both a cocktail each. I had my favorite strawberry daiquiri and we sat next to each other on passenger sun loungers. We held hands while the ship peacefully slipped away from the dock. I could not believe it, but we were actually comfortable and happy and at ease in each other's company for the first time since we had gotten together.

Even Katie commented, "This feels right, doesn't it?" And I had to admit it did. I was kicking myself on the inside that my next sentence would be, "I don't think this is working between us," when it apparently was finally working all of a sudden. It just seemed that Katie's barriers had been lifted and she had finally let me in. We talked naturally and spoke of our feelings. It was then where I had to drop the news. I was honest and told her I was getting back with Suzanne. Unfortunately, Katie did not take it as well as I had hoped, and I found myself covered in sticky strawberry liquid from the remains of my drink. Suddenly, what had been a quiet passenger area had turned into quite a busy one, and I was the clown in the middle of it all. I had annoyed Katie and paid the price, but the job had been done and I really needed to keep that indiscretion away from Suzanne or I could find myself single very quickly.

    I went back to my room and showered off the rogue cocktail, and then as if it was scripted, Suzanne knocked on my cabin door. We made the best possible use of my top bunk that we could without interruption. But the whole time I was thinking that with my luck Ross would burst in and shout, "Not you two again!" when it had not been Suzanne he caught me with the last time. The gods were on my side and we had the room to ourselves for an hour. We were now officially back together and it had been sealed with a kiss.

# Chapter 28: Down to Business

After that wobble, things started to get back into a comfortable routine. I had taken over fully from the newly promoted Sophie in the business center. Ross was the night JAP. Clem had his own showcase slot in the Explorers Lounge once a cruise, and all was right with the world. I was still kicking back and having a decent social life, but I was also paying enough attention to Suzanne that she actually felt like she was in a relationship. I had almost found a balance.

I was really starting to enjoy the business center and building up a decent customer base with the passengers that were on each cruise and with the officers and crew. The rule was that I could allow officers and some crew in if the PCs were not being used by passengers. So, I used that ability to its fullest extent and helped as many people as I possibly could, while my predecessor had done the opposite. I was becoming popular for helping so many people and I learned loads about the internet and computers in a very short period of time. I had my own email address and had started to become a computer geek. Somehow, I was getting away with people thinking I was some sort of guru. The formerly grumpy computer officer that I had previously feared, had turned out to be a great person and very funny. He was very good friends with Katie because they both came from Vancouver and had similar senses of humor. It seemed he was just grumpy before because Sophie was miserable and they fed off each other's foul moods. I was a breath of fresh air with a great attitude and wanted to learn and help people, and it had been noticed. The revenue the business center generated was significantly increasing every cruise.

As well as looking after the business center, another role in my job description was to look after the bookings for the Mexican and Italian restaurants. This was an absolute nightmare because the phone was constantly ringing, and I was very confused with the different spread sheets and tables and capacities of the restaurants. If there was a problem with someone not getting a table and they had a reservation, it was my ass on the line. I hated that part of the job. I had nowhere to hide because both of the restaurants were on Deck 7 and the restaurant supervisors knew where to come if there was an issue. And hunt me down they did. I discovered there was nothing worse than an angry Italian or Mexican restaurant supervisor who had guests expecting a meal in their restaurant and no reservation in the system.

Another part of the my role was to assist the computer officer with the turnaround day duties, which involved getting up very early in the morning and setting up the check in computers and ensuring that the technical side of passenger check-in ran smoothly. We were in Istanbul for turnaround over two days and the check-in was run from the massive terminal building on the dockside; it was basic but functional. We were given two JAPs to assist and on this day it was Martin and Katie, so it was going to be both strange and fun. Katie and I had now successfully ignored each other throughout the ship for a while, but we finally came face to face and she had sarcastically asked me how my girlfriend was. I replied as if I were in a playground in primary school, saying "Which one?" She gave me a disappointed look of pity, as I could not come back with anything wittier than that, and that was the last we had spoken. That turnaround day would be a long day, and I would have to do some growing up and try to be nice. The shifts were from 6:00 a.m. until about 7:00 p.m., depending on how the passengers arrived. We would monitor how many were to arrive throughout the day.

The forty strong check-in staff were all locals who spoke English and, for the most part, were very cute girls—so eye candy was plentiful. It was our job to manage and assist them in checking the passengers in with their personal information, passports, and "all important" credit card details. Each check-in station would be armed with a laptop and the staff would input all the information and then once we sailed the computer officer would extract the information and load it onto our systems for the cruise. If there was any missing info, the desk JAPs would check, so the jigsaw of the PIF and credit card information was coming together in my head and it was all starting to make sense how it all worked. Even though it was a long day, it was better than the desk, as we were out and about and we had breaks. We also got to look at pretty locals, and I was becoming very friendly with one of the head terminal staff, who was this stunning Turkish girl. She seemed like a hard worker and controlled her check-in team and worked with the first purser and computer officer to ensure any needs on the day were met with her professional and local knowledge. We had a new first purser, who was another Brit and reminded me of my wonderful uncle John, and he seemed fun and approachable. I was still quite intimidated by the three stripes, so I was slightly more introverted than normal. When he asked my reasons for coming to sea, the best I could muster up was mumblings about my father being in the Merchant Navy and I wanted to follow in his footsteps in some way. Nevertheless, we seemed to get on and he was certainly friendly with my direct boss the computer officer.

I took my role on turnaround day very seriously because I got to carry a radio for the first time, which made me feel very important. I patrolled up and down the check-in lines, ensuring that all the power leads were plugged in and secure, so that we were not in any risk of losing any of the already processed information stored in the laptops. If we did, then we would have to ask the passengers for all the information again and that would seem very unprofessional. I was enjoying the job even though it was a long day. I could show off in front of Katie, flirt with the check-in staff, and we could even sneak off for a cold beer in the small terminal bar as the day drew to a close.

Once 7:00 p.m. hit and the majority of the guests had been checked in, we could hand over to the night team, and we were free to go. Our mega long turnaround day shift was over. We mostly had differing evening agendas, and I was going out for a meal in Istanbul with Suzanne,

Claire, and Clem. The rest of the team were off for dinner and a belly dancing show with some of the terminal management. I had been with those guys all day and even though they were a laugh, I needed to switch to a different company dynamic. Also, Katie would be present and if I ended up spending too much time with her, we could end up drunk and kissing and that would certainly thwart my plans to build a solid relationship with Suzanne. After a refreshing shower and getting ready as quietly as possible, with Ross sleeping before his night shift, I knocked on Suzanne and Claire's door. Clem was already there helping them empty their fridge of beer, so I dove in quickly and assisted him before we had to get off and explore this exciting city by night.

    Istanbul looked like it needed a good clean during the day, but in the evening it illuminated into an amazing paradise of culture and wonder. It was a very busy city and a cave of street markets, apple tea vendors, and colorful locals. We did feel safe going ashore here, but probably only in numbers. We walked around the loaded streets taking in the evening atmosphere. This was real life without the protective bubble of the cruise ship, and we were in the middle of it. We were a foursome and found a safe looking restaurant to eat, even though Clem and I probably wanted to just drink. We had to eat for the girls' sake. The food and service was nice and we paid in million Turkish Lira notes. We went into a bar where there was local music and entertainment. The amazing thing about a ship in port is that even in a city like Istanbul with over ten million people living in it; most of the crew will end up in one place or locate the place that serves drink the latest. We would all end up there: dancers, shoppies, casino, and spa representatives. The draught beer was cold and the company fun, so we had a great night, but we were not the last to leave as the next day was another busy day, and I did need some sleep. I asked Suzanne if she wanted to stay with me for the evening because Ross was on the night shift and she swiftly accepted. We popped back to the front desk to say hello to Ross, but did not taunt him as he did me when I was the night JAP and he had just got back from Barcelona about 6:00 a.m. We hugged Clem and Claire goodnight and did not enquire what their next moves would be. But I did quiz Suzanne once back in my cabin what the pair was up to. Claire was engaged, but lonely onboard and she got on very well with Clem who really enjoyed the company. I had my suspicions, but knew that Clem was a really straight honest man and would only probably agree to see Claire on any romantic level if she were not engaged. I opened one last beer and poured Suzanne a glass of red while we mused over the evening and the fun we were having, with the soundtrack of Travis, The Man who... playing in the background.

  The next day we set sail for our next cruise, the ship was sailing full and I was going to be busy. We had fourteen nights per cruise so the next turnaround would be back in Barcelona. These long cruises suited me because there were a good mix of port days and only three sea days, so there was a lot to do. As I trekked up the stairs in the crew area, en-route to perform my GES station duty in front of our new passengers before we sailed from

Istanbul, the hustle and bustle was great. One photog said to me I passed him, "Here we go again guys. New cruise, new attitude." It a non-sarcastic motivational way ensuring all around him heard. I felt good and as if I belonged to something special, important, and successful. It was a good feeling and it was special to be part of this massive team of fellow crew members, most of which were pulling in the same direction.

# Chapter 29: Honored

During the next cruise, I was just minding my own business in the business center one busy sea day and SAP Accounts came up to me with an envelope and a broad smile. He handed me the envelope and waited for my reaction as I saw that I had been awarded the August Employee of the Month. I was over the moon and totally excited about it. I had to wear a big badge, have a party, attend the cruise meeting, and have my photo in the atrium. I won $100 too, which was fantastic. I was secretly proud of myself as it was my first ever contract at sea and to get this accolade so early on was wonderful. I could not wait to tell Clem and Suzanne and my friends, and I could hardly contain myself for the remainder of my shift.

I was really finding my feet in the business center and it had gotten so busy that we had to get some chairs for people to sit down on while they waited for a spare PC. Compo (Pete the Computer Officer) was working on a booking system to maximum capacity on our six computers and that it was fair for passengers, especially on sea days when I had long queues. But luckily I had a very patient manner so the passengers never got too irate; 2,400 passengers and six computers is not a great fit, but we made the best of it and smiled and got on with our jobs. I was starting to get on really well with Compo Pete, and we started to spend time in the gym and eating together. He was a strange one to read and work out. He kept his cards very close to his chest, but I treated him as if he was my boss as well as a friend, which he was, and we had a healthy relationship.

I received notification that my duties as EOM would begin shortly. I had to be presented with my certificate by the Commodore, have my picture taken, and pose for a head shot for the atrium. My presentation would be in the back office; the F&B team brought in beer, wine, and nibbles setting up a mini function with outstanding efficiency. I was working in the business center and Pete came to relieve me and told me to go to the back office. I arrived to a round of applause, to which I was slightly uneasy with and went a slight shade of red. Most of the team was there with a drink in their hands as well as the senior pursers. I did feel special and all I had really done was be good at serving passengers with a smile. Some people receive EOM for saving a passengers life or handing in wallets full of hundred dollar bills; the CRUISE committee must have been a bit thin on the ground this month, but I was not going to complain. It was certainly good for me and the pursers department. The Commodore arrived in regal style—cool, late, and loud. His confident, clear, slowly well-spoken words stated, "Where is the man of the moment?" referring to me. SAP Accounts pushed me forward in a camp way, and I received a manly shake from the Captain of the Captains. "You've done very well," he stated. I stood in awe, as if I was in the presence of true greatness.

I was still at the stage of being highly impressed by the power of stripes and even though on land and in the outside world, they were pretty much powerless, within the belly of this steel beast, they were the law. The celebration party impressed me with canapés being distributed by F&B staff and cold beers and glasses of wine on display in a makeshift back office bar. I did not feel bad about the two Coronas I drank; everyone was having a drink but did show moderation in the current company. I kept it all low key and did not make too much of a fuss at what I had achieved as EOM on my first contract, but I felt quietly proud. During the flurry of activity at the office party, SAP PR called me over because I had a phone call. I took the call with a cheery hello only to be welcomed with a grumpy, "Are you ever coming back?" It was Pete, obviously bored with manning my business center post and wanting out. I felt like saying, "Do you know who I am?" or "This party is in my honor, you know." But I just settled with saying, "I will be straight up." I left the winding down party and swiftly made my way back to work. Pete was okay when I got back and he sped off with efficiency as if he had more important things to be attending to than my job, which I am sure he did. I completed my busy shift looking forward to continuing drinking those cold Coronas with a wedge of lime in a few hours' time, even though I would have quite happily drank on there and then.

  The few hours passed and before I knew it I was drinking in the wardroom with the engineers and Tracey showing off my new large blue badge that I would have to wear for the next month as part of my EOM duties. We had a laugh and I was joined by Clem and Suzanne. All of a sudden I was in a happy place: work and social life were gelling well and this moment was one to be savored.

The business center was going to be busy the next day because it was a sea day, and I had awoken with a pounding head and was unusually slightly late, so I had a queue of my regulars who all taunted me with wisecracks and jokes about time keeping and how rough I looked. I felt guilty and worried I would be in trouble, but after an hour there was no trace of recrimination of my poor timekeeping and being socially confused. At lunchtime, Pete relieved me for an hour and I had cheeseburger and chips to soak up the night before and proceeded to my cabin for a half hour power nap. Ross was snoring away as he has exhausted from staying up most of the port days on tour. He said he would make the most of nights he had already, but I advised him to take a few days' rest. He said he would use the sea days to sleep even though there were less of them than port days. I was slightly worried that he would burn himself out; I knew how draining staying up all night was on that shift, let alone staying up most of the day on tour in the company of passengers.

Upon return to my post at the business center, Pete said that we would be looking at extending the hours of the business as a trial the next cruise to try to boost revenue. Great, more hours I thought, but Pete said it would be done fairly and the first purser was very pleased with what we had been doing and how we increased the turnover through my good-natured manner. It was true. Even though I had very limited computer skills and knowledge, I managed to keep all the demanding passengers happy and the six seats filled to full capacity. It was no mean feat as a month earlier, I did not even have an email address, and now I was registered on Yahoo and was getting a good supply of jokes and porn through, which I thought was what it was all about. The passengers liked my genuine way of dealing with them and I was getting tips at the end of the cruise, which had not really happened before in the role. At the end of my shift, Suzanne came and picked me up from work and said we would be going for a drink together. It was not that usual for her to instigate me going for a drink, so I happily went along with the plan. We would be passing my cabin and she said she wanted to pop in and use the bathroom. As I opened the door for her, I almost jumped out of my skin. About a dozen people shouted "Surprise!" at me from inside my cabin. I was in shock as it was not my birthday but I saw the homemade banner saying, "Congratulations on becoming EOM!" I was touched and smiling as I saw Pete, Katie, Ross Clem, Stef, and Tracey all with drinks in hand and nibbles spread around the room in bowls. I was touched that apparently Pete and Katie had arranged this, and I was honored that they would think so much of me to treat me in such a way. A few more department members came and went, including the tour manager who popped in for a swift wine and presented me with an envelope. I was at a loss as to its contents, but soon found upon opening that I had been given two days off by Compo Pete to go on the Rome overland tour. My jaw dropped in amazement that someone would go to all that trouble to arrange such an amazing treat for me. I turned to Pete and asked him about my shifts, and he said that he had spoken to the first purser and that he and Katie would cover the shifts at the business center. I was blown away and excited to be going on an adventure. I looked at the envelope and at that moment realized in horror that it left the next morning. No time to pack! I was in the mood to drink heavily, the party was actually in my room, and I did promise Suzanne a romantic evening and a day out together. As I looked at her and could see that she was pleased for me but also slightly disappointed; she knew about the party but not the two days away on tour. I did not possess the relationship maturity skills to address her concerns at that moment, so I just gave her a kiss and said that it was exciting. She just smiled and said that I deserved it.

After emptying my own mini bar, I managed to get everyone out of my cabin and onto the wardroom as Ross and I cleared up before he went onto his night shift and I got packing for the next morning. I had to report to the crew office at 6:30 a.m. to pick up my passport, so I needed to be on the ball. I was also on tour in the official capacity as ship's escort and would have the responsibility of looking after all the passengers' passports too, as well as ensuring that we did not leave anyone behind and assisting the guide. Suzanne stayed back and helped with the tidy up, and we sat and had a glass of wine and a chat. I grabbed the moment to apologize for our plans over the next few days being ruined by my overland tour. We were still on slightly rocky ground given that we had only really just gotten back together, so I needed to tread carefully with my excitement of leaving the ship and her for two days. To be honest at that moment I could have done without the tour to Rome, but it was such a lovely gesture and a few days off would not hurt.

# Chapter 30: Overland

I awoke with a sense of urgency as I had slightly overslept due to the previous night's excitement. I still had to finish packing and ensure I had all I needed for the two-day trip. We were in Livorno, Italy and I had to get my ass in gear as tour dispatch started in 15 minutes. I still needed to get my passport from the crew office, so I needed to be focused and slick—a bit difficult when all I felt was hung-over and sick. After one of my famous 60-second ship showers, I skipped the shave and threw some clothes in a bag and ran to the crew office. Luckily they were ready with my passport. I just had to sign for it and I was away. I made it to the theatre for dispatch with moments to spare. I was awarded a sticker and an escort badge. Great, another badge. I was already being told off at every opportunity by SAP PR for not wearing my ridiculously oversized EOM badge. I was thinking I was badge free for a couple of days and now I was given two to wear. I was told to sit down and I joined a group of about thirty passengers in the front row. They had paid several thousand dollars to go on this tour, so I needed to look as if I appreciated what I was getting. Our group was called down to Deck 4 and then off the ship onto the already humid and busy dockside. We were led by one of my fellow JAPs who did not even notice me in the group—my anonymity was still intact. At least I would not be bothered by the thousands of passenger questions that they want to ask crew members when they have them trapped on a coach. We were led for about ten minutes around what seemed a labyrinth of doors and round corners until we came upon a line of coaches and we were met by our guide, a very attractive Italian girl. She greeted us and said that she would be looking after us for the next two days, which made me very happy. She had shoulder-length brown wavy hair. She was about five and a half feet tall and had classical Italian beauty queen features finished with the perfect tan and clothes that probably came from Milan. Now was the perfect time to blow my anonymity, and I immediately introduced myself to her as the ship's escort. She gave me a stunning smile and asked me to collect everyone's passport and make a head count as that would be our magic number for the next two days. We were not allowed to lose anyone or leave any passengers behind. I obeyed like a newly trained puppy and was already making plans for our wedding and wondering if she would move to England or if I would live in Italy with her. I was given the passport bag to look after, which was something of great importance and responsibility. If I lost those, all these American passengers would not be able to fly home at the end of the cruise. It had the potential for career-ending disaster.

We set off on our overland adventure leaving the ship and onboard life behind us. It seemed liberating and quite strange, like I was leaving my home and family behind—a feeling I was getting used to. Our beautiful guide gave us commentary as we headed through the countryside to our first stop, Pisa. It was time that I consulted the tour itinerary as I was already bored. I had visited Pisa and the leaning tower a few weeks previously with Stef, and we had pizza and a beer in a local bar. I had not even looked at where we were headed on this tour. I thought it was just Rome, but as I read on, I discovered that we would start at Pisa, and then drive to Florence for lunch and a guided tour. Then onto Rome to check into a hotel and then go out for a dinner and show. After breakfast, we had a full day in Rome seeing all the sights and then coach it back to the ship for the evening sail away. Okay, it did sound interesting, but my mind could not help but wonder where I would get a beer in at all. I did have a couple of emergency cans of beer in my luggage that probably would be warm and shook up by the time I would get to them, but that might be my saving grace. I would be missing my normal evening ritual of going to the crew bar or wardroom with friends and filling my belly up with drink. We arrived at Pisa and had a guided tour of the area and some facts about the tower before a half hour free time to get some souvenirs. I was tempted during the free time to go back to the bar that Stef and I discovered on our last visit, but thought I had better stick with the group and not leave a bag of passports on a bar stool in a high volume pickpocket paradise. Pisa and the area were very clean and it was very busy with cruise ship passengers. It makes the mind boggle on how many ships call at Livorno every year to visit this tower; they must be raking it in. The leaning tower is a decent sight, and I stood again looking at it thinking another box ticked in the world highlights book.

Shortly after finishing taking a few photos, our stunning Italian guide was rounding us all up to get back on the coach to drive to Florence. It was only just after 10:00 a.m., and we had already completed our first visit. She counted the 37 heads onto the coach—that was the magic number—and we efficiently went on our way on the road to Florence. I had my CD player and chilled out and relaxed on the coach. I had a double seat to myself so I was comfortable. My thoughts turned to the ship and what an amazing journey it had been so far. Then my thoughts turned to home and the girl that was supposed to be waiting for me. That's right; I had not made the cleanest break from my past as I should have done. So there was some poor lass sitting back in the UK hoping that I would come back and things would be as they were before. I was not feeling totally guilty. In my mind, if your partner tells you that they are leaving to go and work on a cruise ship for six months, it would be a rather large hint to beg the question, "Is this working?" and just call it a day and finish things there and then. But no, she let me go in the hope that I would miss her and want to come home and settle down. It was having the opposite effect. I was in love with my new life and not wanting to go back on any level—harsh but true. I had telephoned a couple of times and written one letter while I was on nights, but that was only out of good manners really. Looking back, I should have written her a "Dear John" letter on my first day at sea or even on the plane flying over to Miami to join the ship. I had since met Suzanne, my new South African girl, had a fling with a cute Canadian, slept with a mad Scot, and flirted with about a dozen dancers, so I was clear in my mind where the past relationship was headed. I gave her the occasional thought but I had no yearning to go back to England and be with her. I had been quite harsh over the years in relationships and not wasted my time. I had been in love only once with Marie who left me for Swansea University and broke my heart. I had not really wanted a girlfriend but just had drifted in that direction during my last year in England, and that inspired me to get out of there.

My mind drifted back to my current life and the overland tour I was on. We were stopping to take a photo of Florence from a hillside as we had arrived. I was taken aback at how stunning it looked, reminiscing a scene from the past, nothing seemed to have changed and the buildings were all amazing pieces of architecture and the river seemed an excuse to build a number of outstandingly breathtaking bridges. The place seemed like something out of Peter Pan. I was officially impressed. We continued into the city by coach and were let out for a guided tour of the highlights and many statues that adorned the city squares. The whole place looked like a museum, but outdoors. There were iconic statues and outstanding architecture wherever I looked, and at every turn, there was an amazing sight. I was looking for a pub or bar because I was getting thirsty but I had to remember my escort duties. We did stop for a lunch in a local restaurant where we had a couple of glasses of wine, which was appreciated. I was getting to know some of my fellow tour participants and there was a good mix of people. From what I could tell, all were American, mostly late-middle-aged couples and a few families with teenage children and some in their thirties. I sat with a very nice family and their two sons, both in their twenties and we began talking together. They were keen to learn about my life onboard and why I was on the tour. I told them the truth about everything and my EOM status and that this tour was my reward for achieving that. I was on my best behavior and was as charming as I possibly could be. I needed to get good feedback from any potential complainers. I had only been on ships for a short time, but I was very aware of the power the passenger has over the crew in the way of what they could do to make life difficult if there was a problem or personality clash.

    The reason I respected and feared the passengers was that quite a few of the male crew spent time on decks pursuing the female passengers, or even more dangerously, the daughters of passengers. That was not a game I was willing to play as I could see the big neon sign saying "sexual harassment" over any pretty passengers. Most of the young female passengers onboard lied about their ages, and knowing my luck, I would end up with some stunning girl who would be a psycho and send the company a letter saying that I raped her. I could see the potential danger and would not consider jeopardizing my new life for a piece of ass, tempting though it was sometimes. I would sometimes join my fellow JAPs look up "hotties" on the A-Pass security system and that would give us their basic details and, most importantly, their ages. At least in our department we could be warned about any potential underage girls. I always kept passengers at an arm's length. I had so much crew totty to chase that there was no point in taking that career gamble, especially when I was still picking mostly the low hanging fruit from the crew manifest. But here I was trapped with the sexy guide as the only non-passenger, so I made the best of it. Our afternoon saw us finishing our guided tour of Florence, which I had fallen in love with, and we soon found ourselves re-boarding the coach to drive onto Rome. I still had the bag containing the passports so I was performing my duties. I had hidden my blue badge saying escort now even though pretty much all the passengers knew who I was.

    I managed to sleep on the coach in my double seat as the lovely Italian countryside sped by to my left. As I slipped into a half comfortable travel slumber, I again reflected on how my life had differed in the space of a few months. Here I was exploring Italy for free where in my past life I would only go abroad once a year. Most of the passengers on the coach had slept in some form or another by the time we were approaching Rome. It did not take long for everyone to be alert with anticipation as we started to get a sense that we will be seeing some highlights from this amazingly historic city in a few minutes. We got a short orientation tour dipping our toes in the water as we passed a teaser of a few sights: a flash of the Coliseum and parts of Vatican City. The next day would be the big tour day with an early start, but for now we were in route to our hotel with two hours to freshen up before evening pick-up to a restaurant for dinner and a show.

We were dropped off at the hotel, which was just off a square, not a historic famous square as far as I could tell. Our dwelling was a typical city hotel and check-in was quite painless even with our numbers. I found myself in my single room exploring and discovering this new territory that would be my cave for the night. I only semi unpacked because I would only have to repack the next morning. In honesty, I had not fully unpacked my case on the ship either; maybe it had something to do with the fact I had been moved about so much already and did not feel the confidence to claim my turf. To my delight, I found the two cans of beer I had packed for an emergency. I threw then into the overpriced mini bar fridge and dove into the shower with the TV set on MTV loud. I was officially excited. This was truly an exciting city, and it was mine to explore and discover. I was not really a history buff but you just cannot fail to get excited about Rome, it felt like the capital of history. Upon exiting the shower, I grabbed a can of beer and as I opened it and took the first sip out of the can, a video came on the MTV channel that totally captured my imagination, mood, and moment. The song was "Rock DJ" by Robbie Williams and it was some sort of semi-rap verse with a catchy chorus and the video was the coolest I had seen in ages. I was a fan; Robbie was a cool dude who had come up trumps with this. It was just a magical moment and it could have been my state of mind and where I was, but I just know that whenever I hear that song again I will remember that the first time I heard it was my first night in Rome.

Our coach pick-up time was 7:30 p.m. outside the front of the hotel, so I just had only enough time to finish the second warm can of beer and then it was time to hit the city for the evening. Our transfer was only fifteen minutes, and it was an authentic local restaurant that was hosting about three groups, including ours, which made for a decent atmosphere. There were long tables laid out with bottles of wine every second person, so I would not be far from a drink to help me through the night. Our entire group sat together on two tables, and I managed to sit near the nice family I had sat with at lunchtime; they were good company. The wine was flowing before our starters arrived, so it was all quite painless. We were dropped back to the hotel before 10:00 p.m. due to the next day's early start. I was not ready for bed and had three choices: venture out, try to locate our guide for a debriefing on tomorrow's events, or have a beer at the expensive empty bar. I did attempt all three options and only succeeded in one after forking out seven Euros for a half a beer. I took a stroll around the neighboring streets looking for a bar or even better a Italian "adults only" bar (if they existed) but failed on both counts and decided to return back to the hotel before I became too lost or was mugged. I wandered around the hotel looking for the hot guide and failed to find her, so I ended up sitting at the bar on my own nursing an expensive beer, but I was still quite happy with the day I had.

## Chapter 31: Gladiators

My delightful wakeup call from reception alerted my senses at 6:00 a.m., and all of a sudden I was grateful that I did not find the late night watering hole. I felt bad enough as it was. A quick shower and totally inadequate local breakfast later, with passports in hand, we all met in reception ready to be shown the greatest city on earth. All the Americans were like kids about to enter a historical and cultural candy shop. You could hear them chatting about what they were looking forward to, but I had to remember this was more of a unique experience for them. After all, I lived in Europe and the United States was much farther away, I excused them in my mind and granted them their excitement. We boarded the coach in the early morning sunshine and headed for the Vatican to avoid the crowds. It was not a long drive, and we were soon in the smallish queue to get inside Vatican City. Our stunning guide had the help of a Vatican City expert to help us through and to give us more information, but at first, he was most mostly trying to sell us special commemorative coins available in the shop. "Only $99, exclusively yours to own!" Yeah shove it, I thought. I did manage to hold myself back and keep my EOM $100 in my wallet to buy something equally special, such as a Stella Artois.

Vatican City is massive; everywhere you look, you see history and religion. We were given a guided tour of the main highlights by our coin salesman, who pointed out where the Pope lived and the flag that denoted if he was in or out. He was in today, so I would keep my eyes out for an autograph. Next, we were taken inside and shown the stunning Sistine Chapel with its famous ceiling painted by Michelangelo and many amazing sculptures. I took many photos, and suddenly noticed that I was being chatted up by our sexy guide, she was asking about life onboard the ship and a lot of questions about me. I was amazed at her interest and became aroused by her tempting Italian accent; all I could concentrate on was me stripping her off and our naked bodies hard at work on each other. After about ten minutes of this, I was officially walking around one of the most religious places on the planet in an aroused state. My mind had inadvertently run away with itself and it was in a totally different place from the guide and the rest of the tour group. Luckily one of the uglier and older members of the group asked a history question and I was brought back to the reality of where I was. The male body and a vivid imagination are a dangerous combination, I was like an uncontrollable school boy just coming out the other end of puberty. Luckily, no one else noticed my unusual walk and the small bulge in my trousers.

    We were led back into the mid-morning sunshine and given a half hour of free time to explore or buy some souvenirs and coins if we wished. I had a look around and checked out the overpriced shop. It is strange that even though you know it is a rip-off, you are still tempted to buy something as a souvenir. I ended up buying a book about Vatican City that I will probably never open again. It will sit on my bookcase gathering dust for many years. It will move house with me, maybe be upgraded to a box in the loft to be discovered by one of my children in 45 years' time when I have passed on. She will look at it and possibly stick it in a garage sale or it may stay in a box in her loft to be discovered by her children after she is gone.

    We were rounded up again to meet the coach and move on to the Trevi Fountain to throw our three coins over our shoulders like they say you should. It is a unique and ornate fountain and there were many people throwing their coins in. There must a fortune in that thing at the end of every week when they drain it; I wondered who claims the money. We walked around a few of the streets until we reached our destination for lunch, where I managed to get a few wines and still more tiramisu. We were now experts at grading the quality of this particular desert. We were told that we were just five minutes from our next stop, which would be the highlight of the trip for me: the Coliseum. We exited the restaurant and walked at a quicker pace.

    Then it struck us—the first corner of the structure came into view. As we continued, we were faced with the magnificence of this wonder. I was impressed. It was amazing to be standing in the arena and pits and soak up what actually happened all those years ago. Our guide gave us a basic idea of where everything was and how it used to look. I had enjoyed the day and it was time to re-board our coach for the drive back to the ship. I was very lucky to have seen so much of this amazing city for nothing. I had the pleasure of giving all the passengers their passports back on the coach and my role was complete. I wanted to have one last crack at the guide, but what was the point really? I would not be making any plans to meet up with her again, so my efforts would be better focused on rebuilding my relationship with Suzanne. So, that is where my thoughts turned and I was looking forward to being reunited after this impromptu break from each other.

It was strange to see the ship again and think of what I was doing there. I was looking forward to returning to my routine and seeing Clem and my friends again. I had hardly returned when the phone rang in my cabin and it was Pete asking me to report back to the business center. He obviously had requested to be informed by the tour office when the overland returned so he could pounce on me and get me back to work. That was fine. I had just had two days off, so I changed in a hurry and rushed up to the business center and relieved a stressed Pete, who hurried off back to his office. He had a bit of a shorter fuse than I did when it came to dealing with passengers lacking in computer skills. Even though I had a great experience off the ship seeing all the amazing historic sights, I was happy to be back and settled into my routine again. Within an hour, Suzanne popped along to say hello and deliver me a bag of sweets. She looked very pleased to see me and I felt good that I meant something to someone who missed me.

I sunk my teeth into my job over the next few days. Pete and the first purser were having fun with my popularity and advertising my helpfulness in the ship's daily newspaper in an attempt to bolster revenue. They gave the business center more exposure on the front pages and inviting them to come and meet the "Internet guru," which was hilarious because barely one month earlier I didn't even have an email address, and now I was labelled a guru. The role was becoming very busy and with the combination of great customer service and an organized booking system created positive feedback and higher tips for me. I had cleared nearly $250 on just one cruise.

Clem and I decided to go and explore Ephesus one day in Kusadasi when Suzanne was on in port manning. He met me at the business center ten minutes before the end of my shift, I changed quickly and we headed off the ship on our adventure. We walked the length of the long pier at Kusadasi and took a taxi into the historic site, which was about a thirty-five-minute journey. Clem informed me that he had brought his camera to "document the day." That was the first time that I had heard that term and planned on using it in the future. It was a very hot day, dusty and dry; once we were dropped off, hundreds of people were walking about. Most of them were on tour, obediently following guides to try to catch snippets of information they would never remember. Clem and I had no guide and our own agenda to spend some quality time in each other's company and enjoy the sights. We photographed each other at the relics and enjoyed the day; we were disappointed that there was no bar at Ephesus. Clem did seem to be really into the history and culture, but I put that down to him being American. I sort of enjoyed it but was probably too culturally immature to appreciate it. I was a shallow 28-year-old who was more interested in finding beer and chatting up dancers than the history of the world. It was a visit I will always remember though because it was just two friends out for the day enjoying free time.

    I will always clearly remember my return to the ship after Ephesus because Pete came to see me in the business center and said that the new rotations had been released, and I was only doing a five-month contract now instead of six months. Meaning that I would be going home in just four weeks. The news that I would be able to see my family and friends again excited me, but it also scared me because I had established a happy routine onboard. I had established some strong relationships. I had a great job on the ship, lots of friends, the respect of my peers, and a girl who loved me. I had known that it was only going to be for six months, and I knew that it was ending at some stage. I was just having such an amazing life experience that I was in denial that it would end so quickly. Did the decision makers on the rotation know that I was doing a great job, that I was employee of the month? And that I was happy? They probably did not even care, and they just saw us as working units and numbers used to fill resource gaps. I thought about the next four weeks and accepted that I was going home sooner that I thought. I felt nervous that someone else in an office somewhere, who did not know me, was in control of my life and destiny with so much power over me.

    At the end of my shift, I went to find those nearest and dearest to break the news. Suzanne was my first stop and she had news of her own. Her contract had also been shortened and she was actually leaving a week before me.

She would re-join this very ship after a month of leave. We hugged it out as we shared our thoughts on the matter. All the ship life changes were difficult to compute in my brain with so much happening so quickly. I turned to what I knew best—beer. I called for Clem and we wandered along to the wardroom to discuss the day. Clem seemed to be the most traumatized because he was staying on the ship after we leave; he would be left without me and Suzanne during his last month. He had started to get on well with Suzanne and described her to me as a beautiful human being and an artist with huge potential. Being the philistine that I was, I did not see very much of that at all. I was still in my superficial years and just saw someone whose company I enjoyed and who adored me. Clem's hands were shakier than normal as he lifted his glass filled with Bud and expressed his fears of wandering the ship's halls alone for the last month of his contract. I did my best to reassure him that we had both made loads of friends during the last few months and had lots of people to talk to. If it was me in that position, I would be okay, so he should be too. His response will hang with me forever: "It's much easier to leave than to be left."

# Chapter 32: Barcelona Freak Out

The reality of my early disembarkation settled in and I would only have two cruises left sailing the Mediterranean. They were long cruises but when I found myself saying to friends that I only had two cruises left, it did sound like a lot less. I decided to just enjoy the last of my contract. I also realized that I had not saved much money, so I would have to watch what I was spending as I only had two wage payments left. The majority of the crew members were paid cash onboard once a month and had to go through the indignity of waiting in a line outside the crew office and receive their money from the SAP crew in one window. In my case, this was a total of $1,450. Then, in the next window I would have to pay the crew AP my outstanding balance on the bar bill, which had been my downfall. My bar bill averaged $550 a month, which was really far too much for a JAP on my salary especially when a beer was 70 cents and a vodka cranberry was only $1.10. The expensive things were drinking in passenger areas because we had to pay full price, but I did that minimally. Basically, JAP wages were poor, but the actual fact that you spent your life on a cruise ship and paid no tax should offset that. I could see in some of my colleagues where that particular sales pitch had been exhausted and they were wise to it. They either left ship life or worked harder for promotion to AP status where you earned $2,250 a month and got your own cabin.

My penultimate cruise was upon me, and we were in Istanbul where I would be disembarking in a month's time. Claire would be leaving at the end of this cruise in Barcelona, and Suzanne would follow her halfway through my last cruise. Things were certainly being closed off, and I could feel amongst my circle of friends that certain defense mechanisms were being primed. Relationships that had been so valued months earlier were being dissolved and couples living in their cabins together were preparing to return to families and loved ones on land. Suzanne and I had not spoken about how our relationship would play out after our contracts. She was returning to the Grand, and I made a vow to her that I would do everything in my power to get myself back onboard for my next contract also. That was as much as we could promise to each other at this stage, and we both seemed alright with that. Claire had started to panic about the end of her contact and meeting with her fiancé again after her last six months' experiences. She was scared and had no idea how she felt about him anymore. Even though she had not really met anyone else on the ship, she had made some great and solid male friendship bonds that you can only really make on ships. She felt that she had certainly changed and was concerned that might have outgrown her intended. I do have to admit that getting engaged and then going to work on a cruise ship for six months is a strange way to show that person that you are committed, but then again, different people in different countries have different views and ideas on what marriage is. Her fiancé had given her the six-month contact as a gift to show his love, openness, trust, and flexibility. Now that is one hell of a massive gamble—especially if you have no idea what it is like living in a tin can for six months with not much to do except drink, meet other people, and work. It does have its romantic side and the feeling of being isolated away from home. The upside is that cruise ship people are all in the same boat and are a friendly, open, and accommodating bunch, which does ease the pain somewhat.

Claire had one cruise, or fourteen nights, to work out her feelings and what she wanted in life. Her man was meeting her in Barcelona and they were going to go backpacking around Europe together. He had travelled from New Zealand to meet her. The next Barcelona stop would be a relationship-defining moment; it would either make them stronger or dissolve them. If Claire was going straight home, then I would guess that she would suffer from post-cruise shock disorder, but as they were both going on this bonding adventure together around Europe, it could save them.

Suzanne was very aware of this relationship volcano brewing in Claire; she suggested that we all go out for a meal and drinks together on the evening of turnaround in Barcelona. I was always up for going out and obviously asked Clem to join us on this double date, totally forgetting and not even thinking of Clem and Claire's past close friendship. I had surpassed my normal social hand grenade self and not given a thought about what could happen.

Well as it happens, I had nothing to worry about from them causing a scene. Unfortunately, I ended up being the center of attention that evening for all the wrong reasons. It's not something that I had planned or was even remotely proud of, but I certainly made an impression on Claire's intended. The big problem was that it was Barcelona turnaround, traditionally the busiest day for our department, on par with the day before turnaround. I was still working in the business center and was assisting in the terminal, so it was a very busy and long day. We had to set up all of the laptops in their workstations and get the terminal staff up to speed. It was probably the most demanding turnaround we had encountered yet. We had laptop issues, long lines, passengers' were complaining, and there were paperwork problems. I was running around like a "blue ass fly" for the whole day. I barely managed to take a half-hour lunch break, where I changed my white uniform shirt as it was unbearably hot and ate some of the very limited selection of lunch on offer in the mess. By the time 6:00 p.m. came along, I was fit for nothing, especially not going out, socializing, and making an effort to meet new people. I had almost forgotten about the arrangement to go out with Claire. All I wanted to do was have a shower, eat some food, have about three beers, and go to bed. But it was not to be. I had a knock at the door and my friends were ready to go exploring the streets of Barcelona for food and drink. I met Claire's fiancé and he seemed a likeable open-minded guy; they seemed to fit together well. Any awkwardness that they were worried about must have dissipated over the last few hours, and they were back to being a couple and looking forward to the next adventure together. I was very happy for them both and slightly relieved.

I was in a foul mood and not good company. I was grumpy, especially at Suzanne, who seemed to be the happiest. We got taxis though the bustling early evening outskirts and got dropped off at the bottom of Las Ramblas. I was in dire need of food and drink, especially in the form of a large beer. I selfishly made the others aware of this, and we hit a bar where I was presented with the largest beer I have ever had the pleasure of drinking. Clem and I had one each and that did help my mood, but I still had not really eaten properly for twelve hours or so. We found a restaurant swiftly because everyone could see I was being uncharacteristically moody and disagreeable. The venue was halfway up the main strip and everywhere was very busy. The waiter managed to find us a table and we seemed to wait an age to get any sort of service. Now my memory of the next events is a bit of a blur, but reports tell me that I had a mild freak-out in the restaurant where I insulted the waiter, threatened to break things and tip the table over. In my defense, it was exceptionally slow service, and I was hungry and exhausted and had lost my patience. It is not very often that this happens, but it did in this restaurant in Barcelona, much to the embarrassment and amusement of my friends and fellow diners. The manager asked us to leave the premises. Clem managed to grab me when he heard the words "civil police" and we ran away as fast as we could, still not fed. As we made a very swift escape through the busy street, I was coming around to normality and it sunk into me what a fool I was making of myself in front of everyone, especially our guest of honor, Claire's fiancé. As soon as we got our breath back, I started to apologize for my actions but noticed that everyone was doubled up with laughter. Suzanne grabbed me and gave me a kiss, and everyone agreed that I had been a legend; I thought I had been acting like a total tool and I was an epic failure. We all decided to go and eat McDonald's, which seemed to be the nearest and fastest way to get food in me. I was warned that I would not be eligible for a Happy Meal though for being such a moody jerk. Clem gave me a hug and said that it was very funny indeed, and Claire's fiancé said that I had made his evening. He would always remember me, so at least I made an impression.

    I had found my second wind after eating crappy fast food. The only upside is that you can get a beer at McDonald's in Europe, so I enjoyed that. We went for a stroll around the back streets to take in some of the amazing architecture, and Clem was very keen to visit a few churches and take in more culture. I found this to be unusual behavior; normally, we would sit about in bars talking about music, girls, shiplife, and drinking. I went along with it because I was in need of some culture after the evening's stupidity. The evening closed on a quiet note, and by midnight, I was finally in my pit for the sleep I had craved six hours earlier. The moral of the story for me is not to go out when I am tired, hungry, and thirsty, especially not when I might be faced with crap service.

## Chapter 33: Back to Earth

The next morning we were finishing off checking in the last of the embarking coach passengers and would be sailing at 2:00 p.m. It was business as usual, and I did not notice or remember that Claire had left until I saw Suzanne that evening. The reunited couple was off on their adventure to complete the next part of their journey through life together.

The ports flew by during my last two cruises, and I did my best to make the most of leaving the ship and doing something in the places we visited. I was spending a lot of time with Suzanne and Clem and drinking below decks in the wardroom. I was still in shock that my time onboard was ending so soon. Suzanne would be leaving in a few days and was already confirmed to return after one month, so I put in an onboard request to have my second contract on the same ship. I was not really ready for the massive change of another actual ship and having to find my way around all over again. I was told by the crew office that quite a lot of the same people do return to the same ships because it helps with promotions. Over time employees become better known to the ship's management and start to build knowledge of the ship. I completed my request form and Suzanne was happy knowing that I was doing all I could for us to stay together.

My Compo boss did not want to let me disembark on turnaround day when the majority of the crew flew home. He had requested that I do the extra day's work and then fly home on the second day so that I would handle turnaround with him. I was quite flattered to be needed, but I suspected that it was Compo Pete being lazy. He didn't want to have to manage a new person alone on a difficult day. The flight report that was hanging outside the crew office with details of our flights home certainly made it feel official, I would be flying back to London where my best friend would pick me up from the airport. I would spend a couple of days with him before making my way back to the Isle of Wight and to my parents' house to fill them in on what I had been up to for the last five months.

Suzanne was leaving just a few days before me, and even though I would miss her, I have always been someone who could cope quite happily on my own and would default back to single life for a time. There was still uncertainty about where I would end up for my next contract; even though I had requested a particular ship, it was by no means guaranteed. On the day that Suzanne left, those words from Clem—"It's much easier to leave than to be left"—weighed heavily on me. If I still had a few more months to run on my contract it would be difficult, but with my impending exit in Istanbul in a few days' time, I was looking forward to going home.

The last few days were a busy time. I had handed over the business center with reasonable ease to a fellow JAP and was back on the desk for my final few days in the line of fire with the passengers. It was a strange feeling coming to the end of my first contract. I had seen so much, met so many people, and grown up a bit. On the day before disembarkation, I found myself in the leavers' queue outside the crew office where all disembarking crew members would sign off the ship's articles and pay the final bar bill and collect the last of any outstanding pay.

I celebrated my last shift and had my end-of-term report, or officer's appraisal as it is better known, with SAP Accounts, who said that I had done "really well" and I received better than average scores on the report card. I was very happy with that and felt like I had done a decent job. I was told to meet at the gangway at 9:30 a.m. to get a transfer to the airport in Istanbul with one of the deck officers.

I handed my $15,000 float over and was free to go to the wardroom and crew bar for my last night of shiplife. I also had the small matter of having to pack my belongings. I wanted to travel light but had accumulated rather a lot of souvenirs and things from the various ports of call. I ended up giving most of it away or just leaving it in the cabin. I was doing my best to drink my mini bar that I had accumulated from the various parties over the previous months, but it looked like my cabin mate would benefit from that also; so much to drink, so little time. In the end, I stuffed as much as I could into my rucksack and ended up with two extra pieces of hand luggage. Neither was a practical travelling piece, but I was not used to travelling. I was used to an average shared hotel room on a working cruise ship. My last evening was actually almost quite forgettable. I met with Clem and we drank our normal amount of beers. He presented me with a signed CD and a few photos of us on our day out at Ephesus. I ended up in the wardroom drinking with the dancers that I finally was making some progress with, mainly because I was leaving, feeling confident and quite drunk. The evening ended with me getting on like a house on fire with them all and they seemed sorry I was leaving the next day, just as they were just getting to know me—ironic, I know, but that's shiplife.

    I awoke in a panic as I was getting off the ship and I had less than an hour to get ready, finish packing, and go to the crew office to collect my passport and get my transport at 9:30 a.m. to take me to the airport. By some miracle and with the help of Martin, I was on time. I still felt a bit drunk and was touched to see about five of my fellow JAP colleagues at the gangway to see me off with Clem. I gave them all a hug and Martin ran up to the lobby bar and brought me back my favorite cocktail, a strawberry daiquiri, to suck down before boarding my transport. It was just a deck officer and myself leaving on this second day of Istanbul. He was probably half impressed that I had a farewell party at the dockside with a cocktail at 9:30 a.m. I gave Clem one last hug and told a crying Stef to look after him for me, but not to sleep with him – no good could come of that.

    Before I knew it, I was speeding through the streets of a bustling Istanbul, sun blazing through the window on my way to the airport. I felt that I had achieved a job well done. But what now? I had no idea what the next step was, what ship I would be going back to, or if I would be welcomed back. I could see no reason why not after being EOM and having a winning appraisal, but I knew very little of how the company worked. For the time being, I had to make my way home and that meant being sober enough to cope with travel. I was feeling really rough and the parting cocktail did not help. I had made small talk with the Irish deck officer in the van, but I was grateful when he took a different check-in desk upon arrival at the airport. He was flying to Dublin, so I was half relieved I would not have to attempt to be interesting or interested. I had just finished five months of doing that to people I barely knew. Once I had fumbled past security, I sat and waited for my gate to open, which was over an hour away. I sat and reflected and listened to Clem's CD. I became emotional. The music on the CD was the exact same stuff that I had been hearing him play in the atrium over the past five months. I had grown very fond of his rendition of Morel's "Danza in E"; it had become the tune I probably heard him play the most as it normally ended his set. Clem had joined the ship on the same day as me and we had been friends as soon as we met; we stuck together, helping each other through bad, lonely, upsetting, and heartbreaking times, as well as some amazing times. I was very grateful for his friendship and companionship and knew he would be one of my closest friends from what we had been through together on my first contract. I was determined to see him again one day in my life. Hearing his music and closing my eyes, I was transported back into the atrium with me on the desk and Clem playing his guitar.

    Before I knew it, I was transported back to England and waiting for me at the arrivals gate was my best friend who had seen me off five months earlier. I remember at that time feeling very much like the first day of school with butterflies in my belly. It was now over and I had enjoyed my contract very much. I had met so many amazing people and seen so many amazing places. Adrian and I hugged, and he took me back to the heart of London where he was living with his girlfriend's family.

Quite shortly after the welcome back celebrations came the big bump back to reality as well as the unfinished relationship that I had left behind. I had thought that if you leave your girlfriend at home and go on a cruise ship for five months with barely two phone calls and one letter in the interim, it would give a strong enough hint that the relationship was not moving in the right direction. But I guess that I was not forthcoming enough in my intentions, and even though I had been acting like I was single for the last five months, the girl I left behind legitimately thought we were on a relationship break. She had heard that I had returned home and was phoning my friend's house in London to talk to me. I had no idea what to say as I was completely unprepared. I hoped that the fact that I was not taking her calls would give her the general idea and she would give up. But the calls kept coming, and it took a stern telling off from those close to me, to get me to talk to her. I was squirming because I had no idea what to say and was not very good at ending relationships. I sat at the top of the landing stairs and did my best to explain what I had been doing and why I had not answered her calls. It basically ended with me being told what a dickhead I was, which was totally true in this case; I took it like a man because it was an overdue telling off and dressing down. I just tried to end the phone call as quickly and as courteously as possible. I felt a bit sick from being so disrespectful to another person, especially one I had feelings for at one time.

Adrian handed me a cold beer and asked if I needed anything. I said that I needed to write a letter to her to just close things off as clearly as possible. We set about penning the perfect "Dear John" letter to try to give my ex some peace of mind. It started well enough, but we found that being emotionally imaginative was thirsty work and started sucking back a few more beers to get our creative juices flowing and really to get in touch with our sensitive sides. After about an hour and four beers, we had penned what we thought was an acceptable, respectful, and thoughtful letter. We had left about eleven blank spaces, where we were stuck for words and could not find the term we wanted, but we figured that we would fill them in later when Adrian's fiancée returned from work. We went to the pub to play pool for a few drinks in Kensington before heading back to the house for a lovely dinner. Considering I was not a member of the family, the hospitality was so generous and kind. We drank and talked into the night and closed the evening off with a game of cards, where we did our upmost to take as much money from each other as possible.

The next morning, and one hell of a headache later, I stumbled onto the train to make my way back home to the Isle of Wight, posting my letter before I left. As I dozed during the train trip, I realized with horror that I had not filled in the blanks of the letter and there was still a bunch of important words missing from the text. The letter would only make half sense and it would seem like it was written by a drunken halfwit, which is mostly true.

    I had reached the end of a life changing few months, starting a new job, travelling by cruise ship around Europe, meeting some amazing people and experiencing some exciting adventures.

    I felt that I had found where I belonged and was looking forward to the next chapter to begin.

# ABOUT THE AUTHOR

Tobias Biddick first experienced cruise ship life at the turn of the millennium and spent five happy years at sea. Following ship life he then enjoyed many equally blissful post ship years as a Cruise Executive based in Southampton, claiming the Global Seatrade Environmental Initiative Award in 2011. These amusing and mostly true memoirs have now finally come to life sharing at least some small legacy of many memorable years at sea. The crewshiplife series is the perfect read for cruisers and the non-cruising curious that want to know about what goes on below passenger decks, also a great book for reminiscing crewmembers and anyone that fancies a fun, funny, touching and 'nautically naughty' light read.

One last thing............
If you have enjoyed reading crewshiplife please leave a review at the below link
www.amazon.com/dp/B00X7PS99E

Part 2 and 3 in the crewshiplife series are now also available -

The Fourth Induction (Book 2)
https://www.amazon.com/dp/B01GOBT4YG
is the story finding love on the second cruise contract, intertwined with hilarious stories showcasing a melting pot of characters, ships and destinations.

Knights in Whites (Book 3)
https://www.amazon.com/dp/B08CBT1T9H
brings the series to an emotional climatic finale with tales of humour, darker moments throughout the continued quest for a meaningful love connection.

Connect with Tobias below
www.amazon.com/author/tobiasbiddick

Made in the USA
Monee, IL
20 May 2023